PRAISE FOR
THE ASSASSIN GAME

"McKay keeps things ambiguous so that readers will continue guessing until the true culprit is revealed in the climactic scene. Her witty, self-deprecating voice captures the thrill of belonging and the complicated emotions that come with new money. Smart, edge-of-the-seat thrills."

—*Kirkus Reviews*

"Umfraville Hall, an exclusive boarding school on the windswept Welsh island of Skola, is an ideal setting for a mystery that takes a few cues from Agatha Christie's *And Then There Were None*... McKay (*Undead*) pokes a bit of fun at teen angst, using Cate's wry voice to tell this twisty whodunit."

—*Publishers Weekly*

"Fans of elusive thrillers like Gail Giles's *What Happened to Cass McBride* will enjoy this book thoroughly. Lovers of mystery and suspense and those who appreciate a good boarding school story will also engage with this fast-moving and adrenaline-packed novel."

—*School Library Journal*

"McKay's world building is top-notch and the suspense palpable."

—*Booklist*

"Red herrings abound in this page-turner... The fast-moving plot will motivate readers to sort through the many characters, guess at their motives, and spot the real criminal."

—*VOYA Magazine*

"An exhilarating thriller from start to finish, this action-packed book is full of betrayals, mystery, and heartbreak. Both the Game and Cate's love life kept us guessing until the end."

—*Justine Magazine*

"Perfect for readers looking for a good "scary" novel... *The Assassin Game* has the perfect amount of romance, suspense, and action to make for a wonderful read."

—TeenReads

ALSO BY KIRSTY MCKAY

The Assassin Game

HAVE YOU SEEN MY SISTER?

KIRSTY McKAY

sourcebooks
fire

Published by Sourcebooks Fire, an imprint of Sourcebooks
P.O. Box 4410, Naperville, Illinois 60567–4410
(630) 961-3900
sourcebooks.com

Cataloging-in-Publication Data on file with the Library of Congress

Printed and bound in Canada.
MBP 10 9 8 7 6 5 4 3 2 1

For Megan, who is a spark of inspiration

CHAPTER ONE

———

I didn't realize it at the time, but the first clue in my sister's disappearance was the shoes.

Running shoes, in oxblood red, Gaia's favorite color. She's always moaned about her ridiculously massive feet. She's tall, so that's the payoff for the endless legs, I guess. But then she'd scored these gorgeous blood red sneaks, and she loved them.

They were memorable shoes. So you would have thought I'd remember them that chilly morning on the day of her disappearance. I even tripped over the stupid things, nearly broke my neck. You might assume that later, I'd put two and two together. If her blood red sneakers were on our bedroom floor here at the holiday lodge, Gaia couldn't be out running.

But you'd be wrong to assume anything about me.

"Did Gaia stay at her place last night, or here?" Dad had asked, happily frying breakfast leftovers.

I frowned, thinking back to leaving the party. It was at

Gaia's friends' house, a last-night get-together for all the kids who work here at the ski resort, and I'd tagged along. When the party ended, I'd lingered by the open door awkwardly, trying to ignore a couple making out noisily on the deck while I waited. Gaia was inside on the stairs, deep in conversation with one of her work friends, her black, curly hair bouncing as she talked, brown eyes wide and expressive. I'd felt bad for interrupting, but also very ready to ditch and head home.

"Hey, Es, go. I'll be right behind you, okay?" Gaia eventually turned, gave me an encouraging—or possibly snarky—thumbs-up.

"It's snowing again. Didn't this place get the memo about spring?" I remember I shivered, glanced at my watch. It said 10:35 p.m., but the second hand wasn't moving. Dead. I had no idea how long we'd stayed at the party—that's one of my things, time is totally meaningless—but I suppose it must have been well into the early morning.

"Seriously, I'll be fine, Es," Gaia shouted. "I can cope with a lil' snow, ya know!"

True enough. She's been working the ski season at Moon Mountain Resort since last November. It's her gap year, before she goes to college here in America, and me and the folks are visiting from England. Gaia's majorly smart, a scholarship kid. I had to hope she'd be able to find her way back to the holiday lodge.

"I'll walk Gaia home." Craig appeared, blocking the view of my sister with his tall, muscled frame. He's American, a ski instructor, one of Gaia's friends. And, lucky fella, he'd been my teacher on the slopes this past week. I'm so horrible at skiing I think I nearly broke him. Not that I feel guilty about it; he's kind of the worst.

"Skedaddle, Esme. I'm gonna close this door, we're freezing in here." The door shut in my face. *Yep, the worst.*

So earlier today at breakfast, when Dad asked me if Gaia had slept here at the lodge last night, I assumed yes. I'd gone straight to sleep, didn't see her come in. But she said she would follow me home, so that's what must have happened.

"Gaia came back a bit after me." I glanced at Dad over my mug of black tea. "Must be out now, running off her hangover."

Dad grunted, and like that, any nagging doubt about her not being here was gone. If I'd only thought about the running shoes...

But I didn't. I sat shoveling Dad's vegan lentil surprise into my mouth at the breakfast table, taking in the views of Moon Mountain for the last time. It's stunning; the remains of patchy snow glistening on the slopes, framed by the dark, jagged silhouette of pine tree woods on either side. We've never had a holiday like this before. Big stretch for the parents, money-wise, but we wangled the luxury lodge for free and it's been worth it to see Gaia. Not that we've seen as much of her as I would have liked—she's been working, after all.

"Esme, did I hear you say you walked back on your own last night?" Ma swooped into the kitchen, her arms full of clothes. I was tempted to wind her up, but didn't have the energy.

"Addy walked me. She was staying over at her parents' lodge."

That placated her. My sister and Addy Addison have been friends since forever, and Addy's a sweetheart. She's also the reason we got the fancy accommodation free; her uncle owns the resort. She and Gaia scored jobs together—my sis can work here legally because her birth dad was American—and Addy's family is mega rich, so nobody ever tells them no.

"As long as you weren't wandering around alone." Ma's voice had an edge; she's way overprotective of me. That's one thing Addy and I have in common. In my case, it might be justified, but Addy's eighteen and sensible and her dad's *still* all up in her business. God knows what he'll be like when she starts college and he can't keep tabs on her. I think one of the reasons I like Addy is that she doesn't seem tainted by the parental interference. Wish I could pull that off.

"Aw, cut Es some slack," Dad stuffed the rest of his breakfast into his mouth before Ma could whip the plate away. "She's sixteen, after all."

"Not yet she isn't." Ever the stickler for accuracy; my birthday's in a few days' time. "And she's not a *normal* sixteen."

"Julia!" Dad almost spat his sausage out.

"She knows I don't mean it like that, don't you, Es?" Ma bent in for the forehead kiss.

I do know. What she meant was: I'm not super-together like she is, like my sister is. What Dad thought she meant was: I have dyspraxia.

If you haven't heard of dyspraxia, fair. Neither had I until I got diagnosed four years ago. Sounds way worse than it is. Officially, it means I have problems "placing myself within time and space." That sounds kind of sci-fi, but what it boils down to is that I get extra time on tests because I have zero sense of how many minutes have passed. And there's the clumsy: I drop things, bump into stuff. Don't know left from right, can't do directions. Sometimes I talk inappropriately loudly, sometimes I mumble; that's one of Ma's particular faves. Dad makes out he's chill about the dyspraxia, but Ma gets on my case.

"Pack your things when you've finished. And Gaia's too. I don't want us having a last-minute rush, okay?"

I didn't answer her, but it wasn't really a question. Ma runs a tight ship. She'd planned for us to all leave Moon Mountain together and drive to Boston for a final night with Gaia, before we leave my sis and take the sad flight back to London.

So I packed, right after breakfast, to keep Ma sweet. Maybe I didn't realize about Gaia's shoes—even as I stuffed them into a gym bag—because my brain works different than other people's. Or maybe anyone would have done the same. Outside, the sun was bright and the day dripped away like the snow off the roof of our lodge as I packed. All done, I reclined in the big armchair by the fire, finishing the final pages of a book. Dad appeared, fresh from cramming luggage into the car.

"Wasn't Gaia supposed to be saying goodbye to her friends today? At a brunch?"

"Think someone mentioned that last night, yeah."

"Should be over by now." Dad frowned. "She can't still be running around the resort. Text her, will you?"

"No phone."

Dad sighs, remembering how I'd killed my latest phone. Death by ski lift on the third day of the vacation. He should be grateful it wasn't me plunging from the chair, could have totally happened.

"Use mine." He reached into his back pocket, knew I wouldn't make the catch, and carefully placed the phone in my hands. "Ask her when she's coming back. Your mother's gone to check out; she wants to leave on time."

So I texted.

———

Gaia never answered that text I sent from Dad's phone, and she didn't come back. We ate a sandwich, I finished my book and wandered out to the deck. It was still cold, but the sun is so much stronger here than at home. Dad was sitting in an Adirondack chair, head back and eyes closed like it was summer.

"Almost 3:00 p.m.," he croaked at me. "Your mother is not going to be pleased."

Ma was striding quickly up the lane, her mouth set, cheeks flushed with the effort. Even for her, it was quite a pace, walking as fast as possible without actually running.

"Jim!" she called as she got closer. "Jim!" There was a catch to her voice that made Dad open his eyes. "Gaia wasn't at the brunch."

"No?" Dad stood up and walked slowly down the steps. "Couldn't face the pancakes, eh?"

"Jim," Ma grabbed Dad's arm. "Her friends haven't seen her since last night. Nobody knows where she is." Her face flickered. "Gaia *is gone.*"

CHAPTER TWO

——

"Didn't she come back last night?" Dad stares at me. We're in the living room now; my parents pacing up and down and me quietly wondering how much to panic. "I thought you said she'd gone running first thing?"

The damn shoes.

"I...got that wrong, I think."

"We need to call her." Dad turns to Ma. "Where's my phone?" He disappears through the archway into the kitchen.

"Maybe she crashed at a friend's?" I offer.

"She'd let us know, and she'd be here by now. Nobody at the brunch had seen her, none of her housemates or friends."

"Where's my phone?" Dad is shouting in the kitchen.

"Here!" I spot it on the armchair. As Dad comes back, I jog over and go for the grab but somehow end up batting the phone into the metal grate of the empty fireplace.

"Esme!" Dad yells, retrieving it and bringing up a cloud

of wood ash. There are cracks across the screen. "Can't see anything on this now!" He tries to swipe. "Ow!" He shakes his finger and a plop of dark blood drips on to my armchair.

"Jim, you've cut yourself!" Ma says, like he needed telling. "I'll get a bandage."

"I'm fine!" He's not, he's dripping red; it's running down his hand in a totally overdramatic way.

"God, sorry, Dad."

"It's okay!" he says, looking down at his not-okay finger. He shouts through the archway at Ma, who sounds like she's rummaging in a kitchen cupboard. "Leave it, Julia! Just call Gaia!"

"It was the first thing I did, *obviously*." Ma shouts back, reappearing. "Straight to voicemail." She shoves a roll of bandage and tape at Dad. "I called, texted, IM'd, emailed." Pulling her phone from her back pocket she scrolls, searching. "Nothing." The phone goes to up to her ear. "Voicemail again." Ma takes a few steps away and clears her throat, her back to us. "Gaia, love." The voice is casual, everyday. "Can you call us—we're a bit worried that you haven't turned up. We're at the lodge. Love you." She hangs up. "I'll ring Addy. She might know something." Holding the phone to her ear, she moves to the window. "Oh, hell, why do kids never answer?" She goes to the front door and walks out into the cold air. We hear her leave a chirpy-but-taut message for Addy.

Dad has managed to roll the entire bandage around the end of his finger, the tip so fat it looks like a giant cotton swab.

"Let me get this straight, Es," he says, biting tape. "You came home with Addy last night."

"Yeah." I sink lightly onto the armchair, memories of Addy wobbling alongside me, slightly the worse for wear. "It was snowing—she left me, went home to her parents' place." Not entirely accurate. I'd ended up seeing her home, sort of. I was worried she might pass out drunk and freeze overnight, but I don't need to share that right now.

Ma appears at the doorway. "I heard the door unlatch. We'd gone to bed, Jim, but I can't sleep 'til I know the girls are back."

"And you thought Gaia came in shortly after, Es?" Dad is fiddling with more tape.

"Not exactly..." I bite the side of my thumb. "She said she'd follow me, but she was in the middle of talking to someone." I picture her on the stairs with...*who? Can't remember.* "So then, Craig—you know, my ski instructor? Whose house the party was at?—well, he shooed me out and said he'd walk her back."

"Did Gaia actually say she'd walk with Craig?" Ma says. "Oh for goodness' sake, here, Jim!" She slams the door shut, strides up to Dad, and deftly ties the tape off for him.

"Um," I try to remember. "Nope."

"Oh god!" Ma says.

"Julia, she's *nineteen*." Dad says. "She's an adult, and she knows her way around."

"Not well enough, clearly," Ma mutters. "Stay here. I'm going to drive to her lodging. Es, you can come with me, and if she's

9

not there, we'll get her luggage into the car. That way we can leave for Boston as soon as she comes back."

Dad nods, silent. I follow Ma out of the door. She will restore order. That's what she does.

———

When Gaia sent us a pic of her new home, it took my breath away.

I'd watched this old movie called *The Amityville Horror*, and Gaia's house had looked just like it. The movie had been a bit of a disappointment. Dad conned me into watching it, promising spooks to the max, but the actors were over the top, and it was funny rather than terrifying. The house itself gave me chills, though. In the movie, it's this huge, run-down place, and when you see it for the first time it actually looks like it has an evil face, windows for eyes, the whole bit. The pic of Gaia's house had that going on too. Only, when we landed in the United States, I realized that quite a lot of the houses here are inherently creepy. Very different from the redbrick terrace I call home. I don't know if it's the wooden shutters and the crawl spaces, the attics and the basements—and Americans never close their curtains when it gets dark. What's up with that?

The house isn't far away, but I'm pretty sure we take the scenic route because Ma is scanning for Gaia. She drives slowly as we pass holiday lodging interspersed with woods and the ends of ski trails. There's a big leisure complex and pool, and the center of the ski village with its shops and eateries. We do a drive-by, and most of it looks shut. Nobody is around except for a couple of maintenance guys up a cherry picker on the side of the road. We pass only one car going in the opposite direction, and Ma slows down to look over. It's a boy-girl couple in a beat-up four-wheel drive, packed to the gills with luggage, skis on the rack. They're arguing, and they don't look at us as we check them out. I think they were at the party last night, but I couldn't say for sure.

At the turning for Gaia's street, Ma slows to a stop. There's a figure in the distance, walking slowly toward us: head down, a black hat, dark green parka. Gaia's parka is dark green. Whoever it is, is struggling with a large laundry bag. Ma has her indicator on to turn right, but we sit there, willing that figure to be Gaia. As they approach, they look up, and it's not Gaia. A slender, young white man with thin spikes of yellow hair poking out of the bottom of the hat looks back at us.

Gaia's place is at the far end of a street with several large houses, all on one side of the road. They're the oldest buildings in the resort; Abenaki Avenue, "named after the indigenous folk the white people stole the land from," she'd (half) joked. We'd eaten at The Apogee, the revolving restaurant on top of the mountain, earlier in the week, and Gaia had pointed out a framed print on the wall beside our table.

"Check out my crib!" She'd said, brown eyes twinkling. "Back in the day, I woulda had a *deluxe domicile*." And there was her house in the photo, in nineteen thirty-whatever, with plucky folk standing on the deck wearing tweed pantaloons and holding thick, wooden skis.

Apparently, when they were built the houses had great views of the slopes, but they became staff quarters when the resort expanded and newer accommodations sprang up. A line of trees was planted to hide the staff housing from the road and deny their new occupants the view. Gaia reckoned she was lucky because she and Addy shared an attic room and could see the top of the mountain from their window.

Ma pulls to the side of the road. A couple of the houses have people outside, in various stages of packing their cars.

"Looks like everyone is leaving," Ma says. "I wonder how many of these kids stick around for the summer season?"

"Gaia told me not many, mainly waiters and bar staff. She and Addy got asked to stay on in Concierge, but they already had those beach jobs lined up at the Cape."

Ma nods, suddenly throwing her door open and leaping out. I'm left to climb over her seat to exit, as there's a wall of frozen, compacted snow curbside.

"Hey, guys!" Ma is already accosting people. "Anyone seen Gaia?" Nobody is being particularly helpful; most of them know who Gaia is and mention she was a no-show at the brunch, but no one volunteers any new info. As Ma chats away, I can see her surreptitiously checking out the cars, even running up to a house or two to try and get a glimpse inside. She's shameless like that. Normally, it would give me a chronic cringe, but right now I'm glad she's so brazen.

Ma powers up the street to Gaia's place when she's finished her interrogating.

"Addy's car." She slaps the hood of a silver-blue hatchback in the drive of the house. "So, Gaia hasn't borrowed it. I wish she had; Adam Addison probably installed a bloody tracking device, knowing how he monitors his poor daughter's every movement."

"Does Gaia drive it?" I try the car door, but it's locked.

"Yep." Ma nods. "We fumed. The Addisons bought it for the girls in Boston, had it waiting for them in the airport parking lot when they landed." She gives a hollow laugh. "What a stupid idea. Neither of the girls had ever driven on the wrong side of the road before, and then the first time they get behind the wheel is in Boston, home of the worst drivers in North America."

I forget sometimes that Ma lived over here; she barely talks about it. But I've heard about those times from what she's told Gaia. It was quite the love story; Ma was only a teenager when she met a handsome U.S. soldier on the military base near her little English village. I've seen pictures of Ori, Gaia's dad. He was Black, super tall, and extremely good-looking; no wonder Ma followed him back to the United States. Ori was seriously clever too—he'd been in the military to fund his college education, studying to be an engineer—and when Ma got pregnant, they knew it was going to be a struggle, but the future looked bright. Gaia doesn't remember much, but she says Ma tells her they were really, really happy. But Ori died, in their backyard, right in front of them. It was a heart attack—some desperately unfair, previously undetected problem. Because she wasn't married, Ma had to leave the United States and take little Gaia back to the UK. My dad came on to the scene a year later, and me soon after that.

Ma's leaning on the car as though if she listens hard enough, it might whisper secrets. But then her face hardens, and she pushes herself up and runs lightly to the front door, opening it and striding in without invitation.

"Gaia!" she bellows into the hallway.

It's a big house, and the last time we were here it was buzzing with people, but today it stands silent. Ma leaps up the stairs, runs down a corridor, and immediately tackles the second flight, with me hurrying to keep up. On the second-floor landing there's a door that leads to a narrow, twisty flight of stairs to the attic bedroom. Ma pauses a second before going in: Addy and Gaia's room. We almost trip over a trunk, which takes up most of the floor space. The rest of the room consists of bunk beds—one stripped, one unmade—an open closet, and a dressing table. It takes a second to see that Gaia is not here.

"Someone packed this." Ma lifts the lid of the trunk. "The Addisons are going to pay to store the girls' snow gear until autumn."

"Addy's backpack." I point to the gray and pink bag leaning against the bottom bunk. "It's full." I look around. "Where's Gaia's?"

We find it, stuffed into the top of the closet. Very not-packed, which I expected, because I can see some of her clothes hanging, and some on the floor. And there are toiletries, and books and a small saucer of jewelry that I know is Gaia's. I pick up a single earring, an amber stud; I gave her these for her birthday last year. *Where's the other one?* I pocket the one in my hand.

Ma is rifling through the trunk.

"Only Addy's stuff is ready to go." She straightens up, sighs, momentarily closes her eyes. "Right. Gaia wouldn't give us a fright like this. She must have been…held up, or something." She grabs Gaia's empty rucksack. "Help me get things squared away, will you? We'll take it back in the car."

She hesitates, staring at the pack like it's going to bite her.

"Ma?" I look at her. When she doesn't answer, I go to grab a pile of Gaia's clothes from the closet.

"No!" she says, one hand out, stopping me in my tracks, carefully laying the bag back on the shelf where we found it. "Actually…maybe… We shouldn't touch anything." She leaves the closet open and walks past me to the door.

"Why not?"

But she doesn't answer me.

We're sitting in the car again, now parked outside the house, like cops on surveillance. Apart from Addy and Gaia's attic, only one bedroom showed signs that it was still occupied. We checked every room, top to bottom, and we were, as I had suspected, completely home alone.

"We'll wait here a few mins, in case she comes back." Ma stares at the house. "Where the hell is she? Anything unusual happen at the party last night, Es?"

I breathe out slowly. Oh god. *Where do I start?*

CHAPTER THREE

———

It started with a boy.

It was snowing lightly as Gaia, Addy, and I walked to the party at Craig's house last night. On the way over, I'd had a little disagreement with a patch of icy pavement and wiped out. Broke my watch and knocked my head. No biggie, very much business as usual for me, but by the time we got to the party, my head was thumping, and I felt seriously queasy.

"Hey," I'd tugged Gaia's sleeve as we'd walked up the steps to the covered deck. "Gonna catch my breath for a sec. I'll follow you in."

"You'd better." She raised a thick eyebrow, but left me to it, the noise of the party enveloping her and Addy as they went through the front door.

Oh god, a wave of nausea hit as the door closed. I staggered across the deck, grabbed the rail, and hurled my supper into the darkness below. *Wow. Didn't see that coming.* Sinking to my knees, I clung to the deck, inhaling the freezing air like that was going to fix me.

"You done?"

A voice from below, from the direction of my hurl. I pulled myself up and leaned over the rail. A curly blond head looked out from the shadows.

"Need to barf again?"

Argh, a boy. Maybe a year or so older than me. Not one of my sister's friends. He stared up from below the deck with worried eyes. No, I definitely didn't recognize him.

"I'd help ya." He gave me a wonky smile. "Only I can't move right now."

I blinked, tried to focus. "You can't move?" My voice came out like a gasp. The boy nodded, his hair ridiculously curly, almost ringlets.

"See the backpack?" He pointed off into the shadows. "Pass it to me?"

Oh man, I thought, *I'm being lured off the safe deck into the night by some weirdo.* You hear about how kids are tricked into the back of vans on the pretext of helping someone. This was totally that.

"Sure."

Head pounding, breath sour, I carefully walked down the steps and around to the backpack.

"Thanks," the boy said, reaching to take the bag from me.

I nodded, gently. "So… How exactly are you stuck?"

"Huh? Oh—snare." He opened the pack, searching for something. "Raccoon trap. And I stepped in it."

I looked down to see a tight-looking piece of wire looped around his boot.

He rummaged in the pack again. "Gotcha." The silver of a small blade flashed in the moonlight. Crouching, he began to saw away with the knife.

I shuddered, suddenly cold. *Well, this is different.* I wanted to ask him what he was doing underneath the deck in the first place. Part of me was wondering if Gaia would come out to rescue me, and part of me really hoped she wouldn't.

"Could you cut the wire? Kinda awkward to reach."

I hesitated a second, but then…*aw, to hell with it.*

"I should warn you…" I gingerly took the blade and crouched down. "I'm lethal with knives…"

"Got thick boots." He grinned.

"Good." I pressed the blade carefully against the wire and sawed very slowly, using every ounce of concentration I poss-essed. Amazingly, after a few seconds, *ping!* and I'd freed him.

"Thanks," he said, as I handed him the knife. "You missed me, by the way."

"What?"

He pointed at the ground. A pile of my very yellow sick lay about a meter away from where we were standing.

"Oh god. Sorry." *Does he think I'm drunk?* "I bumped my head, but I feel better now. Don't worry, I'll warn you if you need to dodge again."

He chuckled. We walked up the steps to the deck and sat on a bench against the wall.

"You Gaia's friend? Saw you walking with her."

"Sister. We don't look alike… We have different dads." This felt like way too much information, but the boy nodded.

"Blended families, I get you." He leaned forward, looked at his boots. "You guys came over from England?" He made a face. "Well of course they did, Bode, you dummy." He shook his head and grinned at me. "Thought I'd seen you around. Staying in the fancy lodges on Hillview?"

I nodded. "You're called Bo-dee?"

"B.O.D.E., but yeah, pronounced Bo-dee. Like the skier, only Mom says she had the idea first."

This meant nothing to me, but I didn't let on.

"My name's Es, by the way."

"Thanks for freeing me, Es." His eyes are nice. Crinkly. He's messy-looking, but I like that. "Short for…Esmeralda?"

"Almost. Esme."

"Cool." Bode said. "Never heard that name before." He sat up quickly. "Wait. I have. The Stepford Cuckoos. Esme's one of the sisters. You read comics?"

"Yeah!" I said. "Wow, I'm impressed you know that."

"Well, Marvel's all right. But I'm more of an Eisner fan, Alan Moore, old school."

"Me too!" My head was beginning to clear. "I mean, I'm no, like, aficionado or anything."

"Me either," Bode side-eyed me. "I just like a good story."

19

"Yeah!" I said, racking my brains to come up with something more intelligent and failing. "You work at the resort?"

"No," Bode leaned back, crossed his arms. "Not officially, anyways. I live with my uncle over there," I followed his gaze across the close to a small, detached, wooden house on the other side of the close. "See the barn, in back? That's my space."

"You live in a *barn*?" It came out way more full-on than I meant, like he just told me he lived at the city dump.

He laughed. "In the attic. Kind of chilly sometimes, but nobody bothers me. My uncle's good that way. He's super here at Moon."

"Okay. Er, what's he super at?"

Bode laughed again, his eyes doing the crinkly thing. "Resort superintendent? Like, head maintenance guy?" He cracked his knuckles. "I help, a little. I'm finishing up high school in town. That's the idea, anyways."

I waited for him to offer more, but nothing came. There was a flurry, like we were sitting in a snow globe. I got to my feet.

"I better go in or my sister will think I've got lost."

Bode looked up at me from underneath the curls. "Out here on the deck?"

"Oh, it's entirely possible."

He grinned. "So, you wanna hang later? Or tomorrow. I'll give you my number."

"I don't have a phone. And we leave tomorrow."

"Oh." He got up, crossed the deck to the door. "Shame."

But of course, when my mother asks me if anything unusual occurred at the party last night, I don't tell her about Bode. He was only the beginning of it.

"Nothing happened," I say. "Just party stuff."

Ma frowns. "Gaia's been a bit…distracted since we've been here. Don't you think?"

You could say.

When we were at the party, she'd kind of ignored me. Okay, not ignored, exactly. She was…preoccupied.

I'd weaved my way through people in the lounge, glancing over to see Bode sit down with a couple of boys by a woodstove. Gaia was nowhere to be found, but eventually I thought I heard her raucous cackles and wandered down a corridor to the kitchen. The smell of sweet and smoky hit me as I entered the room.

"Hey, sis!" Gaia was sitting on the countertop, half-leaning out of a window. She grinned and passed a joint to Addy. "You okay?"

Are you?

I tried not to stare. Normally, my sister has to be persuaded to have a glass of wine on Christmas Day because she hates feeling out of control, and yet there she was, smoking something. I mean, it's probably legal over here and I'm certainly no goody-goody, but it was just…*not her.*

"Falling over again, I hear?" Craig, the beefcake ski instructor, was wrestling a metal keg and pouring frothy liquid into red plastic cups on the table. "You know you're dangerous, Esme. If you think I'm giving you a drink, forget it."

"Not interested." I smiled. "Beer tastes like sweat."

"Not really one for parties, are you?" A voice came from the corner.

Like it could get any worse, Craig moved and I spotted my least favorite person in the world: Eli Addison.

Eli is Addy's brother, but more than that, he's Gaia's ex. I guess everyone's allowed one big mistake, and he's hers. Eli's twenty, handsome, smoldering … and indisputably basic. You know how TV magicians are? Like they try to be all enigmatic and intense, but are clearly compensating for being kicked around the playground? Anyway, these days Eli reckons he's big news because his uncle owns this mountain. Apparently, Eli works here too, when it suits him… If you consider "working" strutting around with two phones and pissing everyone off. He hates me, because he knows I'm not fooled. Eli's problem is I remember him when he was still a loser who blubbed when my sister dumped him.

"Way past your bedtime, isn't it, Es?"

I ignore him. It's my default way of being with him; no one would expect any different.

What is different is that normally my sister would be all over Eli and Craig's snarking. She'd be jumping in to defend me. But last night in the kitchen, she let it go, grinning a slightly baked grin from the countertop, letting me battle it out for myself. Which, *normally*, I'd be very happy to do. But I guess I was feeling needy, knowing this was the last time I was going to see her for ages and wanting her all to myself.

And Old Gaia would have known that. But this one didn't.

"Would you say being over here has changed Gaia?"

Ma's question jolts me out of the memory, and I stare at the car dashboard. It sounds like the sort of thing she'd ask Dad, not me. I do a sort of feeble laugh.

"She's started sounding American. That's embarrassing." Ma doesn't join in the laugh. I try again. "I suppose… It's weird because she's been off for months having a life that we don't know anything about."

"That's exactly it," Ma says quietly. "It's the strangest thing, once your children begin to exist entirely without you." She starts the car. "You'll know what I mean when you have kids."

"Yeah, that's not happening," I mumble into my coat.

Ma's phone pings from somewhere; she fumbles to get it out quickly.

"Gaia?"

"Nope." She shakes her head. "Text from Addy."

"What does she say?"

Ma looks at the phone a moment longer.

"Craig…the ski instructor? He was the one who was supposed to be walking Gaia home, wasn't he?"

I nod.

"Okay," Ma inhales sharply. "According to Addy, Craig is missing too."

CHAPTER FOUR

———

Dad is lounging on the arm of the big armchair in the lodge, looking like a weight has dropped from his shoulders.

"Julia," he says, trying not to laugh, "I'm not thrilled about it either. But at least Gaia's not dead in a ditch somewhere."

Through the archway to the kitchen, a cleaner pauses to look quizzically at us before hurrying away with a shocked expression on her face. When Ma and I arrived back at the lodge, we were greeted by a whole team of ladies dressed in white overalls and armed with buckets and vacuum cleaners.

"Don't say that, Jim!" Ma hisses furiously. "And of course I'm upset. Craig is closer to your age than Gaia's!"

Dad snorts. "Massive exaggeration." He turns at me. "How old would you say Craig is?"

Uh-oh. Wrong person to ask.

"Old-ish." I shrug. "But not nearly as old as you. Early thirties?"

"That's bad enough, she's only nineteen!" Ma shouts.

One of the cleaners enters the room very tentatively, holding a cloth and a spray bottle. She makes for the first window and begins cleaning the glass with a series of loud squeaks.

"Look," says Dad. "Just because they are missing together doesn't mean they are…" he glances at me, like I'm still nine or something, "…*doing anything else* together."

Squeeeeeak. The cleaner pauses.

"I don't think for a moment that they are!" Ma glares at Dad, totally contradicting herself. The cleaner moves to the second window very slowly, as if she thinks that makes her invisible. "Because it's not like Gaia. Not like her at all."

We all stare into space as the cleaner begins on the second window. She's trying to be quick and silent, and it turns out that you can't be both. With each squeak I can feel Ma coming closer to losing it.

"I have Craig's number!" she shouts suddenly. "Because of Esme's ski lessons."

"Er, Julia—should we?" Dad says. "We don't want to sound like we're…accusing him of anything. Especially if Gaia is about to roll in, red-faced an' all."

We look at the door as if that's going to happen. But it stays shut.

"We're only calling to ask him if he's seen her. It's perfectly all right." Ma shakes herself and dials. "Voicemail," she swears, then puts on her sweetest voice and leaves him an oh-so-chipper message. "His phone must be switched off. It didn't even ring."

"Guys," I say gently. "Why don't we go to Craig's house? I dunno, maybe they got stuck in the basement or something?"

Ma stares at me in horror. "Is that possible?"

"I have no idea!" I hold up my hands. "I mean, maybe."

Ma looks fraught. Dad thumps the arm of the chair. Upstairs, the vacuuming is reaching fever pitch. *Oh, this is too much.* Suddenly, I feel a Gaia-like power surge through me.

"Ma, call reception." I fetch the cordless landline phone. "Let them know we're looking for Gaia. They might be able to check places we haven't thought of. Maybe they have security guards who could have a look around."

Ma gulps, and nods.

"Might be something silly like she's shut herself in a bathroom or a gym changing room." I'm totally pulling this out of my ass, is that even feasible? But Ma is buying it, and I'm giving her a *plan.* She understands plans. "Message Addy again—she can put the word out to everyone Gaia and Craig know." *God, I'm on fire here.* "And I'm guessing we're not going to Boston today. We need to arrange to stay another night." As if to make my point, a huge bundle of bedsheets is tossed down the stairs, landing with a thud.

"Not go to Boston?" Ma looks incredulous. "Of course we're going to Boston! As soon as Gaia gets back!"

I put a hand on her arm. "Contingency. Let's have the option." I'm chancing it, but it is the language she knows, and unbelievably, there's a nod.

"Okay, Es. You're right. Clever thing."

I turn quickly, totally thrown at how choked up that compliment makes me feel.

"Come on, Dad, we'll go to Craig's. I know the way."

Well, kind of.

"Everything looks different in the light." I grit my teeth, the stiff breeze making my eyes water as I scan the road ahead.

We'd trotted down the lane past the lodges, our heads swiveling from side to side like we're expecting Gaia to suddenly shinny down a pine tree, or jack-in-the-box from a garbage bin and shout, "Surprise!" I'd had a minor victory remembering there was a tunnel under the road we had to walk through—that's where I'd slipped last night—but now we're at a crossroads, and I'm stuck.

I can hear crows cawing in the distance. It seems like everything is dripping; the remaining snow melting fast in the bright sun. And then I see it through the trees. The rounded, red roof of a barn, looking completely out of place among the other buildings. That boy Bode's barn. And opposite a sign saying *Bluff Point*, and the party house.

"There it is!"

Oh bloody hell, what will we find at Craig's? This is going to be awkward AF if she's there. Ma is right, the Gaia she knows wouldn't have hooked up with some slightly creepy, older ski instructor. But we're all playing catch-up; after everything that went down at the at the party last night, I'm still processing the revised version of my sister.

Dad bounds up the steps to the deck, his face grim when he raps on the door. When that doesn't immediately work, he grabs at the handle, and turns it.

"Should we wait…?" I say, but Dad has already gone in. *Okay.* This is our new normal.

The living room seems much smaller than it did last night, and dingy, blinds drawn. The detritus of the party—cans and bottles and a bunch of plates—are strewn on the coffee table and the floor by the fire. There's the slightest whiff of smoke and I wonder if Dad smells it too.

"Hello?" Dad opens a window blind; light streams in, dust particles flying in the air like fairies. "How many people were here last night?"

I do a little mental count and instantly lose track. "Twenty? Sorry, I didn't know most of them."

Dad walks over to the shabby sofa by the woodstove. There's the indentation in the cushions where I'd sat most of last night.

After I'd escaped the kitchen, I'd slunk back into the living room, feeling sick at heart. This party was going to be a write-off. I sipped the kiddie drink that Craig had sarcastically dumped in my hand, managing to spill it down my top. While I was trying to nonchalantly wipe it away, I saw a movement out of the corner of my eye. It was Bode, beckoning me over.

"Hey, you find your sister?" He turned to a boy on his right, a huge guy with a padded shirt straining at the buttons and a black beanie pulled down around his full face. "Scoot down, dude; Es needs a seat."

"No need, it's okay." I protested, but his friend balanced precariously on the groaning arm of the sofa, making it rude to refuse. The cushion was warm where he'd been sitting. "Sorry if I'm squashing everyone."

"What, compared to my man Giganto there?" Bode laughed. "No need to apologize. You're so British." His friends laughed too, but not in a horrible way.

"Guilty."

Bode threw up a hand. "Not a bad thing." He gestured to "Giganto." "This is Jai," and to a lithe kid with a baby Afro, baggy jeans, and an oversized sweater. "This is Keith." He leaned in and fake whispered to me. "We're the persona non grata kids here, in case you hadn't noticed." He grinned and chugged a beer. "We're not cool, we're locals. Only reason I get invited is so they can bribe me to keep my uncle off their backs for all the stuff that goes down in these houses."

"Does that work?"

Jai and Keith guffawed, and Bode smiled at me under his mop of curls.

"So long as they don't burn the place down, my uncle doesn't stress much. And if I have a beer with them, it means he's got eyes on the ground."

"Win-win!" said Jai.

"Win for you, brother!" Keith laughed. "You wouldn't be getting your ass invited any other way!"

"Whaddya talking about?" Jai raised his arms in a shrug. "These rich chicks love me!"

"Dream on, bud." Bode chuckled.

"Yeah, trust fund hippies," Keith said, turning to me. "No disrespect."

"None taken." I took a sip of my drink. "Although, FYI, we're not rich. Addy's family paid for us to stay here."

"That Addison family, they own everyone in Moon!" Keith shrugged. "Your sister, though; she's not like the rest of these fools."

"True," Jai said. "It kinda helps that she looks the way she looks, also."

"Jai, man!" Bode leaned across me and hit him on his massive arm.

"What?" Jai's face crumpled. "She's a whole lotta woman! I'm just saying!"

"What he is trying to articulate," said Keith. "Your sister, she is a *class act*."

And then the thing happened. With Gaia. The thing that made me want to disappear down the back of the sofa like a pocketful of change. The thing that I'm not going to tell my parents about...yet.

"Somebody there?"

The shout brings me back to the present with a start. I look at Dad. For a split second, I'm sure we both think it's my sister.

"I'm in back!" *Nope.* Definitely American, male.

Dad and I hurry down the hall to the kitchen.

By the window, right where Gaia and Addy had been

smoking the night before, a figure leans against the counter, hunched over a phone. He turns and dazzles me with a smile that makes my heart skip a beat.

Scott.

Scott.

Oh god, Scott.

My sister's boss. Her new BFF. And—I remember it now, how could I forget?—the person who she'd been talking to on the stairs when she told me she'd follow me home last night.

Scott smiles, and I feel my face on fire. I can't help it. Every time he looks at me, I want to Actually Die.

You see, even though we only met in person a week ago, Scott and I have *major* history.

CHAPTER FIVE

———

Scott "Hot" Mazzulo was in my bedroom when I was nine years old.

That sounds way worse than it was. Scott Mazzulo stared down at me from posters ripped from *Tween Girl* and *Gl!tter* magazine. Scott Mazzulo was my first crush. Scott Mazzulo was bye-bye Barbies, hello mood swings and sweaty armpits.

I discovered him one week when I was sick with chicken pox and my harassed parents were using TV as a babysitter. Scott was on a short-lived reality show called *Rival Roomies*, about a house of teens auditioning to be in a boy band. I lay on the couch that glorious week, itched my spots, and binge-watched Scott's every move. He was the oldest of the kids, dreamy-looking and funny but kind of, I dunno, misunderstood and wise beyond his years? He was vegetarian too, which started me off on my whole vegan track... Anyway, I identified. I had all the feels by the end of the first episode and thrilled beyond all reckoning when he made the final cut for the band.

Gaia delighted in becoming my enabler—she downloaded the band's hits, printed out pictures…and had a good laugh at my expense. The band didn't last long, though; they faded away with my chicken pox scars, and I mourned Scott with an intensity that had previously been reserved for the death of our cat, Mop. But I moved on. And I didn't think of Scott again until five months ago.

It was an evening—I was lying on my bed reading—and Ma burst into my room in a way that is entirely unacceptable. She was holding her phone and wearing the biggest smirk.

"It's Gaia calling from America!" She thrust the phone at me, bubbling with way too much excitement, and I should have known something was up. But there's no way I could have guessed *what*.

"Hey, Esme." A face beamed at me from the phone. "Great to finally meet you!"

I blinked. Not the right face. Not my sister's handsome, brown face with the thick, arched eyebrows and the bouncing hair. A smooth, shiny-faced man stared back at me, blushed pink, with high cheekbones and startling blue eyes. The same blue eyes that had twinkled down on me from my bedroom wall all those years ago.

"Don't you recognize me?" Scott laughed in that cute way he does.

I was holding the phone and for a split second, I actually thought that this was all Ma's doing, because, let's face it, it's so easy to blame your mother for everything. But then Gaia came into view on the screen, laughing and jostling with *my childhood boyfriend* (yeah, I know that sounds wrong), and worlds are colliding and minds are being blown and *aargh* my skin is spotted with zit cream and I'm in my oldest pj's with the rabbit pattern and this was *not* the way I would ever intend to meet Scott Mazzulo.

Scott, it turned out, was my sister's new boss at the resort. After his fifteen minutes of fame, he'd gone back home to Moonville and gotten a real job. *He's lovely*, Gaia said, *so down to earth, hilarious, we get up to mucho mischief!* Oh, but *we're not dating*, Gaia assured me—Scott wasn't into girls, a fact which hurt my nine-year-old self's heart.

Me? I was jealous. Scott was my pinup, not hers. So stupid—like I should even care anymore!—but that's what I felt. Now I've met him in the flesh, all I feel is embarrassed. Gaia actually told him I'd crushed on him. *Mortifying.* That was years ago! Okay, yeah, so six years ago. But as Scott should know, that's a lifetime.

When Scott realizes it's Dad and me coming into the kitchen, the smile vanishes, and his expression switches to stricken.

"Mr. Gill—Es—has Gaia turned up yet? Please say yes." He fiddles with his phone a second, holding it up as if he's trying to get a signal. "Oh my goodness, Mr. Gill, have you hurt your hand?" He nods to Dad's bandaged phone finger. "You guys should sit, can I get you something?" He opens the fridge and grabs a can with his free hand. "Soda?"

Dad shakes his head, but it's too late, I've already taken the can. It's so ice cold it's almost burning my hand off, but I can't return it now.

"You don't live here," Dad frowns.

"God, no!" Scott says, quickly. "I have a place in town. Lost my phone last night, came back to find it." He's standing with one arm bent, holding his phone up, as if to show us.

"You were at the party."

"Sure!" Scott says. "But Mr. Gill, I left before your daughter did." He glances at his phone. "Pretty much after Esme went home."

"Did Gaia look like she was going to leave soon after? She told Es she'd follow her."

Scott flicks a look at me. "Oh yeah." He smiles, quickly, then back to serious. "Honestly, I could not say for certain, Mr. Gill. I remember someone offering to walk her home— back to your lodge."

"Craig," I say.

Scott breathes out, heavily. "I do believe it was."

"Who is also not around today," my dad mutters.

"True." Scott grimaces at my dad. "It's kind of odd for Craig to be a no-show for a free brunch though."

"Yep…" Dad is glowering. His eyes are darting back and forth to the phone Scott is still holding up. "Scott…?" Dad says slowly, taking on the tone that Gaia and I call his Shit List Voice. "You're not…filming this, are you?"

"Do you think something could have happened to them?" Scott ignores the question.

"Scott! Your phone!" Dad is clenching his hands, even the one with the poorly finger. I really hope he's not going to wallop Scott. It would be completely out of character, but that seems to be how my family is rolling today. "Are you filming this?"

"Say, Lucille lives here," Scott beams at us and pockets the phone. "She might know something. Lucille!" He rushes past us, out into the corridor.

Dad leaves the kitchen in hot pursuit and I finally ditch the can and follow. Scott whips around.

"Lucille's staying for summer. I thought I heard her come in when I was in the kitchen, but maybe that was you guys." He looks at us with those heavy-lidded blue eyes, each eyelash well defined. He's clean shaven, product in his hair. So out of place among these scruffy snow bunnies.

"Let's be sure," Dad flings doors open—a bedroom, a closet, the toilet. He finds the basement and practically throws himself down the steps in semidarkness, only to emerge a few seconds later, his face a strange mixture of grim disappointment and relief. But he doesn't pause; Scott and I follow as Dad takes the stairs two at a time. "Hello?" He opens the first bedroom. It's been emptied.

"Greg and Shantay's room, they've left for Canada." Scott says. "They're engaged, though Lord knows that won't last."

Greg and Shantay. The couple in the car Ma and I passed earlier.

Dad sighs, impatiently. The door to the next bedroom is stiff. He gives it a shove and finds out why. Clothes, books, ski gear. A camping stove, makeup, and food wrappers. As small as the room is, there's so much crap it takes us a second to establish there's no human inside.

"Lucille." Scott tuts. "Yeah."

I've moved to the next door. As I open it, a strong smell of cleaning fluid hits. It's a bathroom, no room for anyone to be hiding here. There's a bucket on the floor by the toilet, with rubber gloves beside it.

"Yeuch," Scott wrinkles his nose. "Guess someone got a little sick last night." He shakes his head, backing away. "Some kids can't hold their drink."

"Some *kids* shouldn't be drinking," my dad corrects him.

"Absolutely, Mr. Gill." Scott nods. "But Gaia and Addy are old enough to be legal in the UK, right?"

"You think it was Gaia who was sick?" Dad says.

Scott shrugs. "I would not have said so, Mr. Gill, but I left the party earlier than her, you know?" Before my dad can say anything, Scott points to the final door. "Craig's bedroom. He has the master. Of course."

Dad pushes the door open with way more force than necessary.

It's a large, airy room with a view of the woods. There's a desk with a *Ski USA* magazine, some toiletries on a windowsill, and a huge—seriously massive—zipped sports bag on the floor.

My father coughs, walks over to the bag, and unzips it. We've all seen the movies and we all know why he does it.

It's almost embarrassing when there are only ski boots and helmets inside.

Better than a dead body, however.

"God, it's freezing in here!" I shiver. The far window is open a crack; Dad goes over and shuts it. He tries the double closet next, flinging the doors open like he's expecting someone to be hiding there. Ski wear, neatly folded. A pair of jeans hanging, a couple of checked shirts. Socks, balled, on a shelf. Underwear actually laid out flat on another shelf.

"Orderly fellow, isn't he?" Dad growls.

I notice a metal beer keg, standing by the bedside table, and frown. Craig had that in the kitchen last night. Did he carry it upstairs to enjoy by himself...or with someone else?

Crouching by the immaculately made bed, I pretend to fiddle with my sock. If my sister was here, maybe she dropped something, a hair tie or her lip balm? And then I get a sudden urge... *I'd recognize her scent on his sheets.* I lean forward, and sniff. Laundry detergent, with a low note of male ski instructor. I clock Scott watching me and know in an instant that he gets what I'm doing. Dad is staring out of the window, but Scott looks appalled, and also, somehow, in awe. I straighten up, feeling my face flush hot.

"Are they dating, Gaia and Craig?" Dad is still fixated on the trees. "She hasn't mentioned it, but then again, why would she?" He looks supremely awkward and a little sad. "You'd tell me, Scott?"

"Of course, sir." Scott's eyes grow big.

"How old is he, actually?" Dad does an embarrassed half laugh. "Thirties? Quite an age gap. Got to wonder why an adult is still hanging out with a bunch of teenagers." *Hmm, that's shade, Dad.* Scott's in his mid-twenties.

"I hear you," Scott says evenly. "It's the lodge lifestyle, Mr. Gill. Attracts all ages."

"Uh-huh," says my dad. "What did Craig *attract*, eh?" His phone rings. He fishes it out of his back pocket, looks at it, puzzled—I think he's forgotten the smashed screen. "Damn!"

"Can you see who's calling?" I lean over.

"Es, out of the way! I can't swipe, the screen's too cracked!"

"Let me, I've got smaller fingers." I go to take the phone and bungle it, and the stupid thing hits the floor. Dad gives me a furious look, bends to pick it up; small pieces of glass fall off.

Downstairs, the door slams.

"Gaia?" Dad shouts, and all three of us run out of the room to the stairs.

In the living room, a small blond with a goggle tan looks up at us.

"Lucille!" Scott runs down the stairs.

"Hey, Scott," she says lazily.

"Have you seen Gaia and Craig?"

"What?" The girl goes over to the sofa and throws herself down on it. "Holy cow, I am beat." *Where do I know her from? Yes*—I think she was one half of the couple making out that I bumped into on the deck when I left the party.

"Did you see my daughter last night? Did she leave with Craig?"

Lucille peers at Dad from behind a wound-up scarf. "You Gee's dad?" She rubs her face. "Can't say I remember anything much about last night, dude. But don't worry, Gee knows how to handle Craigy."

"What does that mean?"

"Whatever, hon." She yawns. "Maybe she's giving him a sweet goodbye."

"Come on, Es." Dad growls, flinging the front door open. "That was probably your mother on the phone. We're wasting our time here."

CHAPTER SIX

As we reach our lodge, I can see Addy's car and a large four-wheel drive parked outside. My heart leaps. *Gaia?* Dad breaks into a run. The front door is open, and we clatter up the steps of the deck.

My mother and all of the Addisons—Addy, Eli, and parents, Adam and Claire—are standing in the living room like a miserable welcome party. I can tell Ma's trying not to pace. By the window, Addy looks as if she's been crying. My chest tightens.

"News?" Dad tries to sound casual.

"She wasn't there?" Ma's face is sheet white.

"No." Dad goes to hug her, but she's not giving off hugging vibes so he squeezes her arm instead. "We saw Scott and one of Craig's housemates, Lucille..."

"And nobody knows anything." She finishes off Dad's sentence. "No news here either. I tried calling reception... They weren't too helpful, initially."

"But then I had a word!" Adam Addison claps his hands together. "Came as soon as I heard, Jim."

"We were planning to stay another night anyway." Claire Addison bats her long lashes. "So don't worry about that." Ma and Dad smile politely, but I can see that was the last thing on their minds. "And I brought wine! Can't hurt!" She flourishes a bottle and clacks off to the kitchen in her heels. Eli has the decency to look a little embarrassed by her remark, and for that I decide I can tolerate him.

"You folks are all set to stay too. No charge, we've got you covered. Helps when you are related to the owner," Adam Addison says, for about the hundredth time this week. It makes me want to crack him over the head with his wife's bottle of wine. "The resort is a little short-staffed, given its changeover week and a Sunday, but I'm assured they'll get people out searching. Got the head of security—man called Seymour, ex–chief of police, no less—coming over to speak to you. Pulled him in on his day off, specially."

"Oh, great, that's great." Dad leans on the back of a chair as if he's suddenly very tired.

"Now there is a sheriff's office in town," Adam continues, "but it's only manned until 4:00 p.m. on a Sunday, so we've missed it. Otherwise, you're looking at the police in New Lanchester, thirty, forty minutes away. Don't think you want to pull the trigger on that, so to speak. Wiser to wait until morning rather than drag the city cops out here."

Ma and Dad look completely befuddled.

"Cops?" I say. "Is it… I mean, are we there yet?" Suddenly, this feels way too serious. "Dad, don't we think she's just with Craig? Don't we have to wait twenty-four hours or something?"

"Exactly!" Adam Addison jumps in before my parents can reply. "It's premature to be calling the police. Chances are the two of them are fine! I'm sure you don't want to attract bad attention for the resort, cause a fuss unnecessarily." He smiles. "Let's keep this in-house for the time being."

Wow. Did he just say that? By the look on Ma's face, she thinks he did. Things are about to go nuclear.

"Addy!" I'm not sure what's going to come out, but I have to say something to stop Ma before she blows. "Gaia never said anything to me, but is Craig her boyfriend?"

Addy sniffs. "I want to say no."

"What does that mean, you *want* to say?" Dad's eyes narrow. "Yes or no?"

Addy looks at me and I nod encouragingly. She turns back to Dad.

"It means *no*. But I think—I know—that he would *like* to be her boyfriend."

"Was he, like, putting the moves on her?" I ask.

Addy shrugs. "Sometimes, I guess. I mean, Craig can be a pest, but Gee has dealt with *way* worse," I feel Ma tense up again. It can hardly be news to her that Gaia gets hit on, but for sure she doesn't want to think about it. "I don't think he'd do anything bad—be violent or anything," Addy says quickly, "But…" She crosses her arms, defensively. "If you're wondering if they have…gone off together…" she looks at the floor, "for the night…well, yeah. Gee might have been down with that."

"Gee!" Dad mutters. "When did my daughter become reduced to 'Gee'?"

"Excuse me, Jim." Adam Addison's voice is ice cold. "It's not my daughter who's done something wrong here."

"And mine has?" Dad looks at him sharply.

"No! Stop!" Addy gets between them, a blush spreading across her pale cheeks. "I'm sorry. I should have told you when Gaia wasn't at the brunch, but I didn't think it was important."

"It's okay, Addy." Ma purses her lips. "When this head of security person gets here, you can tell him all about it. And *everything* that happened at the party last night."

"Julia." Adam Addison holds his hand up. "Don't forget, the girls are underage in the United States as far as drinking goes. Let's not get into anything that could taint their college records before they even start."

My mother pauses, but only for a beat.

"Adam, my daughter is missing. Right now, my only concern is that we get her back. I couldn't give a *flying fig* about anybody's college record."

She doesn't say *fig*.

Fortunately for everyone, Addy's phone beeps, and she jumps, tucking a strand of her red hair behind her ear nervously.

"I literally pinged everyone at Moon…" We all hold our breath as she checks her messages. "It's one of the guys from the equipment store." Addy shakes her head. "Gaia was supposed to pick up her skis this morning, but she didn't show."

Dad digs out his phone. "Did you call me before, Julia? The screen's busted."

"Wasn't me," Ma says. "But it could have been Gaia."

"The truck," Eli says suddenly. "You went to Craig's house—did you notice if his truck was there?"

"Didn't know he had one."

"Piece of crap Chevy pickup," says Eli. "*Orange*."

"It's vintage, a classic—he's restoring it," Addy says. "And it's 'Burnt Sienna,' kind of rust colored."

"Yeah, you got that right!" Eli says. "Rust bucket. Idiot thinks it's an investment, but I bet it broke down somewhere."

"Sharp thinking!" Adam Addison slaps his son on the back, as if Eli's totally cracked the case. "Vehicle like that can't stay hidden long. When security gets here, they'll be on it straight away." He looks around at us, beaming, as though expecting a round of applause.

"Who do we call to track the vehicle...?" Ma pulls out her phone. "Highway Patrol? Is that the same as the police?"

Mr. Addison wags a finger. "Seymour—head of security—will advise. Best to wait." He moves to the window. "Should be here any moment."

Ma looks unconvinced.

"Pop," Eli jumps in. "I've got to go collect Addy's luggage. Why don't I swing by Craig's house and check for the truck?"

"Great idea, Eli! Get on it." Mr. Addison says.

"The parking lot is at the back of the cul-de-sac." Addy grabs her coat. "It's kind of hidden—I'd better show you."

"Addy." Ma puts a hand on her arm. "Please stay. You have all the friends' numbers, you know Gaia's routine, the places she goes. I want to put a list together…"

"I'll come with you, Eli. We'll find it," I suddenly find myself saying. Not that I'm overly anxious to spend time with him, but anything is better than staying here.

"That's decided," Adam Addison says. There's a knock on the door. "Oh—perfect!" He opens the door and there's an old man sporting a ginger mustache and an oversized Scout hat. "Officer Seymour!" He shakes the man's hand. "Adam Addison, come in. Do we call you 'Officer'?"

"Chief'll do it." Seymour coughs, takes his hat off, and stamps imaginary snow from his boots. He doesn't look too thrilled to be pulled away from his Sunday afternoon at home to deal with us. "Mr. Addison, pleasure to meet you." Seymour nods to him, then turns to my dad. "And you're the father of the girl?"

"Jim Gill." My dad stretches out to shake his hand. "This is my wife, Julia, my daughter, Esme."

"Oh, she turned up!" Seymour smiles, visions of dinner and TV sports reruns restored.

"No," Ma says. "It's our elder daughter, Gaia, who's missing." She flicks the screen on her phone. "She's nineteen, she works at the resort, you may have seen her around. Here's a picture."

Seymour squints at Ma's phone, then his eyes dart to Dad and me.

"She adopted?"

Dad's jaw tenses, but Ma's an expert at dealing with this.

"No. Gaia is my daughter from my previous relationship."

Seymour's face relaxes. "I was gonna say, she don't look like her folks or that's some suntan!"

There's a stunned silence, where we collectively pinch ourselves.

"Right," Eli says. "I'm going."

"Me too!" I chime in.

"Anyone for pinot?" Mrs. Addison reappears from the kitchen with wineglasses aloft, and Eli and I get the hell out.

CHAPTER SEVEN

———

Eli is hunched over the steering wheel of Addy's car; I sit in the passenger seat as we drive achingly slowly to the party house on Bluff Point. Some narcissists drive too fast, but Eli makes you want to get out and push.

"She's not *with* Craig," Eli says suddenly. "And if I see him first, so help me god…"

"Er, *okay*." I shift in my seat. "That makes no sense. She's not *with* him, but you're going to kill him." Eli's face tenses, but he won't let himself react. "How do you know they're not together, anyway?"

"Pah!" Spit flies out of Eli's mouth as he crawls round the corner into the cul-de-sac. "She would never."

Irritation buzzes through me. "What do you even mean by that, Eli? Gaia can do what she likes."

Eli glances at me. "You've noticed she's changed."

"So?" He may be right, but I wouldn't let him know it bothers me. "People do, don't they?"

Eli doesn't speak for a moment, pulls over at Craig's house, turns the engine off. "Craig's a loser, a waste of space. And Scott's fake, a totally moronic reality star has-been. She shouldn't be hanging out with people like them."

"Well, she won't be," I unclip my seat belt. "She's finished working here, she's moving on."

"Yeah, but they're going with her. Didn't she tell you?"

My hand is on the door. "What do you mean?"

"To the Cape!" He shouts at me, like I'm completely dumb, which I definitely feel right now. "Scott's got some made-up 'social media ambassador' job at the beach resort Gaia and Addy are working at, and Craig—god knows what he's doing, but he's tagging along for the ride, hoping they'll pay his way, no doubt."

"Pay?" I stare at him. "Are you loopy? Gaia doesn't have any money." I'm hurt that she hasn't mentioned any of this to me, but maybe Eli is full of it. And yet… "This is stupid. We need to find the truck." I get out of the car. "Are you coming?"

He doesn't look at me. "No. You can walk back. I'm going to her digs. There might be something you've missed."

"Sure, Eli." I shut the door heavily. He starts up the car and crawls down the lane, still hunched over the wheel.

I walk slowly around the perimeter of the cul-de-sac, anger and upset cramping my stomach. Eli's *wrong*, Gaia would've told me if Craig and Scott were going with them to the beach job. Or would she? Either way, does it matter? Only now she's missing. Suddenly, every little whim or half plan she might have made seems massively significant.

Where's this parking lot, anyway? The silent houses of Bluff Point look down on me, seemingly empty. It's very quiet here. The woods surrounding the cul-de-sac feel claustrophobic, like they're closing in on me. I shudder, crossing my arms across my chest tightly, telling myself I'm shivering because it's chilly. I can feel my heartbeat quicken beneath my coat. I suddenly feel very alone.

Don't be stupid. Get on with it.

Clambering up onto a messy pile of compacted snow gives me a better view.

Suddenly, there's a bang and I lose my balance, arms windmilling, feet slipping, narrowly saving myself from another ass-planting on the hard sidewalk. What the hell was that noise? Crouching behind the snow pile, I peer out. At the house at the bottom of the cul-de-sac, a door has been flung open and a figure wearing a hoodie and hat with earflaps runs out and disappears around the back of the building. Can't tell if it's male or female, but it's not my sister, nor is it tall enough to be Craig. I make myself walk toward where the person disappeared and a car emerges from a lane that was hidden from my view by a fence. The car is driven by a boy maybe Gaia's age; it stops and a window jerks down.

"Yo, Sean! We rollin'."

A second guy comes out of the house, slamming the door shut behind him. I hurry to meet the car.

"Hi!" I say. "Do you live here?"

"Not for much longer." The driver looks at me quizzically, as his friend gets in the passenger seat and cranks up the dubstep on the stereo. "You lost?"

"I'm looking for someone." I bend down a little. "You weren't at the party last night, at Craig's house?"

"No way," laughs the driver. "Wouldn't be caught dead at that dude's place. Who ya lookin' for?"

"Do you know Gaia? Gaia Gill?"

"Sure, English chick!" says the driver.

"That's right." I nod. "Have you seen her today?"

"You wish you'd seen Gaia!" The passenger speaks for the first time, laughing at his friend. "Man, I'd like to *see* her!" They both laugh, then the driver punches his friend on the arm.

"Shut up, man!" He nods at me. "You her friend?"

"Sister. She's kind of *gone missing*"—the words sound fake in my mouth, like I'm making this up—"so, um, if you see her, can you call us?" I scrabble around in my pocket for a pen. "Got a bit of paper?"

"Got a bit of paper!" The passenger parrots my accent, sounding like Mary Poppins.

"Shut up, asshole!" Driver punches him again, he yells and leans back in the seat, laughing. "What's the number?"

Oh god. My mother's number. I can't remember numbers, it's one of my dyspraxic things. I rack my brains.

"Shoot!" Driver guy is waiting.

"We're in Lodge 11, up on Hillview, you know it?" Driver guy is putting his phone away. "Do you know Addy Addison, her friend? Could you call her if you hear anything?"

"Hmm, I'd really like to *know* Addy," guffaws the passenger.

The driver laughs and pulls away. "Good luck, sweets! Hope you find your sister."

"Craig too!" I shout after them. "He's gone! If you see him, let us know, they might be together—"

The car speeds up, turns the corner, and disappears.

Damn, so not good at this.

At least I know where the parking lot is now. I run down the lane between two houses and see a paved area, hidden from the road by trees and surrounded by a chain-link fence. It's big enough to hold…twelve, fifteen cars at most? There's a quad bike and a huge snowplow at the front of the lot, parked beside some massive dustbins and a recycling thing. Behind the bins there's a white van with Moon Mountain's logo on the side, and a couple of cars toward the back. I walk toward them—a silver car called an Oldsmobile, a navy Subaru, and—bingo!—a Chevy pickup truck, in the corner. It's covered with a thick crust of ice, and there are little borders of snow around it on the ground; this is not a truck that's been anywhere recently. I run my hand over the hood, scraping at the ice; the paint is faded red, not orange, and although the truck looks like it's seen some miles, it's definitely not what I'd call vintage.

So, Craig's car isn't here. What does that mean?

I decide it makes me feel better. Casting my eyes across the lot for any signs of where a car might have been recently, I spot an outline where it looks like water has dripped down. There is a skid mark near the entrance too, and oil drips, but what does that tell me? Nothing useful.

The sun has moved behind a swath of gray, and the air is definitely getting chillier as the afternoon begins to think about jacking it all in for the evening. I jump as a crow drops onto the pavement in front of me and pecks at a burger wrapper.

"Gaia and Craig have probably eloped in his crappy orange truck," I say, my voice sounding too loud. The crow puts its head on one side and looks at me. "That's gross," I tell the crow, "but as Dad so touchingly put it, it's better than her being dead in a ditch somewhere."

A voice calls from behind me.

"They don't talk back. I've tried."

CHAPTER EIGHT

"Crows."

Bode is standing a few feet away in the entrance of the parking lot. "Not too chatty."

His dark blond curls look even wilder today, like he slept in a hedge. He's wearing jeans and a fuzzy sweater, and big boots with laces trailing as he walks slowly toward me.

The crow hops on to the hood of the frozen truck and caws, bang on cue. Bode laughs.

"Hey, what do I know? He probably likes your accent."

"Caw! Caw!" I join in. *I can't help myself.* I actually flap my lil' wings. Bode's eyes widen.

"Right on, you speak his language!" His head bobs as he laughs, the curls doing a dance.

I laugh too, lower my arms in a kind of hey-I-do-this-all-the-time way, while simultaneously making a mental note to never, *ever*, do a crow impersonation in front of a boy that I like.

How do I follow that?

I sniff. Bode scratches his neck.

"So, I'm emptying the trash, and you're…communicating with the birdies?" Bode squints at me.

"Not exactly." I take the plunge. "Although I wish crows *could* speak. He might have seen what happened to my sister. She's missing."

"Whoa!" Bode's mouth drops open. "That was some conversational one-eighty."

"Sorry," I kick at a loose stone, feeling cheap, and try to walk it back a little. "She's probably fine, but we can't find her. Did you notice her leave the party last night?"

He crosses his arms. "That when she was last seen?"

"We think so."

"And you guys are flying home later?"

"Actually tomorrow, but we're supposed to be driving to Boston today." I sigh, pull my coat around me. "It's not like her to be a no-show. That's normally my trick."

"Oh yeah?" He raises his eyebrows but doesn't question further. "Man," He walks around in a little circle, eyes on the ground. "Okay, so, I'm thinking, last night… You musta left the house around one?"

"No idea, unfortunately. I'm not great with time."

"I guess I didn't stay too much longer. Half hour? Whatever, I was out by two." He pulls a face. "But yeah—a bunch of people left the party same time as me."

"Was Gaia one of them?"

"Let me think…" He shuts his eyes for a second. "Nope. There was me and the guys, and most of the kids your sister works with, but not Gaia." He stares at the pavement for a moment. "You know what? She was long gone."

"Really?"

"For sure." He looks at me. "Scott? He left after you. He freaked out because he'd lost his phone, and I helped the guy look for it, searched most of the rooms in the dang house. No sign of your sister then."

"Scott said he left before her." I frown.

"Maybe he thought he did." Bode shrugs. "He was all wrapped up in finding the phone. Major drama."

"Okay," I breathe, trying to work out what it all means. "How about Craig? She was supposed to be walking home with him."

Bode gives me a look. "They together? Together-together?"

I feel my cheeks get hot. "You tell me. You've probably seen them more than I have."

"I mean, I would say just friends on her part…" Bode hesitates. "Dude has got a rep with women, though." He rubs the back of his neck.

"It's fine, I just want to find her."

He glances at me. "They hung out, but she kept him at arm's length. Gaia and Addy had those ski lift jerks they live with chasing them, and sometimes Addy played." He holds a hand up. "No judgment!—but I never noticed your sister being that interested in anyone…" He breathes out heavily. "This is coming out weird—sounds like I've been stalking them, but I haven't! I guess I just notice things."

"It's okay, it's useful!" I believe him. I can't completely work him out, but I don't get any creeper vibes.

"What I'm saying is—" he shrugs, "—I wouldn't have guessed she'd be, er, involved with Craig, but anything's possible."

"I came to look for his truck." I turn around to the assorted vehicles. "And it's not here."

"No, it is not. Man, your folks must be losing it."

"Yeah." I walk in the direction of the houses. "I should really get back. They've got some head of security bloke talking to them at the moment."

"Old Man Seymour?" Bode follows. "That dinosaur. He was an okay cop once in town, but I don't think he's dealt with more than extremely petty-petty crime, up mountain."

"Thanks for the info." I turn and shoot him a brief smile.

"Anytime," Bode says, returning the smile, but his is way nicer; it's warm and his teeth are really great and those hazel eyes with flecks of amber... I start walking again. *Wow*, I cannot have distractions like *that*. He follows. "I can help you look, you know, if she doesn't show?" We reach the end of the road. "My uncle will be home later." He cocks a thumb to the house. "Knows the mountain inside out. We got wheels too, if you need 'em." He fishes in his back pocket and brings out a pen. "Hey, do I remember you saying last night you don't have a phone? Or was that just letting me down easy?"

I gulp. "No. I dropped it. From about fifty feet."

He looks at me in disbelief. "You bring a tablet or something?"

"Nope." I shrug. "It doesn't bother me. My parents are like the only ones in the world who are worried their kid doesn't spend all day staring at a screen. I don't really do socials. Hate it."

"Wow." Bode nods. "Impressive. Kinda think that makes you more evolved. You got some paper on you?" When I shake my head, he grins and rolls up my left sleeve. "This okay?" I nod a little too enthusiastically, and he writes a number on the back of my hand in black Sharpie. His hand is warm on my wrist, and the pen tickles. "Call if you need help. Heck, she probably got stuck in town. I've heard Craig pulls lame moves. He'll be like, 'Hey, babe, it's late, guess we'll have to stay in this cozy motel.'" He rolls his eyes.

"He does that?"

Bode looks embarrassed, like he's shared too much. "Sure. My friend Jai, you met last night? He works at the Eazy Stay on Route 16. He's seen Craig there, more than once."

"Could you possibly call him? Jai, I mean? Ask him if they're there?"

"Right on." Bode nods. "He's working today." He makes the call, holding the phone up to his ear for a moment before hanging up. "Guess Jai's MIA too." He smiles ruefully. "Sorry, bad joke. He'll be cleaning the john. Know what? Easier for me to buzz down there. It's like fifteen minutes." He turns and runs back down toward the parking lot. I stand for a moment, not knowing if he's going to appear again, but then I hear the growl of an engine, and Bode zooms toward me on a quad bike. "Wanna come?"

I stare at him, mind racing. "With you? To town? On that?"

"We could take the plow, but it's kinda sloppy on corners." He pulls a beanie on his head, grins, and slaps the seat behind him. "Hop on!"

I hesitate. My parents do not need me disappearing on them. But... They've got their hands full with Chief Seymour, and I won't be long. They won't even notice. Plus, as much as the idea of finding Gaia with Craig in some seedy love nest makes me feel like throwing up, it would mean I could prepare her for the fallout.

And at the end of the day, a cute boy is asking me to ride on the back of his bike. What am I supposed to say?

"Is this even legal?" I shout in Bode's ear as the engine roars and we fly up the road. The air feels freezing on my face. I tuck my head in and loop my arms around Bode's waist to stop myself from falling off as we go around a corner. I can feel his stomach muscles tensing slightly, through his sweater—hey, I don't want to fall off, okay?

"Meh," Bode shouts back. "We should have helmets, but I'll try not to crash."

As he takes the bike down the mountain, I remember Mr. Addison saying the cops weren't around after four. I guess right now that's a very good thing.

CHAPTER NINE

Okay, so I promise I've never been the kind of girl to fantasize about hanging off the back of some guy's bike, but this is *fun*. Exhilarating-slash-terrifying. A couple of times I close my eyes as we veer a little close to the edge, but I don't feel like Bode's showing off and that makes me like him more.

Is it bad to be enjoying this? Well, it's not going to help Gaia at all if I hate it, is it? And the farther down the mountain we go, the more I become convinced we're going to find her at the motel, maybe hungover with a broken-down truck and no phone signal. It makes total sense.

"Motel's on the far side of town," Bode shouts at me, when we eventually level out and begin to see the buildings of Moonville.

I'm guessing this place looks better in snow, but down here the white stuff has long since melted, the tourists gone. From what I've seen from our visits over the week, "town" is really only made up of one main street—the road we're currently on—with a stretch of bars, restaurants, and kitschy shops, mainly ski- or outdoor-living-themed. There's a bunch of small hotels, faux-Alpine in style. Behind either side of the main street there are houses; tucked in the midst I can see the white spire of a church and a sign pointing to a school, maybe the one that Bode goes to. Must be weird living in such a small place, where everyone knows who you are.

"Not long now," he says, as we approach an aging strip mall with a supermarket, factory outlet store, and taco place.

Eazy Stay Motel has the kind of retro, shabby chic neon signage that would make me want to Insta a selfie, if I was into that sort of thing. I recognize it. When Gaia was first over here, Ma showed me a pic of her and Addy standing in front of this very sign, along with random shots of them grinning at yellow school buses and *wow*ing at outrageously huge plates of food. It all screamed, "America!" and I thought it was pretty cool. Now I'm thinking that the pic with the sign is evidence she's been here before—significant?

Bode turns off the road into the motel. There's a main building straight ahead with a glass-fronted reception, and it's flanked by two buildings of two stories each. There's a single car parked outside reception, and I think I can see the shape of someone sitting behind a desk inside.

"No sign of the truck." Bode has slowed almost to a stop. "Let's hunt this sucker down." He hangs a turn and accelerates around to the back of the first building. Immediately, I spot a large guy in overalls and rubber gloves, poking at a drain with a stick. We screech to a halt.

"Yo, Jai!"

Jai looks up as we dismount from our beast, Bode with a leap, and me all jelly-legs.

"What's happening?" Jai flings down the stick and takes off his gloves. There is something green and swampy hanging off the end of the stick, and an acrid, throat-stripping smell hits me. "Come to help me clear my blockage, man?" He and Bode do a broshake, and he gives me a nod.

"What is that smell?" Bode holds the back of his hand over his nose and peers down into the drain.

"Dead body," Jai looks serious and I feel my heart jump into my mouth. "Nah, man!" he laughs. "Skunk. Blown up like a frickin' balloon. Can't reach him."

I absolutely have to look down the drain, but immediately wish I hadn't. Several feet below floats a huge, bloated mass of black and white fur, surrounded by a soup of the same green that is covering Jai's stick. I feel the bile rising in my throat and back off hurriedly, the smell making tears prick my eyes.

"My uncle has a hook, if you wanna borrow?"

"Much obliged." Jai grins and hauls the grating back over the drain. "Mañana. End of my shift, anyway." We follow him as he walks toward a hut against the side of the building. "So, what brings you to the *Eazy Lay*?" He looks me up and down. I feel my face get hot.

Bode fills him in, keeping it kind of light and not too dramatic, which I appreciate. Jai's expression turns serious.

"Oh man, it's tragic if Craigy's gotten his paws on your sister."

"Yeah," I say, my eyes on the ground. "Bode says sometimes Craig comes here with his...dates?"

"True!" Jai says. "Dude has a season pass!" He chortles, then remembers he's talking about my sister and apologizes. "So, I haven't seen him today, but I'll ask Kelly-Anne if he checked in." He picks up a walkie-talkie and turns a knob. "Hey, Kelly-Anne, you hear me, baby girl?" There's static, then a click.

"Jai, I told you not to call me that, you total incel," a girl's voice drawls back.

"Aw, babe; don't be mean to me." Jai looks at us, big grin firmly in place. In the static that follows, I can practically hear Kelly-Anne's eye roll.

"Whaddya want, Jai?" she says finally.

"We got that player, Craigy boy, staying with us? My friend's here trying to track him down."

"Don't tell me you got friends?" She claps back.

Jai winks at me. "She knows I got friends."

"What's in it for me, Jai?"

"Tomorrow I bring you caramel latte from the good place in town." Jai beams into the walkie.

"There's a good place?"

"Screech Grill has the best latte." He sounds personally insulted she would think otherwise.

There's a pause. "Okay. Throw in a double breakfast sandwich with egg and cheese, you got a deal. Wash your hands first, though." I can hear the click-clack of fingernails hitting a keyboard in the background. "I wasn't here last night, only came on this afternoon." There's another pause, a few more clicks. "Yeah, there's a Craig. Room 29. No key here, so your guy's still snoozing."

For the second time, I feel my heart leap. "Ask her if he's with anyone!" I urge Jai, who nods.

"Party of two, Kelly-Anne?" He says into the walkie.

"That an invitation, Jai?" she drawls back. "How would I know? Just says Craig Wilks, paid cash. According to the computer he hasn't checked out, but that doesn't mean much. Mary worked first shift, and that doll can't deal with anything more sophisticated than a Post-it."

"Thanks, lover," Jai croons.

"You wish," Kelly-Anne snaps. "Latte, tomorrow. And don't forget the breakfast sandwich."

Jai grins, switches the walkie off. "Room 29, far side of the building, second room up the steps." He looks at Bode. "Need backup?"

Bode shakes his head. "We got this. Thanks, man."

I thank Jai profusely, and practically run back to the quad, Bode behind me. He fires up the ignition and as we lurch off again it hits me for the first time that Craig might not be too pleased at us turning up unannounced. I wonder if we should have accepted Jai's offer.

We see the truck first.

There, parked right outside Room 29, is an old-fashioned pickup. The half-light of early evening is making the truck glow a weird amber color, a beacon, drawing us in. Slowly and cautiously, we roll into the slot alongside it, and Bode kills the engine.

I've already hopped off the quad. I glance inside the truck—empty—and keep going toward the external staircase up to the second floor and the door of Room 29. The door is off-white, with a peeling, red 29 sticker, the paintwork spackled with dirt. There's a window, blinds are drawn. I go to knock, then stop. *Huh?* Door's not completely shut. Moving a little closer, I put my ear to the door, straining to hear voices, a TV, something. Silence. A knot forming in my throat, I stretch out a finger and push the door open a crack.

"Hello?"

No answer. I push the door a little wider.

"Craig? Gaia?"

The room—what little I can see of it, a chest of drawers and a TV—is gloomy and still.

"*Craig!*" I yell and Bode jumps about a foot into the air beside me.

"No one's home." Bode pushes the door fully open, but hangs back. I step inside.

It's empty. The bed is made, and the carpet has lines on it like it's been vacuumed. There's a remote by the TV, and a fresh box of Kleenex on the nightstand. It's actually a lot nicer in here than I'd imagined from the outside. Tired, but clean and serviceable would be my travel review. There's an open door at the back of the room, and I look inside: a toilet, sink, and shower. It all smells of bleach only just winning the battle over pee, but I can't fault the effort.

"Gone." I feel heat rising and a tightness in my chest, like I'm going to cry. I was so sure she'd be here. I would restore her to our parents, bask in a little unaccustomed glory, and then we could all return to normal. Gaia would be safe, and I could go back to being clumsy, truculent Esme.

Bode exhales. "At least we know he was here."

I nod, brush past him, my head down, making for the outside. Gotta fight the tears, they've completely taken me by surprise. I lean on the stair rail and look down at Craig's truck below, sucking in deep breaths so that I don't howl. *Breathe, breathe.*

And then I notice something.

"Door's open."

Doesn't anyone shut anything anymore? The passenger-side door, although closed, has a tiny gap like it's been closed but the latch hasn't caught. I run down the stairs to the truck and open the door. No keys in the ignition. All very tidy; there's a coffee cup in the console and some dark material balled up on the passenger seat, but none of the usual junk you find in people's cars. I grab the material; it's a Moon Mountain hoodie in XL, navy. Not Gaia's, at least I don't think so.

"Dead battery?" Bode says, from the other side of the car.

"That's what I'm thinking. Door got left open, the light stayed on all night."

"There's a lockbox here," Bode jumps up onto the flatbed. "No jump cables."

I stand on my tippy-toes and squint at the large, silver box bolted to the back of the pickup. "Does that open?"

Bode waggles a padlock. "Not without my lockpicks."

"I wonder what he keeps in there." I frown. "It's not big enough for skis." *Or a body,* I think but don't say. "Keys would be great."

I walk around to the front again and have a feel beneath the seats. Under the passenger seat, my hand closes around something cold and metallic, and for a second I think I've struck lucky, but it's the wrong shape entirely. I pull my hand out and stare down at the thing glinting in my palm.

"Bloody hell."

CHAPTER TEN

———

"Fancy." Bode peers over my shoulder.

Fancy doesn't begin to cover it. It's a woman's watch; slim silver links with a rose gold face and diamonds instead of numbers. "Rolex."

"Daamn." Bode whistles. "Gaia's?"

"Not unless she won the lottery and didn't tell us." I can't imagine her buying one of these even if she had a million bucks. "And it's not exactly Craig's look."

Bode takes it from me, turns it over, and studies the back. "Reckon whoever it belongs to has to be missing it. These things cost more than the truck." He hands the watch back to me. "Think it's real?"

"I know someone who'll know." I pocket it.

He raises an eyebrow. "O-kaay...and after, I guess you'll hand it over to the cops?"

"Sure. Why, do you want it?" Breaking eye contact, I glance

around. "So, if my sis and Craig were stuck without wheels, how would they get back to the resort?"

"Moonville don't got Uber. They could walk it?"

"How long would that take?"

Bode thinks. "They're hungover, but in shape. Couple hours, max?"

I sigh. "But then why didn't she ring Addy, or even Dad, get a ride?"

"Keeping it on the down-low?" Bode offers. "Figured she'd be back by the time you guys were leaving for Boston."

"But it's way past that!" I say. "What time is it, actually?"

Bode looks at his phone. "Quarter of seven."

I'm not sure if "quarter of" means before or after, but the important bit is *seven*. Late. Like, sun-going-down-soon late.

"Shit." I thump Craig's truck with my hand. "I shouldn't have stayed out this long, Ma will be wearing through the floorboards."

"So call them," Bode says.

"No phone!" I shout at him, frustrated.

"No problem." He holds up his.

"Sorry," I sigh. "It *is* a problem, *I'm* a problem, I can't remember my mother's number, it's this, well, disorder-thingy that I have, I'm awful at stuff like that."

"Still no problem." Bode taps on his phone. "Who remembers numbers anyway? D'you know what lodge you're at?'"

"Eleven," I say. "Ma drilled that into me at the beginning of the week. "Legs Eleven," she said, she even did the cancan, gave me a handy, embarrassing mental image to make me remember. I guess it stuck."

Bode chuckles, taps his phone some more. "And by the power of Moonville's patchy Wi-Fi… We have success!" He holds the phone up to me; there's a telephone number.

"What, did you hack into something?" I stare at him.

"Not exactly." The hazel eyes twinkle. "I remote accessed my uncle's database. He has the numbers of the accommodations in the resort because of his job. They gave him a computer but he never got around to setting it up 'til a couple weeks ago. Hates tech, he's always been more of a paper-and-pencil kinda guy."

"Know how he feels," I say. "Thank you."

"Meh," Bode shrugs. "Truth be told, we coulda phoned reception and gotten transferred." He hands me the phone. "But I guess I'm trying to impress you."

My heart does this horrendous little flutter thing, and I take the phone, trying to avoid his gaze. "Um, okay," I mumble, tapping the phone and holding it up to my ear, my stomach twisting as I brace myself for Ma's inevitable screeching or Dad's terse disappointment. But I don't get either. I get a robotic-sounding voicemail inviting me to leave a message.

"Er…hi—it's Es." I blink at the sky for a second, wondering how much to tell them. "I'm fine, I didn't want you to worry because I'm not back yet. We found Craig's truck, but they're not here, um, I'm in town, Moonville… Anyway, I'm with…" I pause, "one of the resort employees," I wince at Bode, who grins back. "We're coming back now so—"

The beep cuts me off and I hang up. Oh well. I got the main bit out. At least they know I'm not Dead in a Ditch, TM. Better get my arse back on the double.

"Thanks." I hand the phone to Bode. "For everything. You didn't have to do all of this."

"Anytime." Bode actually blushes a little. "I had a full list of chores my uncle gave me; this is way better."

"Oh, really?" We get back on the quad and he switches the engine on. "Will you get into trouble?" I shout in his ear. "And what about the bike? Can we give you money for petrol, um, gas or whatever?"

"No sweat," Bode shouts back. "He'll be stoked I could help you."

With that, we move off, past the front of the motel, with no sign of Kelly-Anne behind the desk, or of Jai. The sky is dimming, and Bode flicks some lights on the quad. There's more movement on the street as we pass through town, a few people coming and going from the bars and restaurants. I check out the faces as we pass, scanning for a Gaia or a Craig, but no, that would be too easy. There's a red light ahead and we stop at the crossing.

"So, where do your parents live?" I ask Bode.

"They're in the city now."

"Right. Is that…New Lanchester?"

"Boston."

"Oh, okay." I say. "That's hours away. Wouldn't you rather be there, with them?"

"Nah, I'm a country boy." Bode replies. "Okay, *honestly?* Country boy with Wi-Fi." He chuckles. "Cabin in the woods miles from anywhere, solid internet, and a drone bringing me Chinese food, that'd be perfect. How about you? You're a city kid?"

"I guess; we live just outside London. But the cabin idea sounds pretty good." I lean into his back as we drive off again. The countryside isn't so bad if you have someone to enjoy it with. I indulge in a little Bode-Cabin-in-the-Woods fantasy for a moment. I'd have the big armchair from the lodge there, and a floor-to-ceiling set of shelves, bursting with books. Maybe get the drone to bring vegan Indian food sometimes. Have one of those steamy tin baths on the deck that cowboys lie in—or no, even better, we'd hike through the woods and find an amazing waterfall, and bathe naked...

Oh god, stop it, Esme! Your sister is missing and you're having filthy thoughts!

Actually, Gaia would think it was so funny that my mind is in the gutter while looking for her, she'd totally approve.

And what about that? Has Gaia run off to her own version of Cabin in the Woods with Craig? Or on her own? The thought of her disappearing on purpose is so preposterous it hadn't even crossed my mind until now, but people do it all the time, don't they? People up and leave, get a new life. But not people like my sister. She has everything going for her. She's loved, she's having a great gap year in America, she's starting at one of the most prestigious universities in the autumn...*hmm.* That's kind of terrifying. College: super expensive, a lot of pressure. Is she having second thoughts?

"Got an idea," Bode shouts. We've left the town behind and started the ascent up the mountain via sharp, dogleg switchbacks. He pulls into the side of the road so we can talk properly. "There's a shortcut, see that trail?" He points to a gap in the trees a few meters up the road from us. "Used to be a maintenance road, but they don't use it anymore, because there was a landslide. It's the most direct route back if you're on foot. Craig would definitely know it, maybe your sister too, because when the snow's deep, you can ski it."

I stare through the trees trying to see farther up the trail, but even if the light wasn't fading, the trees are so tall it would still be too dark to make much out. A little voice in my head warns me that going into the woods close to nightfall is all kinds of wrong.

"Landslide? Can we get up there on the quad?"

"It's what they're built for," Bode slaps the beast on its shoulder. "A little steep in places, kinda wild, but hold on good and tight and we'll make it."

Ooh, don't have to ask me twice. Argh, stop it, Esme!

"Okay, then," I try to not sound too excited at the prospect.

Bode does a *yahoo*, and we take off at top speed, instantly making me doubt I've made the right decision. But although he's faster off road, I get the feeling he's done this more than a few times. He seems to know when to slow for a corner or dodge a ditch. And yay for that—it is so much darker in here with dense forest on either side. I'm grateful we're traveling at speed. On the trail you get the feeling that someone could be standing only a few feet back in the woods and you wouldn't see them. If Gaia is somewhere in the middle of all of this, I hope she has Craig with her. It would be a scary as hell place to get lost in on your own.

After skidding around a boulder, Bode slows to a stop. "Ready for the big one?" he turns, grinning.

I take a deep breath and nod, but we're going for it already. I cling on for dear life, we lean forward as the engine screams, the mountain rises in front of us, and we throw ourselves up the steepest slope yet.

"Come on!" Bode urges. The grass below turns to shingle, and the wheels begin to spin as we reach the brow of the hill. "You can do it, baby!" Bode yells, and for a moment I think he means me, but then he swears colorfully at the quad, revving the engine again. "Don't let me down, girl!" Just as I think we're sliding backward, something catches, the bike lurches, and we've made it.

Bode whoops, I yell "Yes!" and punch the sky, the engine stalls, and we both collapse over the quad with laughter and sheer relief.

"Oh my god!" I haul my leg over the bike. "I have to get off for a minute. Please tell me that was the worst of it!"

"I swear!" Bode looks at me, a huge grin on his face. "You did great. I thought I was going to lose you there for a second."

"I did nothing! I just hung on!"

"Tell you a secret," Bode says. "Never made it up that stretch before."

"What?" I say, horrified. "Never? Bloody hell!" I laugh and go to mock-hit his arm with my hand, but he catches it and holds it firmly. His hand is warm and strong. There's a moment, and we look at each other through the haze, and for a sec I think he's going to kiss me. Or maybe I'm going to kiss him. And then suddenly, I'm spooked because I'm in a forest with a boy I only met last night *and I don't even know him and worse than that there are random feels and this is not my thing at all.*

"You survived." He laughs softly, letting go of my hand.

"'Course I did," I nod, breathe. "Got your phone?"

He looks at me, all serious. "Wanna call your folks? Might not be a signal here—"

"No, I need it, because it's dark in them there woods."

He flicks the phone flashlight on and hands it to me, confused.

"I've got to pee." I stomp off toward the tree line. *Good job, Esme. Way to put him off.* And that, of course, is entirely what I meant to do. This is all completely ridiculous, these palpitations in my chest are not entirely due to the near-death experience of scaling a slope on the quad or being in the middle of nowhere at nightfall, and that is *bad news.* So, let's knock the oh-no-romance on the head before it even starts.

I find a spot, as deep into the woods as I dare, behind a fallen tree. Bode, bless him, is whistling.

"Not looking, not listening!" he hollers at me.

"Good!" I shout back. "Sing a song."

"Ninety-nine bottles of beer on the wall! Ninety-nine bottles of beer!"

"Louder!" I do what I have to do quickly and stand up again; Bode has fallen silent. All I can hear is the wind gently blowing through the treetops. I make my way back toward where I think the trail is, but wait—I've got turned around. *Huh?* I flash the phone around me, pick my way through the undergrowth in a different direction. "Bode?" I call, trying to see through the trees. My chest tightens when he doesn't reply. "Bode!"

"Are you lost?" he calls back from somewhere behind me. How come I ended up facing completely the wrong way?

"I'm okay!" I start back toward his voice. "Hey, at least if Gaia and Craig are anywhere around here, they will have heard us, we were loud enough!"

"No kidding!" Bode shouts back. "Hello!"

I stop in my tracks. The sound of his voice echoes around the woods, bouncing back at me from multiple directions. *Cool.*

"Hello!" I try. "Can you hear meeee?"

A few feet away, the undergrowth moves. I thrust an arm out, pointing the phone to light the patch of trees. Big brown, startled eyes stare back at me and I gasp.

"Bode! Come here!"

An animal, on thin, spindly legs, stands up, shakily.

"Quickly, Bode!"

"Es?" He approaches, a few feet behind me.

"Oh my god!" I turn to him, smiling. "Check it out!" I shine the phone and the animal stands there, looking at us, not scared at all. "Isn't it adorable, it's so tame!"

"Es," Bode says, his voice low and calm, his hand curling around my arm. "Move back to the trail with me, real slow and quiet."

"Why?" I rasp. "It's not scared of us."

"No," Bode says, pulling me backward. "It's a baby, Es."

"What do you mean?" I shine the light on it again. "Kind of big for a baby, isn't it?"

"Not for a baby moose."

Suddenly there's a crash, and a huge, dark shape comes hurtling toward us.

CHAPTER ELEVEN

"Run!"

I pelt after Bode toward the quad, but as we hit the tree line, something catches my foot and I fall onto my belly in the mossy undergrowth. The ground is thudding; instinct tells me *stay down.*

"Moose!"

Looking up, I see Bode standing on the trail, next to the bike. He's waving his arms, yelling, jumping up and down.

"Hey, moose! Get over here!" He's found a thick stick and he's banging it against the side of the quad, making a loud clanging. I stay still, lying flat on the wet ground. The thudding stops—there's a rush of air—and the thing that was chasing me crashes through the trees and joins Bode on the trail.

She's bigger than I ever would have imagined. I'm not well versed on the woodland fauna of New England, but if you'd asked me, I would have guessed that moose were probably about the size of, I dunno, a fairly modest cow? But this thing is huge, taller than a cart horse, thick neck with a long ugly face, a muscly body on ridiculously skinny legs. And what's more, she's really, really pissed off.

"Stay there!" Bode hisses at me from the other side of the quad. The moose pauses, puts her head down, and rolls her eyes at him ominously. He turns on the ignition, and I scramble to my feet, hiding completely ineffectually behind the closest tree. Bode has one hand revving the engine, but he's hedging his bets about getting on the bike, the moose eyeing him from a few feet away. Should I make a run for it to join him? I hesitate, but Mama Moose has made her decision. She runs at Bode, hackles standing up along her back like a furious wild dog. Ears back, she rushes the quad, her front feet mounting the bike. Bode slips, the engine roars and the quad rears up, as if defending its owner. The moose hefts her bulk against our trusty steed, which falls over on its side, wheels spinning. This seems to anger Mama even more, she runs at the bike again, shouldering the quad and pushing it back down the hill we conquered.

"Es!" Bode waves desperately at me from a ditch on the other side of the trail. He points up the trail and starts to run. I glance at Mama, who is still staring, head down, at the quad halfway down the hill. Now's my chance. I make a break for the trail, leaving my hiding place behind, thankful it's easier to run on the mix of gravel and grass, rather than the forest floor. But my relief is short-lived as I see someone else has broken from the trees and joined me on the trail: Baby.

Under any other circumstances I'd be delighted to make Moose Junior's acquaintance. But this is not most circumstances. When Gaia and I were little, my mother always told us she had eyes in the back of her head when it came to her kids, and Mama Moose seems to be similarly gifted. I hear an infuriated "harrumph!" and sure enough, Mama's turned away from the quad and is glaring at me and her offspring, side by side.

"Move!" yells Bode, and I don't need further encouragement, turning and propelling myself up the trail toward him. I run as fast as I have ever run, it scares me how fast, all the time hearing Mama's hooves—or whatever moose have—scraping on the ground somewhere behind. I'm gunning it up that trail, Bode's terrified face coming into sharp focus ahead of me, his arm brandishing the same stick he somehow managed to keep hold of all this time.

And then I can't see him, because something has got in the way, like a black cloud moving in front of the sun. Something that stops me in my tracks. Something that stops Mama Moose too.

A gigantic bull moose is walking down the trail toward me, antlers spread like huge hands grasping at the sky. Mama is huge, but this male is immense: elephantine, hairy, and built like some Ice Age beastie that should be long extinct. But he is not extinct, he is very much alive, and plodding, slowly but surely, my way.

My head whips around; the female is a few feet behind me, head down in what I now know is her bad mood posture, licking her lips. Her calf is at her heels and she no longer cares about me; there's a way bigger threat in town. I swing front again. All I see is moose, this monster steadily bearing down on me. Nowhere to run, nowhere to hide.

Suddenly, something pops into my head. Gaia, surfing on her phone, back in England last summer.

"I'll be lucky to make it out alive!" she had said, her mouth hanging open in horror. We were lounging on the floor in her bedroom at home, the rain lashing the windowpane like only an English downpour in August can. I was making my way through a much-thumbed Stephen King and the end of a packet of vegan chocolate cookies.

"Say what now?" I pretended to be pissed off that she was disturbing me, but actually this was my favorite kind of family coziness.

"According to this," she pointed to her phone, "there are black widow spiders, two types of poisonous snake, and ticks that give you deadly diseases." She was loving it. "Plus," she giggled, reading, "bears, moose, wolves, coyotes, bobcats, and...vicious wild turkeys!" This last one tickled her especially.

"Seriously?" I reached for another biscuit. "Fake news."

"It's an actual thing." Indignant, she thrust the phone at me, and I put my book down to see a video of some unfortunate man being chased by a massive turkey. "And this is where I'm going to be living!" She groaned. "God, I better get prepared. Don't they make anti-bear spray or something? Do you think it works on turkeys?" Then a few seconds later, "Mountain lions?! A jogger got attacked last year."

"Always said running was bad for you," I quipped. "And if the wildlife doesn't get you, the other-dimensional creatures from the nearby military installation will." I tapped my Stephen King.

Gaia had continued to read to me from her phone, totally horrified, totally rapt, and eventually she read out the thing that she said could save her life one day. The thing that might save my life right now.

"If attacked by a wild animal, stand your ground. Make yourself larger by spreading your arms wide; make noise to scare the animal away."

And so, I do. As Daddy Moose and I meet face-to-face, I follow that advice to the letter.

"Waaaaa!"

For the second time today, I find myself flapping my arms up and down like a deranged crow. "Waaaaaaaaaa!" I do jumping jacks. I scream, "Ooh, ooh, ooh, ooh!" like a baboon. And then with the jazz hands. "Wooooooooooo!"

"Snort," says Daddy Moose, and walks around me, the tip of one enormous antler grazing my shoulder.

I stand there. Blink. Feel slightly insulted.

A hand grabs me, and I'm running again, being half-dragged up that trail, running and running until my lungs feel like they are going to incinerate but still we run on, around a bend, up a hill until oh god my legs kill and my heart is going to bang right out of my chest and I drop to the soft grass once more, unable to go a step farther.

"You are…a wild woman." Bode is panting out the words, bent double. I can't see any moose, but then again it is suddenly so dark that I can barely see Bode. "What did you think you were doing?"

"Scaring…the…moose away," I gasp. "Obviously."

"Obviously," Bode curls into a ball, his panting turning into a kind of gulping laughter, unable to stop, rolling on the forest floor. "Obviously!"

I lean against a tree, trying to look mad, but then he looks up at me, and I can't help a snort escaping, and it sounds just like the way that bull moose snorted, and we both collapse in laughter again.

"Will they follow us?" I say, once I've recovered enough to breathe.

Bode shakes his head. "No. Female is only concerned with protecting her calf, she's real early to be giving birth, that thing could only be a day old."

"And I think we know the male wasn't bothered by me."

"No, males are only ornery in fall, when it's mating season."

"Ornery when hornery," I guffaw, and we're giggling like loons again.

"Rather meet a horny bull than a mama moose any day. Nothing beats a mother's love," Bode says, dusting himself off. "Those mamas will do anything for their babies, nothing was going to stop her. Although she might have thought twice when she saw you throw down like you did. Come on, it's only another mile to your lodge; need to get you back before your folks freak."

I crash back to earth, come down hard from the adrenaline of running from wild animals and laughing hysterically. Gaia is still missing, and my mother and father will be in bits. *Nothing beats a mother's love.* Bode's words ring in my ears the rest of the way home.

Lights are on in the lodge, and our car is the only one outside. As we get closer, I can tell that someone has unpacked it. My heart sinks. If our suitcases are back inside, she hasn't returned.

"Want me to come in with you?"

"No." I make myself walk to the steps. "Thanks. You've done so much."

Bode grins. "Dead skunk and moose attack, I'll show you the best Moon has to offer." He looks up at the lodge, takes a couple of steps away. "I hope…everything works out okay."

I watch him walk down the lane for a few seconds; he turns once to look back. Maybe he smiles, but it's too dark to see. I take a deep breath, and go in.

CHAPTER TWELVE

Immediately, I sense Gaia's not here. The lights are on, the fire cold; there's no noise or movement. Then suddenly, I hear footsteps.

"Oh!" My mother appears at the archway to the kitchen. "Es!" She's holding a glass of water, sloshing it as she rushes to put it down on the table and give me a big hug. It feels so good to have her arms around me, and I have to work to stifle a shudder of relief. "I'm so glad you're back!"

"Me too." I squeeze her. "You got my voicemail?"

"Yes!" Ma looks at me, tears pricking in her eyes. "Thank you, love. You found Craig's truck? Where? Tell me everything."

"I didn't want to give you any more worry." I pull away, kicking off my boots.

"To be honest, we barely noticed you were gone," Ma picks up her water and presses a couple of pills out of a silver blister pack. "Oh god, that sounds bad, doesn't it? But we assumed you were with Eli. Why did he leave you?" She knocks back the pills with some water, sitting at the table. "Urgh, headache. We were so involved with Chief Seymour, then Dad and Addy went to search the woods with a few friends. After they left and Eli came back from Gaia's house with the note, something just clicked in me and I phoned the police."

"A *note*? From Gaia?"

"It's her handwriting." Ma delves into her back pocket and passes me a piece of paper, which I unfold.

We cannot tear out a single page of our life, but we can throw the whole book in the fire.

"Okay, weird." I frown. "Profound with a side of ominous isn't really her."

"Much more you, no?" Ma gives me a look. "Googled it. It's out of a book by some old French novelist called George Sand, know him?" I shake my head and give back the note. "Eli said he found it in her bedroom, but we didn't see it, did we? Must have been hidden." She waves a hand dismissively. "Probably nothing. But it got me thinking, why the hell are we messing around? I got straight onto the police in New Lanchester; that's probably when you phoned." She exhales loudly. "We got your message. Such a relief you were safe with an adult. Did they drop you off?" She springs up, moves to the window to look.

"Er, yes." I don't correct her on the "adult" part. "You called the police? What did they say?"

Ma motions for me to sit down with her.

"They were rude, to be frank. Totally unhelpful. We reported

Gaia missing, and they told us because she's nineteen, she's an adult and they don't consider her at risk. They're sending someone tomorrow to interview us, but they're not going to search tonight. Oh god, what a nightmare!" She puts her head in her hands. "We mentioned that Craig was gone too, and it all went downhill from there, because they're assuming that they've run off together. And who knows? Maybe they have! It's better than the alternative." She sits up, suddenly remembering that I'm her teenage daughter. "Gaia will be fine, Es. I don't want you to worry. She's strong and sensible and they're both outdoorsy, so if they've run into trouble it's only a matter of time until we find them." She pauses to catch her breath, forces a smile. "Dad's looking in the woods, the resort security is searching buildings, they said they'd go 'til nine at least." She glances at her watch. "Where was Craig's truck exactly? I can phone Dad and they can check that area."

I tell her the whole story. Of course, what this actually means is that I give her the edited version: the motel, the empty room, Craig's truck with the dead battery. Ma takes notes. There's *no way* I'm going to raise her blood pressure by telling her about the Rolex, or the bike accident and the moose. She phones Dad (Adam Addison apparently has given him one of his phones), the Eazy Stay, and the police again, telling them about the truck. She has a little shout at them, which seems to make her feel better. The final call is to the local hospital, "just to check"; that's when I have to get out of the room.

In the kitchen, there's a tray of cold meats, cheese, and

vegetables. With compliments from the Addisons, says a note. Sympathy catering. I suddenly feel starving and make a lumpy carrot and baby tomato sandwich, while trying not to eavesdrop on Ma asking if my sister is lying in a hospital bed.

When I return to the lounge, Ma is staring out of the window into the darkness.

"Nothing from the hospital, so that's a relief," she says.

I nod. *Is it, though?* At least if Gaia had been mildly knocked over or something, we'd have found her.

"Craig's got a mum too, presumably." Ma says, almost dreamily. "We should try and let his family know. I rang reception, asked for a contact number, but they said to try tomorrow when HR is in." She takes out her phone. "Maybe Addy will know?" She taps away, frenetically, waits and watches the screen for a second. "Es?" She looks at me, and her face seems somehow much younger than I've ever seen her. "Now you're back, I'm going to have to go out and look for her. I can't sit around."

"Totally." I nod. I haven't been here long and already I'm feeling antsy.

"Good." She gets up. "I packed your night things. I'll drop you with the Addisons. Claire is at the lodge. She's had a few drinks,. She winces. "But you'll be ok."

"What?" I say, appalled at the thought of an evening in with Addy and Eli's haughty, pickled mother. "No! I'm coming with you!" I'm strung out, exhausted with leaden legs and a pain down one arm from when I fell, but there's no way I'm not searching for my sister. "I'll help!"

Ma's face softens. She goes for her car keys. "On second thought, if we both leave and Gaia comes back, she won't be able to get in." She bites her lip, wrestling with the options. "This is what would help, Es. Stay here, I'll get Claire to come over and sit with you, okay?" She doesn't wait for me to protest, scribbling something. "My number, and Dad's new phone." I nod, knowing her mind's made up. Most of the time I'd fight her anyway, but she doesn't deserve that at the moment. "Lock me out." Ma kisses me on the head. "And don't answer that door unless it's someone you know!" She puts on her coat, opens the door, and waggles the key at me meaningfully.

A memory. Last night. I gasp.

"What?" Ma freezes in the doorway.

"The key." I stare at it. It's a flat, silver key, and hanging off the ring are two finger-length pieces of wood, carved in the shape of little skis. It looks nice and everything, but the lock is stiff, and when you turn the key, the "skis" flip over and whack you on the knuckles. Annoying. *Memorable.* "I locked the door last night when I got in from the party." I put my hand on my chest, as fear and guilt grip me. "I felt pleased, because normally I forget." I look at my mother. "Oh god, I locked Gaia out."

"She would have banged on the door, shouted for us." She pats me on the shoulder. "Don't worry, love." She leaves, starts up the car, gestures for me to go inside.

We both know she's wrong. Gaia wouldn't wake us up if she couldn't get in at stupid o'clock in the morning. She'd shrug, laugh, walk back to the party, or her place. Or maybe get persuaded to take off with Craig and sleep over at the Eazy Stay.

I lock the door, stare at it for a while, chewing a fingernail. There's nothing to do but wait. I'd love a shower, but if Mrs. A is going to show up, I should put a hold on that until she gets here. And Gaia might come back. Is she coming back? She totally still could. I shake myself. Change of clothes would be a good thing, though. These are really wet. *A plan.* I run upstairs and throw on sweatpants and a sweatshirt and am just hanging my damp things over the door when something hits the windowpane. *Shit!* I yelp, hugging the wall.

Was that a bird? Not at this time of night. And too sharp a sound.

As I stare at the window, I flinch as there's a crack against the pane. Someone's throwing stones! I flick off the light in my room, like that's going to totally fool them. But could it be Gaia? I gather up my courage and peer out of the window. All I can see are trees and dark shapes. And then one of the shapes moves, the outline of a person. *Shitity-shit!* I duck, and back into the room.

Okay, okay, what to do? Could that be my sister? Nope, she'd knock on the door. And I can't imagine Mrs. Addison chucking a piece of gravel, somehow. I creep down the stairs. Burglars don't throw stones; they break in. Has to be someone who wants my attention but doesn't want to announce themselves. *Oh god, I hope I'm right about this.* I turn the key. *Please don't let it be a psycho killer.* What if someone got Gaia and has come back to get me? I open the door and gingerly poke my head out.

"Es!" a voice hisses. I step out onto the deck. Bode is at the bottom of the steps, grinning at me. "Sorry if I scared you. Didn't want to disturb your folks."

"There's no one here but me." *Oh whoops.* Probably not something I should be advertising. "Mrs. Addison is coming over in a bit. My parents are out looking for Gaia."

Bode's brow wrinkles. "She's not back? Man, I'm sorry. I guessed as much. My uncle went out searching and I hadn't heard anything." He bounds up the steps. "Wanted to give you this." He hands me a small box. "Burner. Should make things easier."

Burner? I stare dumbly at the object in my hand. "A phone? Where did you get this?"

Bode shrugs. "I've got a few of them, prepaid and reconditioned. I use them for electronics, mainly. They're nothing fancy, no internet, but they'll call and text okay."

"I can't accept this!"

"Sure you can," Bode says. "No big deal, it was gathering dust in my barn. Give it back when Gaia turns up."

"Wow, thanks." I beam at him.

"Know how to use it?" he teases. "You got my number?" I glance at the back of my hand, and the marker's still there. "Great. Phone's charged. Number's written on the back. Ask your mom and dad if you can't figure out the rest."

I snort with derision; he laughs, turns, and lopes away into the night.

Later, I'm getting ready for bed, and Claire Addison is downstairs by the fire, watching TV and working her way through a big glass of something. I feel utterly useless, but short of sneaking out into the night—and giving my parents more grief—there's literally nothing I can do. Hope mixed with fear feels so painful, it's eating my insides like I drank bleach. I lie down and try to distract myself with a book, but the only thing left on the shelf is an epic tale about a wild hike along the Appalachian Trail. I think I could probably write that one myself after today. I painstakingly program Bode's number into my phone before washing it off my hand. As I'm about to turn my light off, a message pings.

"Text!" I have never been so psyched to get one in my life.

Good night, good night... Don't let the moose bite ;)

I try to think of something witty back, but the longer it goes, the worse my replies get. I end up simply typing:

Thanks :)

God, I must work on my banter.

Anytime :) is the reply. I grin, feel good. Feel bad. I put the phone on my nightstand and kill the light. The wind is picking up outside. I shut my eyes, *will* Gaia to be okay, and listen out for the door like my mother had the night before.

CHAPTER THIRTEEN

———

Morning light is streaming in through the blinds I didn't want to shut, and I can hear noises somewhere beyond my room, people talking, downstairs maybe.

She's not back.

If she was, someone would have woken me up. *Oh god, my chest feels tight.* I'm not sure I can deal; the oblivion of sleep is way more attractive.

On the bedside table, my phone beeps. *Bode.* At least I have a distraction, although the thought instantly brings guilt.

Any news?

I feel a little squeeze of pleasure. Sweet of him. Competing emotions of excitement and dread swirl around my stomach, like when I was a kid at a party and ate too many platefuls of sweet and savory food all at once. The screen says Monday

April 16, 7:15 a.m. He's up early. I wonder if he's got school, he didn't mention it yesterday. Maybe they're on break?

I'll leave it a while before I text back, don't want him to think I'm too keen. *Oh, I'm a horrible person, why does any of that even matter?* I brush my thumb over the chunky buttons. This phone is a damn brick, similar to my own: cheap and basic as hell with a battery that lasts a fortnight. Owned only by people over seventy, drug dealers, and me.

Why does Bode have burner phones lying around his house—sorry, barn—anyway? "Electronics," he said. What, like remote detonating homemade bombs? He's way too nice to be a terrorist.

As I pull myself out of bed, the full weight of Gaia not being here drapes over me and I stand, legs aching. Up until now, I think I'd assumed she'd suddenly show up. I'd thought, okay, it's out of character for her to go AWOL, blow off her friends, screw up our plans, *but* not completely beyond the realms of possibility.

But now it's morning, and enough time has passed. This is not late home; this really is Missing.

I dress, scrub my teeth, take a deep breath, and walk toward the noise.

At the top of stairs, I get my first glimpse of the living room. It is absolutely filled with people. At first, I can't see any familiar faces, and for a horrible second I think that a huge bunch of randoms have moved in, and my parents have forgotten me and left—but then I spot my mother. She's sitting at the dining table surrounded by people I don't know, plus Eli and his dad. Adam Addison moves a little and I get a glimpse of a young man in a police uniform, nodding. The sight of the cop hits like a punch to my stomach; shit just got really real.

Ma's ignoring everyone, head down, writing something, phone in hand—like she's incidental to all of this. Where's Dad? I scan the room but can't find him among the bodies.

There's a cluster of Gaia's friends by the archway to the kitchen—Addy, that Lucille person who lives with Craig, and a pair of twins—two girls from the party with straight, inky-black hair. Next to them are the boys that Bode called the Ski Lift Jerks. They're all talking, glancing at phones, a couple of them sniggering, uncomfortably.

In the center of the room are adults wearing snow gear. There's a tall, white-haired guy setting out walkie-talkies on the coffee table, and an older woman stuffing a silver blanket into a rucksack balanced on my armchair. The front door is open, and as I descend, I can see someone pacing on the deck with two sniffing Labradors in hi-vis coats. *Wow.*

As I reach the bottom stair, Scott's blocking my way. He's filming, panning the room with his phone.

"Hi." I tap him on the back.

"Esme!" The phone is a few inches away from my face. "How are you doing? God, I don't know how to say this, hon, but your sister is still missing."

"I guessed," I hold my hand up to my face, hoping he'll get the message and stop filming.

"Hang on in there," he says, grabbing the hand that's shielding me and squeezing it reassuringly. Can't help but feel he might be doing that just to zoom in on my face, though. "Oh, sweetie—these people are here to help, we're going to find her, don't you doubt it!"

"Thanks, Scott." I give him the briefest of smiles, extract my hand from his, and edge past, my eyes on a pathway to Ma at the dining table.

Before I can make my move, the crowd parts for a man in a suit, Chief Seymour, and a policewoman. My eyes are drawn to the cop immediately—she's very tall for a woman, even taller than Gaia, with a long, serious face. Her gray-streaked hair pulled back into a ponytail. My mother spots the new arrivals and stands up. Adam Addison shakes the suited man's hand, then Chief Seymour's. For some reason he doesn't bother with the female police officer; her expression is blank, but her eyes linger on him in a way that leaves me in no doubt what she thinks of that.

"Listen up, people!" The cop holds her hands out, and for the most part, everyone shuts up. "My name is Detective Graff, and I can see that y'all have already met my colleague, Officer Hernandez." Her voice has a southern twang to it, not like the locals I've heard around Moon. Detective Graff clears her throat. "Along with Head of Security Chief Seymour and Mountain Rescue, we are going to be coordinating today's action to find Gaia Gill and Craig Wilks."

"Yeah!" One of the Ski Lift Jerks yells, and a couple of them clap.

"All right," Detective Graff says. "Mr. Huckey here is the manager of the resort," she indicates the suit, "and he has kindly facilitated for us to have the property adjacent to use as our command center today, Lodge 12. If y'all could congregate there, Mountain Rescue will advise how to proceed." She licks her lips. "We have copies of photographs of Gaia and Craig in case anyone needs familiarizing with our two missing individuals."

Detective Graff holds up a sheaf of paper, and I see Gaia's face in close-up. I don't recognize the picture; she looks like she's stifling a laugh. She's got a zit, and her face looks way rounder than it actually is. Who the hell gave them that photo? She'll be mortified when she sees it.

"Now, I need y'all to search safe." Detective Graff looks over at the group of kids by the kitchen archway. "Even if you know this mountain well, don't be thinking y'all can do your own thing. We're in the melt, and that makes for rivers where last week there was none. Got ideas? We wanna hear 'em, but follow the rules. We can get this done!"

There's a smattering of applause and people begin to troop out of our lodge and to the "command center" next door.

"Gill family, close friends, stay if you please," Detective Graff says. "I know you're gonna want to get out there, but the more information we get from you now, the better chance we have of finding Gaia. And Craig Wilks," she adds, as if an afterthought. "It'll take but a moment to set up."

My mother hasn't seen me yet; she offers to make the cops

coffee and disappears into the kitchen. Officer Hernandez sets down a small recorder and a clip file on the table and chats to Mr. Addison and Addy, making notes. Eli looks over, but slinks out of the door before anyone can say anything. Through the window, more people are beginning to gather; I had no idea Gaia was so well known, or maybe they do this for all their missing people? Is this, like, a thing? The thought gives me shivers.

"Esme?" Detective Graff is suddenly beside me.

"Yes." I have no idea how she knows who I am.

"How you holding up?"

I nod, for some reason not able to form a sentence. The detective nods back.

"We'll talk, okay?" She's warm, with full lips, and there are creases around her friendly, green eyes. I wonder how old she is? Maybe my mother's age? The height makes it hard to tell, somehow. "I know you must be wanting to get this over. Let me clear the room first." She strolls past me and around the end of the stairs, where Scott is lurking.

"Sir, what's your name?"

Scott's eyes go big. I'm guessing it's the first time in a while someone has asked him that. "Scott Mazzulo, Gaia's best friend."

Detective Graff nods. "Mr. Mazzulo, I'm going to need you to put that phone away, do you understand?" she says quietly. "And delete what you just filmed. The only recording we'll be doing today is official police recording, you get me?"

"Yes, ma'am." Scott nods. "There's nothing on here, I'll show you." He holds it out, scrolling for her to see, but I know he must be lying. "Hey, I took a bunch of pics and footage at the party. That could be helpful, couldn't it?"

Graff studies him for a moment. "Maybe so. You have a chitchat with Officer Hernandez and tell him all about it later. Wait in the command center for the time being."

Scott smiles, but I can tell he's pissed off at being dismissed so quickly. As he lingers by the door, taking his sweet time putting on a coat, Dad walks in. He looks exhausted and completely confused as to why there are a load of people here.

"Dad!" I run up to him and give him a hug; he's freezing. "Have you been out all night? Are you okay?"

He hugs me back, face in my hair. "Where's your mother?"

"Kitchen," I reply. "The police are here, obviously—the woman in charge seems good—and there's a search party, dogs—"

Dad breaks away as Ma comes out of the kitchen. She pauses when she sees him, and on her face there is an expression that I have never witnessed before on anybody, a horrible mixture of questioning, of fear, of unbridled hope painted over with barely contained despair. His face shows failure, *I have let you down, I cannot find her*. The wordless exchange is like a knife to my gut. They embrace, my mother lets out a couple of tight gasps; it sounds as if she's gulping for air.

I glance at Detective Graff; she's watching all of this silently. Scott, still by the door, is easier to read; he's itching to reach for his phone. And as for me... I'm torn between grief and sheer embarrassment that we're having to play this out in such a public way.

Detective Graff signals to her partner, and suddenly all those last extraneous people are whipped away with Officer Hernandez to somewhere else; the door shuts, there's no sound except my mother, steadying her breathing, and my father's long sniffs. They are still in each other's arms. It's so intimate even I feel like I'm intruding.

"Mr. Gill," Detective Graff says finally. "I'm going to give you a spell to get coffee, a bite to eat, a change of clothes. We have a big crowd come to look for Gaia. When you're ready, we'll talk."

Dad nods. "Just the coffee." Ma goes off to the kitchen again. "And first, I should tell them." He points to the lodge next door. "Tell them where I searched."

"We'll do that straightaway, don't you worry." Detective Graff nods. "I need you to take five and refuel, you're going to need your strength."

"No, you don't understand." He feels around in his pocket. "I marked it on a map. Chief Seymour gave me it, I marked everywhere I looked." He holds up the map; it's limp with damp. The sight of him tightly gripping this pathetic, floppy piece of paper, like it's the most valuable thing in the world, makes my throat clench.

Okay, a voice inside my head says. *No more messing around. For better or worse, time to tell them everything.*

CHAPTER FOURTEEN

———

Before I can do anything, Addy appears at my shoulder; I hadn't even noticed she was still here.

"Got a sec?"

"Sure," I say, automatically. *God, she looks dreadful.* Big, dark circles under her eyes, the gorgeous titian hair unwashed and scraped back off her small, pale face. "Are you okay?"

"Fine," she says, taking me under the arm and maneuvering me up the stairs. "I heard you found Craig's truck last night?" We reach the top landing and she keeps going, toward my bedroom. "Broken down?"

"Yeah, it's at a motel in town." I follow her into my bedroom. "The Eazy Stay, you know it?"

"Nope. You told the police yet?"

"Ma did." I sit on the end of my bed, but Addy seems

too wired to stay put. "We—Bode and me—we came back through a trail in the woods because we thought if Craig and Gaia were together they might have tried to walk back."

"That makes total sense," Addy says. She rakes a hand through her hair. "Where exactly did you search?"

"The landslide shortcut." I pause. "Not really searching though, it was dark, and we were on the quad bike—well, at least 'til the moose chased us—"

"What?" Addy looks at me, horrified.

"Wild, eh?" I rub my legs. "The parents are going to be thrilled about that one."

"You know what?" She looks out of the window. "We need to search around there. Yesterday, when I went looking with your dad, we were mainly around the staff houses, but you finding that truck in town changes everything."

"Yeah, I suppose they'll realize that." I nod. "Oh! I'm so stupid, how could I forget—" I jump up and scan around for yesterday's jeans—there—damp pile in the corner. I pluck them out and delve into the back pocket. "I found this under the seat in Craig's truck, thought you'd be the one to know if it was real." I thrust my hand out for Addy to see.

"God! A watch!" She laughs. "I didn't know what you were going to show me! A severed finger or something!"

"Sorry," I shake myself. "Do you think it's genuine? What would Craig be doing with it? Could it be *Gaia's*? Aren't these things worth, like, thousands?"

"Totally." Addy stares at the watch. "And yep, it's real."

"Aw, hell," I sigh. "I should probably give it to the police, could have something to do with her going missing—"

"Wait!" Addy reaches out and swipes the watch from my hand. "Listen, Es; I have to tell you something." She glances at the door. "Sit down."

"What?" I plunk down on the bed again.

"Okay, this is not easy." Addy inhales slowly. "Es, Gaia did have this watch." She sits next to me on the bed and lowers her voice. "She...she stole it."

My stomach lurches. "Are you kidding me? Gaia wouldn't do that. From who?"

"From my mother, Es." Addy is half-whispering now. "When my folks and Eli were over in February, Mummy lost her watch. Well, we thought she'd lost it. She's half-drunk most of the time." Addy rolls her eyes. "Pop *kicked off*. He'd given it to her for Christmas; he warned her about skiing in it, figured she'd lost it out on the slopes, even got people out looking." She sighs, chews on her lip, and fixes me with watery eyes. "A week after they went home, I found it. Went into Gaia's drawer to borrow something, and there it was, wrapped in a pair of socks."

I sit there, stunned, not knowing what to say.

"I couldn't believe it, Es." Addy puts a hand on mine. "Didn't want to. But Gaia *admitted it*. I confronted her, and give her credit, she fessed up straight away."

"But why would she steal it?"

"She needed the money." Addy's mouth turns down at the corners. "Even with the scholarship and the jobs, she said she'd be struggling to pay for college, said she saw the watch on the bathroom sink at my folks' lodge one night and grabbed it without thinking. She reckoned it was insured, but hey, it's Mummy we're dealing with, so no win there." She rolls her eyes and sighs deeply. "It's not the money, really—but it's caused a shedload of friction between my parents."

"God, Addy." I find my voice at last. "I'm so sorry."

I *am* sorry, but mainly for Gaia. She felt so worried about money she'd steal her best friend's mother's stuff? After all they'd done for her?

And I'm sorry for myself as well. Another thing Gaia didn't—couldn't—share with me.

I stare at my hands. "What did she say she was going to do with the watch after you found it?"

"I told her, 'Look, give it to charity.' That way neither of us has the guilts. She agreed. That was, like, two months ago. But she obviously kept it and dropped it in Craig's car on Saturday night. So," Addy sits up, "here's what we're going to do. I'm going to take the watch, make sure it gets back to my mother. Slip it into a pocket, like it was there all along. Not now—there's way too much going on—but before they head home to England. And when Gaia comes back, Es," she looks at me, her eyes beginning to mist over, "you can't say anything about this, okay? I know what she's like. She'll tattle to my parents, and the shit will hit the fan." Addy exhales loudly. "Pop will take it very seriously; I won't be able to protect her. Trust me to make this right, won't you?"

I nod because there's nothing else I can do. Addy squeezes my hand, shoves the watch in her back pocket, and we walk downstairs, my mind reeling, the object of my agony outlined in the tight denim of Addy's jeans. She turns and smiles briefly, as she collects her coat and leaves.

Damn, I forgot to ask her about the weird note. Maybe Ma already did. If not, it will have to wait.

By the fire, my dad has a sandwich in one hand, a mug in the other, and he's staring at them like he doesn't know why they're there. Detective Graff turns to me.

"We're ready for you, Esme. Do you need anything before we start?"

Not to be here? Yes. A reboot on this day? Yes. To have never come to Moon in the first place? Please, god, yes.

I shake my head, walk over to the armchair, and sit. It feels hard and deflated today. Ma comes back from the kitchen with more coffee, and Detective Graff starts recording.

So many questions. We begin with the party. I try to give them every detail I can muster. How many people were there, names, what time everything happened—although we already know I'm bad at all of that. Then it gets interesting. Detective Graff asks me if there was alcohol, and I say yes. Was *I* drinking? No, I don't like the taste. What about Gaia, Craig—were they drinking? Yes. I glance at Ma apprehensively, but she doesn't flinch. How much? Neither of them seemed drunk when I last saw them…true enough.

"And what about drugs, Esme?" the policewoman asks me,

her moss-colored eyes staring straight into my soul. "Were there drugs at the party?" She says it like it's no big deal, like she's asked me if there were chips 'n dip.

Ma and Dad have stopped breathing because it's The D word. Parents, even the ones that think they're down with the kids, tend to freak when it comes to The D word.

"I'm not really familiar." *Unconvincing.* "There were joints, but I don't know what was in them."

"If you could guess, what would you say it was?"

Damn.

I shrug. "Um, weed? But I don't know."

She nods, making a note. "And were Gaia and Craig smoking?"

"No," I answer quickly, blocking out Gaia, picturing only Craig, thinking about him awfully hard, about how I never saw *him* smoke.

Argh, so much for telling everything. I refuse to rat on Gaia about the blow, and after what Addy said, I'm keeping schtum about the watch too.

But there is the other thing that happened at the party...

"Gaia ran around the house with her underwear on."

I blurt it out, like a kid telling tales.

"Sorry?" My mother's eyes look like they're about to pop out of her skull.

Dad barks out a shocked laugh. "What are you talking about?"

I close my eyes. I remember we were sitting on the squashy

sofa. Bode's friend Keith had just called Gaia "a class act." And then, with a squeal, she ran into the lounge. In her matching polka-dot bra and panties.

"Okay, enough!" Gaia had been laughing as she frolicked through the partygoers. She turned to Scott, who was following, filming her. "I took the stupid dare!"

"All season!" Scott turned the phone on himself. "I have been waiting for Miss Gee to honor her debt to me, and finally she delivers!"

"We are all square!" Gaia shouted at him. "I owe you nothing!"

"That was only half of it." Scott beamed into his phone. "Get your cutie patootie tush out the door, Gee! One lap of the house!"

"Noooo!" Gaia groaned. She trotted to the window by us, and I remember feeling the boys on either side of me stop breathing. "It's proper snowing!"

"*Proper snowing*!" Scott affected her English accent. "Then golly gosh you better get a move on, toodle pip!"

"Gaia, no!" Addy cried from somewhere. But my sister was never one not to follow through. She giggled, dipped her feet into someone's boots and flung the door open, shrieking as the cold air hit her. "Oh my god, it must be ten below!"

"So move!" Scott was still filming. The whole room emptied onto the deck.

Only Bode stayed put.

"It's okay," I said to him. "You can go too."

"I'm good right here." He side-eyed me. "Think she'll step in your puke?"

And that was the moment I decided I liked Bode very much.

"This was a dare?" Detective Graff has been scribbling notes. "And everyone saw it happen?"

"Yes."

"And how was your sister afterward?"

"Fine. She was fine."

But I wasn't. I was judgy and uncomfortable with Gaia's underwear run, I'll admit, but what really bothered me was what Bode told me next.

"You must follow them, right?"

I didn't get what he meant at all, and he must have read it on my face.

"Scott's channel. *Mazzulo and Miss Gee.* They pull pranks. He films everything. They're getting real popular."

I didn't ask him anything more, just nodded vaguely. Like I knew all about it, but didn't care. When in reality, I knew nothing and cared very much indeed.

But I don't tell Detective Graff that. I don't tell her about the channel. Gaia's done nothing wrong, but I can't bring myself to break it to my parents that their daughter might be all over the internet.

But what if it could help find her?

CHAPTER FIFTEEN

———

Hi sorry I didn't get back to you earlier. She's still missing.
Police here.

I've snuck upstairs to text Bode. After what seemed like forever, Detective Graff announced she was done talking to us, for now. I'd suddenly remembered that I hadn't replied to Bode. *Okay,* so I'd thought about it ages ago, and it gnawed away at me, but I couldn't exactly get my phone out and start texting in the middle of the police interview, could I? My parents don't know about the phone. They've only just learned about Bode, and I can tell that it's not sitting too well with Ma.

Detective Graff asked about how I'd found Craig's truck, so of course I had to come clean about Bode…and the quad bike, the shortcut, and *kind of* about the moose. All the time I could see Ma's eyes widening as my crimes mounted with each new revelation.

The phone beeps a reply.

Uncle out with the search. Want me to come help?

I think about it a moment, then text back.

Can I come to you? Need to escape.

I wait a minute and fire off another message.

Got a couple of ideas about something you could help me with

Urgh… Does that sound too full-on? I do need help, though.

No problem come over

Yes! I rifle through Gaia's bag on her bed, looking for something I packed the day before…her tablet. Her phone is missing, obviously, but Detective Graff said they were going to take her other electronics in case it helps find her. *Yep, well… They're going to have to wait.* I quickly stuff the tablet into my backpack.

"Es!"

I trot out onto the landing and my mother's standing at the bottom of the stairs, phone in hand. My dad and Detective Graff have gone, but Addy and Claire Addison are here, sitting awkwardly in the lounge. I grip the backpack, holding it against my side as I come down the stairs, hoping no one notices.

"Dad's gone out to search again," Ma says, her eyes steady. "I'm going to go too, Es, after I've made some calls to rearrange our flights home; the airline is being difficult."

"Julia, I've told you—if it means buying new tickets, we'll take care of it, relax!" Claire Addison calls from the armchair, like we're all having a jolly holiday.

"Thanks, Claire." Ma is doing her best not to get irritated, I can tell. "Hopefully, they'll reschedule us, under the circumstances." She looks at me. "Es, there's still time for you to make the flight home this evening. Eli has offered to drive you to Boston. It would mean you wouldn't miss any more school, love."

I blink. That was quite literally the last thing on my mind. I was going to miss a couple of days anyway because of this trip. Ma had to negotiate that with the school. I have exams this term and they weren't happy about it. Come to think of it, there was probably some revision I was supposed to do, but that conveniently slipped my mind until this very moment.

"I can't go back!" I feel myself getting hot. "Not without knowing she's okay!"

Ma hugs me. "I understand. I think it's best we all stick together too."

"Thanks, Ma," I cross the room to my boots and coat. "I'm going out, I won't be long."

"Where to? Oh, my head." Ma sits at the table, like she's going to faint. "I don't know that I can have you out there."

"Don't worry. I'm going to see Bode." I decide to take a chance, reach into my pocket. "Look, he loaned me this phone to use. In case you need to call me, I'll write the number down for you." I copy the digits on a scrap of paper and hand it to my mother.

"He gave you a phone…?" Ma stares at it.

"Bode's totally solid, he's lovely, in fact." Addy chips in from across the room, her eyes darting at me. "Here, I'll put your number in my phone too." She gets up and looks over my mother's shoulder at the note. "You don't need to worry, Julia. He's a good kid, his dad works here."

It's his uncle, but I don't correct her, just shoot her a grateful look.

"All right." Ma makes up her mind. "Keep in touch, Es. I'm going to ring that number now, so you have mine stored." She shakes her finger at me. "And no more quad bike trips into town! God, did you actually say that you were chased by a moose? This whole thing is a nightmare." She stands up, leaning on the table. "Right. I have to call the Foreign Office. Apparently they might be able to help. This is so surreal." She takes a deep breath. "And the hospitals, again."

I get out of there before she can change her mind.

I'm standing outside the big red barn behind Bode's uncle's house. It's so American, with its bell-shaped roof, it's like being at a theme park or inside a kids' picture book. There are two huge wooden sliding doors at the front, and a person-sized door-within-a-door on one panel. No bell, no knocker. Should I just go in?

It's warmer today, much warmer, but it's beginning to drizzle. On my way over here, the "command center" in Lodge 12 was looking quiet. I hadn't seen any sign of the search party until I reached the main road and went through the tunnel; when I emerged, there they were, off in the woods by the guest apartments. People walking in a line, slowly, eyes to the ground, using long sticks to poke undergrowth and prod the few remaining drifts of snow that dot the woodland floor. The realization hit like a hammer. *They're looking for a body.* A wave of nausea passed over me and I stuck out a hand and steadied myself against a wooden fence. *No. She is missing, but she's alive. Don't panic—they're looking for her stuff.* Her phone, her purse, a scarf, gloves, her beanie. Detective Graff says Craig's phone and wallet are gone too. The searchers are looking for those things. I pushed off from the fence and kept walking.

When I got to Bluff Point, I glanced over at Craig's house, as if I expected him or Gaia to suddenly appear, smile, wave at me. I'd nearly jumped out of my skin when the door opened and somebody walked out. It was Lucille, mess of blond hair hanging in front of her face. *Hmm, you didn't search for long, did ya, hon?* She was holding a steaming mug and laughing, as if someone inside had cracked a joke. I watched her sit on the bench on the deck and notice me. She didn't call, or wave. Just sipped her mug of whatever. Weird girl.

Drizzle is turning to rain. I look up at the barn. This is ridic. *Just bang on the door, already.* There are two small windows up there, but they're too tiny to see anything. I fish my phone out. Should I text him?

"Hey."

I whip around. Bode is standing behind me; it's kind of becoming his signature move.

"Didn't the butler answer?" he grins, reaching past and opening the small door, gesturing for me to go in.

I step through and nearly slam into a huge, green tractor.

"John Deere has the ground floor, I'm up top." Bode flicks a switch and I see two more monster-sized tractor things parked behind the first one, another quad and some kind of little digger. The air is thick with the smell of oil. "Stairs over there."

Through the dim light I can just make out a slightly rickety-looking set of stairs, and as I squeeze past various machinery and a huge lathe on a workbench, I hear music coming from up there, somewhere. James Taylor, echoing through the barn. We climb the stairs, which groan a little, and I hang on to the banister without making it seem like that's what I'm doing. The music gets louder as we climb up, and as I reach the top, I emerge into a large, open-plan room.

"This is where I live," Bode says proudly.

"Great," I say, and I think I mean it.

There's a wide sofa, with its back to me, and a couple of tatty armchairs around a large, beaten-up wooden box that serves as a table. At the far end there's a bed, unmade, and in the opposite corner from that, a tiny kitchen area with a sink and burners.

The most surprising thing about the room is a long counter running the length of one wall of the barn. On it sit screens of varying sizes, a turntable and speakers, at least two games consoles, computer hardware, tools, and machinery parts, big and small. The room is part NASA control room, part *Scrapheap Challenge*. And it smells of hot metal and PopTarts.

"Hey," A head pops up from behind the sofa. Okay, correction, so *this* is the most surprising thing in the room. A girl, late teens. Curls, pretty.

"Uh, this is Hayley," Bode says.

"Hi," I smile at her, shyly, my heart sinking. *Damn, I didn't want company.* I want to break into my sister's tablet and get it back to the lodge before the police or my parents realize I've made off with it.

I think Hayley knows I don't want her here; she looks me up and down, smiling at Bode, who rolls his eyes and stomps past to the kitchen part of the room.

"Wanna soda?"

"Thanks," I say, taking a can from him and sitting down on one of the chairs. The girl is stretched out in jeans and a stripy sweater, her boots on the wooden box. She's twiddling a strand of her curly hair, smiling at it.

"Hey, sorry to hear about your sister," she drawls, kind of more to her hair than to me. "That sucks."

"Er, yeah." I pull the ring on the can of pop, and it spurts out, over the table, over Hayley's boots. "Oh god, sorry." I get up and hunt around for something to mop up the wet, while Hayley giggles like I'm ridiculous, which I probably am.

"No problem, Es." Bode grabs a towel and cleans the mess. "Didn't go anywhere important."

"Except me!" Hayley is now laughing way more than this whole thing warrants. It makes me feel like emptying the rest of the can over her curly head.

"Do you know Gaia?" I ask, partly because I want to know, partly because talking about my missing sister might make her stop laughing.

"Not really," Hayley says. "Sure, I've seen her around, but you know, new faces here every season and then off they fly." Her voice is singsongy, and she's not looking at me directly. "But truly, I hope you find her." She makes a sympathetic face, stands up. "Gotta bounce, Boad." She glances at him. "You got your hands full here."

He nods at her.

"Oh—I got your homework assignment, Bode." She says it like she's making a huge joke, one that I don't get. I'm sure I'm not supposed to. Bode sighs, a flash of frustration on his face.

"Sure, Hayley... Listen, I'm gonna get you that hook. You'll take it to Jai, yeah?" He runs to the stairs and jogs down them, the whole staircase rattling.

"Hey, Bode, dontcha wanna bring it into *school*?" Hayley shouts after him.

"I'm telling you, not now, sister!" Bode shouts back. "And get down here. No point in my hauling this hook up, I'll put it in your car."

Sister. She's his sister. Relief floods through me. I should have known. The curls. They do look alike. Not that it matters, of course, but I'm really completely, stupidly glad she's his sister. He never mentioned he had one, but then again, why should he?

Hayley leaves. No goodbye, not a look. That's cool. I listen to them saying something downstairs, I can't hear what, the music's too loud. Bode sounds grouchy. Sisters will do that to you sometimes. *Wow*, I feel guilty when I have that thought. After a minute or two, I hear the stairs groan and Bode appears again. He runs his hands through his hair, turns the music down.

"Sorry about that." He smiles at me. "She's…well, Hayley's just Hayley."

I smile back. "I get it."

"Great." He rubs his hands together, sits down.

"No school today?" I chuckle. "Or are you bunking off?"

"Bunking?" He looks at me aghast. "Oh, maaan!" He covers his face with a cushion and rolls back on the sofa, legs in the air, dead bug style. "Brit-speak. I thought that meant—no, never mind what I thought. *God.*" He throws the cushion aside, sits up again, face straight. "Yes, you are correct. There's no school today. Spring break."

I reach into my backpack, take out my sister's tablet, and hold it up for him to see.

"Fancy hacking into this?"

CHAPTER SIXTEEN

Bode does not look as excited as I thought he would. In fact, he looks worried. Is it screwed up that I had him pegged as Hacker Boy?

"It's not hacking, actually!" I say brightly. "I know her password. She lets me borrow her tablet all the time. Thing is," I'm being overly casual now, "she stays logged into all her apps, so we can have a look around, see if there's anything suspicious."

"O-kaay," Bode does not sound convinced. "But you know, I'm thinking the police might wanna take a look…"

"Yep." I nod. "That's why I've got to do this now. If anything was going on with Gaia, I want to know first. And I know it's weird, but I really have no clue about social media, so I was hoping you'd help."

Bode's eyes look dark in the dim light of the attic. "You seriously don't have any online stuff?" When I shake my head, he chuckles, examines the floor, and makes a kind of strangled sound. When he looks at me again, I can tell he's made a decision. "All righty, freako. Let's do this." He sits in a chair on wheels at the long desk, slides across the floor, and grabs another chair for me. "So, Ms. Esme, I'll play accomplice. I mean, whatever. I hear juvey in New Lanchester's got good food." I frown at him and he fixes me a deadpan gaze. "We get caught? You get deported, and me? Maybe they'll just gimme the ankle bracelet."

I laugh, nervously, because I have no idea if he's exaggerating or if that's anywhere near approaching the truth. I'm sure the police won't be super thrilled, but it's a chance I'll have to take. I open the tablet, and as soon as the prompt for the password appears, I tap in the numbers: 04–19

"April 19. The date she found out she'd been accepted into university," I explain.

"That's in three days."

"God, a year ago." I watch as the operating system pings to life. "Seems longer. It also happens to be my birthday."

"No kidding!"

"Dunno if I'd remember the date otherwise," I shrug.

Last year's birthday had been gobbled whole by Gaia's acceptance. Dad had taken me out for an early breakfast at the new vegan café that had opened near us. Ma was working in town, and Gaia was staying at Addy's palatial house in the suburbs. Halfway through my eggless omelet, Dad's phone rang. It was an ecstatic, screaming Gaia, and that was that, birthday over. I mean, we still went through the motions. Carrot cake and presents with the family after school, a trip to the movie theater with a couple of my friends, but my family were only there in body, not spirit. I couldn't really blame them; it was a huge deal. Addy had been accepted too, and in August the Addisons hosted a party in the girls' honor, with lobster and champagne in a big white tent on their enormous lawn. I hid in a corner most of the night, feeling like I was visiting from another planet.

"Okay." Bode rolls his chair closer to me, our arms touching. "Wi-Fi password." He hands me a Post-it, with NOstr0m0 scrawled on it, and I get online. "So, all of the usual apps… messages, texts. You comfortable looking at all of this?"

"Got to be." I open one up and scroll through. There's a whole load of people trying to ping her since Sunday morning to see where she is. I skim the earlier ones—jokey, a few slightly pissed off she missed the brunch—to the later ones, the mounting concern, gathering desperation. "She hasn't texted anything after Saturday, 9:09 p.m." I show Bode. "Telling Scott she'd see him later at the party. Let's try email."

I open her inbox. A Moon Mountain staff memo about the end of the season, a few unopened promotional emails, a newsletter from a charity, and confirmation of her entry to a 10K run next month. I click on that one. "Looks like she signed up for this a few days ago. You don't do if that you're planning on going missing," I murmur. "Unless you want to put people off the scent, I suppose."

"Is that a possibility, she's cut loose?"

"No," I say quickly. "At least, I can't be 100 percent sure, but

I seriously doubt it." I take a breath. "There was this weird note Eli found at her place, Probably nothing, but I can't stop thinking about it…"

Bode's eyebrows rise into his curly fringe. "Go on."

I put the tablet down. "Some quote about throwing out the book of your life…?" Bode says nothing, but I can tell he's thinking that sounds pretty spot-on for someone who's gone missing. "Look it up for me, will you?"

"You got it."

"It goes something like: '"You can't tear out a single page, but you can throw the whole book.' Oh!" I almost shout. "It was written by some bloke called George. Wow, I remembered a name! That almost never happens."

"Don't be so tough on yourself; you've remembered plenty." Bode taps away. *"We cannot tear out a single page of our life but we can throw the whole book in the fire."*

"That's it!"

Bode nods. Taps again. Studies the phone.

"What?" I say, when I can't stand it anymore.

"He's a she." He scrolls. "The writer. George Sand, French novelist born 1804, real name Amantine Lucile Aurore Dupin."

"*Lucile*? Like Lucille who lives with Craig?"

"Think that's significant?" He reads some more. "Says here George Sand was one of the most popular writers in Europe, back in the day."

"Why did female novelists always pretend to be a George?" I frown.

"This George committed." Bode reads more. "Dressed as a man. Smoked in public, was into women's rights, had a *bunch* of affairs…"

"Okay, so she sounds amazing. What book is the quote from?"

"Something called *Mauprat*. Twenty bucks says I'm not pronouncing that right." Bode chews his lip. "Apparently the story's like 'Beauty and the Beast' but 'a reappraisal of the passive female role.'"

"Nice one. George has my vote."

"As for what the quote means…" Bode stares at his phone.

"Well?"

"Aw, this is just internet crap."

"Gimme!" I hold my hand out for the phone. Bode hands it to me reluctantly. I look at the screen, see the quote, and written below:

Tag: Suicide.

I give the phone back to Bode, return to the tablet and Gaia's emails.

"Es…?"

"No way," I say, not looking at him. I barely allow myself to breathe. "Not Gaia, I know it." I keep scrolling. There's a couple of emails from Ma and Dad—I glance through, the words dancing before my eyes—details of our impending visit, sent a couple of weeks ago.

"Could there be any reason? Are you sure she wouldn't…?"

"I *know* it. And I don't want to talk about it anymore."

I find two emails from me. I don't open them. I know what they say. Me moaning about my life. Telling Gaia that I'm beyond sick that one of my friends at home has started seeing the only boy in my school I even vaguely liked. God, I was so devastated about that, only a couple of weeks ago; it is *nothing* now. Gaia had replied with all the right words, but I remember feeling like her heart wasn't really in it. She was supportive, but distant and brief. I was a little hurt, but told myself I'd be seeing her soon, and could spend time poring over every little painful detail. Not that it had worked out that way.

"There's nothing here." I click to see the sent file and the trash, but it doesn't show anything significant. I shut the email down and open IMs and texts again. I rub my face. So many messages; there could be clues here if we go back far enough. "It's too much. How am I going to get through everything?"

Bode hesitates, a muscle in his jaw twitching. "Okay, I can do something, but it's not strictly legit."

"Go on,"

He skids his wheelie chair over to a filing cabinet with a key sticking out of it, opens a drawer and comes out with a small black box and a dangling lead.

"Copy her messages to my machine, run word searches for anything…sketchy."

"Like what?"

Bode reaches for a pen and raises an eyebrow. "*Craig, Motel, Party?*"

"*Watch. Rolex. Money.*" I grimace. "*Trouble, fight…hide?*"

He nods, writes them down. "It means I'm reading your sister's private messages. You down with that?"

"It could help find her, and we only have a short time."

"I look good in orange. Gimme twenty minutes." He pulls a laptop over from another corner of the desk and shoves it in front of me, typing and opening an internet browser. "Enough time for you to enter the twenty-first century."

"Eh?"

"You're joining the digital revolution and you're friending your sister." He begins to open multiple social media apps. "You know how to do that, don't you?" He looks up at me, bats his lashes.

"I get the concept."

"Great. I'll hold your hand while you sign up," he snarks back. I stick my tongue out. "I'm going to set you up on this laptop, change the password so you can access it anytime." He goes into settings. "Let's see…EsmE_R0x. Can you handle it?"

"Got to hope I'd remember that."

"And here's a doc where you can save your passwords, because let's face it, who can keep track of all of them. Hey, we'll call it…" He types frighteningly quickly. "EsPasswords. So fire up those socials. Friend Gaia's friends. See what everyone's conversating about. What the buzz is."

I hesitate. My stomach clenches.

"You should really talk to your mom and dad about creating a missing page; something people can share, post tips on, sightings, whatever. Look, I know it sounds kind of dramatic, but with someone like Gaia—popular, good-looking—it'll get shared, you'll get some media coverage, and it might get her found." Bode looks at me. "What's wrong? You okay?"

I'm not okay. Truth is, I'm not *that* big of a weirdo. I used to have social media. But I hated it. Kids posting videos of brutal practical jokes was bad enough. Girls and boys I knew, hung up about their appearance, posting bathroom pics with fake tans and photoshopped bodies. It felt like everyone was in a love-hate relationship with themselves. Friends bitching and shaming and arguing and bullying, or lying about their perfect lives and shoving it in your face—and then you block all of that only to find a constant barrage of images of plastic in the sea, dead babies in war zones, and animals going to slaughterhouses. I didn't want any of that in my head.

But now I don't have the choice to opt out. If it will help find Gaia, I'll do it.

"I'm fine." I run my fingers over the keyboard. "Does this thing have a camera? Gotta have a profile pic, don't I?"

Bode shows me how. Normally, the idea of a boy showing me how to do anything would make my skin crawl, but he manages not to be obnoxious—he doesn't even poke fun at me anymore. Once I know what I'm doing, we both tap away, side by side. It's oddly soothing, and I can hear him breathe, and the creak of his chair when he moves, the rain on the roof. The music has changed to low, melancholic, comforting blues that matches my mood exactly. I log in to my email, reactivate accounts that haven't seen action for years but rise

KIRSTY MCKAY

from the ashes because *nothing on the internet ever truly goes away.*

A few songs later, Bode jumps up from his seat. "That's our twenty minutes."

"You find anything?"

"Craig's got no game. Scott *loves* exclamation points. Addy has whole conversations in emojis. But nothing suspicious, no."

I sigh, disappointed. "Okay, well I need to get back. I've friended as many people as I can. The kids at home won't know what got into me. I guess they'll soon figure it out."

Bode leans back in his chair, arms above his head, knitting his fingers together and stretching until I hear knuckles crack. "Es? You're going to have to be straight up with the police. If they see activity on Gaia's accounts, they're going to think it's her doing it."

I nod. "Thought of that. But hey, I'm her sister. They might slap me on the wrist, but who cares?" I smack my forehead. "Oh, just got your joke about looking good in orange. Orange jumpsuits. *Prison.* If it comes to that, maybe I'll disappear off the radar too." I give him a weak smile.

Bode doesn't smile back. His face is blank like someone hit Pause.

"I've been so stupid!" He leaps up from the chair, snatching the tablet from the table, and swipes until a green radar icon appears on the screen. "Es," he says, his voice shaking. "Tell me you did Find My Phone already."

"What?" I stare at him dumbly. "Oh my god."

"You didn't?"

I grab Gaia's tablet from him and tap the Find My Phone app. Instantly, there's a map, showing the street and surroundings at Bode's barn. There's a tablet icon pinned over our location. There's also a grayed-out phone icon at the side of the map, with the word Offline below …

"If your sister's phone is switched on, it'll show on the map." Bode is hanging over me. "Sometimes it takes a couple minutes." Nothing. "*Come on, Gaia,*" Bode says, his voice low. We watch it, nothing changes. Finally, Bode groans. "Nada. Shit."

"Why didn't we do this yesterday? God!" I slap the table; the tablet topples over, but for once, miraculously, I make the catch. "None of us even thought about it." I set the tablet upright again. "Do you think her battery ran out? Or she's switched it off for some reason."

I won't let my head go to what that means, exactly. What if the phone got broken? Gaia had an accident? Or somebody else switched it off? As I'm pushing that thought from my mind, there's a little flicker of color out of the corner of my eye. Bode sees it too; we both lean over the tablet. The phone icon has appeared, in full color, on the map.

Online.

Right over our location.

"Bode…" I whisper, as though if I make too much noise, it will go away again. "What's happening?"

Bode is staring at it too; we're hardly breathing.

"How can that be?" I look at him. "It looks like the phone is right here!"

Bode takes two fingers and gently zooms in closer on the map. As the image gets larger, I gasp.

The little phone icon isn't hovering over Bode's side of the street, it's over Craig's house.

We run.

CHAPTER SEVENTEEN

"Nobody's home."

I bang on the door again.

It's raining hard. Bode and I are standing on the deck, trying to see through the window into Craig's house, but the blinds are drawn. Lucille and whoever she was laughing with earlier have rejoined the search? Or are ignoring us. I try the handle, but we're locked out.

"I know a way." Bode runs down the steps and I follow him into the downpour and around the side of the house. Gaia's tablet is in my backpack and I hug it to me. Bode stops in the yard, looks around for a second, and rolls a tree stump in front of the kitchen window that Gaia and Addy were smoking out of on Saturday night. "Craig told my uncle about this. He hasn't got around to fixing it yet. Least, I hope not." He stands on the stump, reaches up and holds the window frame, jiggling it up and down until the latch on the inside works its way around and unhooks. "Might as well add breaking and entering to our list of misdemeanors." He pulls himself up through the window and I climb onto the stump, determined not to need help. Scraping my belly on the sill, I tumble onto the kitchen floor.

"Anybody here?" Bode yells. I follow him into the hallway, getting the tablet out of the damp bag. "Got a signal? She must've used her tablet on Craig's Wi-Fi before."

"The phone icon is directly over where we are. Do we have to search every room?"

Bode leans over me. He taps the screen, puts a finger to his lips, *shhh*… I hold my breath.

A beeping noise, quiet at first, getting louder.

"Where?" I whisper.

Bode runs lightly out into the lounge; I'm right behind him.

"Upstairs!"

The beeping is louder, it's coming from a bedroom…not the first one… I race toward Craig's room, beating Bode to it, flinging the door open. The beeping stops.

"Near the far window." I hand Bode the tablet, treading softly across the floor as if too heavy a step will make the phone disappear for good.

"Closer to the bed."

There's the window, the beer keg, the bedside table, and the bed. Nowhere to hide. I looked here before!

"Make it beep again."

He taps, we wait. Nothing.

"Last gasp," he says. "Battery's dead."

I'm already on my hands and knees, scrabbling to look under the bed.

And there it is, Gaia's phone.

I'd sent her a Snoopy cover for Christmas, but when we'd arrived at Moon I was upset that she didn't have it on her phone. The next day, Snoopy was in place. And here he is now. Hot tears spring to my eyes as I extend an arm and claw the phone out, skimming it across the floor. The tears won't stop. I lean over, and sob, my body shuddering, ridding itself of so many hours holding back.

"Sorry," I gasp at last.

"You don't have to apologize."

"Bode, she wouldn't leave her phone behind." I rub at my face, wanting the tears gone.

"Maybe we shouldn't touch it."

"Sod that, I'm her sister, my prints are probably on it anyway." I pick it up, fingertips on corners. I try to switch it on, but he was right, the battery is dead. We both stare at it in silence for a minute, then I open my backpack and carefully put it in the inner pocket. "I'll give it to the police with the tablet. How the hell did her phone get under the bed? I looked there yesterday when Dad and I were here with Scott."

"Could it have dropped down from somewhere?"

From the bed, he means. But haven't we decided that if she was rolling around on a bed with Craig, it was at the Eazy Stay?

"The ringer must have been on mute, otherwise someone would have heard it. We've been blowing up her phone." I shake my head. "Okay, say somehow I missed it yesterday. Maybe she and Craig came up here on Saturday night to drink; there's a keg over there."

"Is there anything else of hers around?" Bode stands, surveying the room. "The police will want to search the whole house. I'm kinda surprised they haven't already."

"Yeah," I sniff, looking around. "I can't see any of her stuff." I go to get to my feet, but something catches my eye. At first, I think I'm imagining it; I lean closer to get a better look. "Bode." I try to keep my voice steady. "Is that paint?" I point to the beer keg. On the metal rim, there's a streak of color. Brownish red.

"Could be anything." Bode says.

"It looks like blood."

"It could be blood," he agrees. "But, Es, it could be anything."

"It's not a splash." I look at him. "Not spatter, more like someone has got blood on their hands and touched the rim."

"Yeah," Bode says. "But even if it is blood, it could be anyone's blood."

I nod, trying to hold it together, trying to reason with myself. If it *is* blood, it's not enough to be concerning. *But* we have just found Gaia's phone, and *oh gosh*, here's a keg that I saw Craig with, and *will you look at that*, there's dried red stuff on it. Not good.

"I think it's time we got out of here, Es." Bode says quietly. "Tell the cops, let them deal with it."

I rise slowly, eyes stuck on the keg, willing it to change, for the smear of color to fade like it's a trick of the light and we're spooked and imagining things that aren't there. But it doesn't disappear. Even when I've moved to the other side of the room by the door, I look back one last time and I can't not see that stain on the metal. *How come I missed that yesterday too?*

As we reach the top of the stairs, there's thumping at the door.

"Open up! Police!"

We freeze in our tracks. Bode swears.

"Want to get out through the kitchen window?" I whisper. "I'll distract them."

Bode shakes his head. "No." He reaches over and squeezes my hand. "I got you."

I nod, and we run down the stairs.

If Detective Graff is surprised to see us, she doesn't show it. I introduce her to Bode, because even in extremely heightened situations I still have my manners. I come clean about the tablet and reveal the star prize: Gaia's phone. Detective Graff gives nothing away. She dons gloves and takes everything out of my backpack, writing down the password for Gaia's tablet. She asks where we found the phone and we take her to the bedroom. The bonus is, of course, that potential bloodstain, and this is where she excels. I can tell there's a whole range of something going on behind the eyes, but her expression stays completely neutral, her voice calm as she radios for backup.

"Let's have you wait in the car." She escorts us out of the house and through the pouring rain, opening the door to the back seat. "Sit tight for me."

She pops the trunk and takes out a small briefcase. As she returns to the house with the case, the central locking clicks. It's not a patrol car—there's no wire grating or glass divide, it looks normal apart from the radio and a flashing light on a curly wire—but it's locked.

The rain is rattling on the roof.

"I'm sorry to drag you into this. I'll say it was all me, you only came along because I asked you to."

Bode looks at me; there are water droplets on his hair, like little gems. "Don't worry 'bout that. If it gets them closer to finding her, totally worth it."

"Thanks. But don't admit to the computer stuff, okay?" I grip his arm. "We need to keep our stories straight. I came to you with the tablet, I went into Gaia's accounts, and we pinged her phone. I made you come over to Craig's to help me look." I let go of his arm. "Honestly, I'll feel so much worse if you get into trouble over this."

He nods, looks away.

"We don't need to say we read her messages. The good thing is they'll go through them now, right? Search them for clues? So no need to confess—I can't have you being locked up." I smile. "Otherwise, who am I gonna call when I want to do the next bunch of dodgy stuff?"

He chuckles. "*Dodgy*. I live for the dodgy."

The windows are steaming up. When a cop car arrives, I wipe the condensation with my hand to see Officer Hernandez and another policeman get out and meet Detective Graff and her briefcase. I can't hear what they're saying, but the new cop goes back to his car, takes out yellow tape, and begins fixing it around the entrance to the house. *Oh god, it's like a movie.*

Over Bode's shoulder, I watch Detective Graff make a phone call, and by the way she's glancing over at us, and the expression on her face, I can't help but think she's talking to my mother. Call finished, she says something to the other cops before getting into the front of the car, briefcase on the passenger seat.

"Esme, I'm going to drive you back to your lodgings and your mom and dad." She starts the ignition. "Bode, I haven't tracked your uncle down yet, he's still out with one of the search parties, but when I do, I'm going to ask him to meet us at the lodge also. We'll take y'all's statements."

"Detective Graff…" I take a breath. "Is that blood on the beer keg?" She says nothing, her back to us. "Did you test it with something in that briefcase?"

She sits there a couple of seconds, turns around and looks at me through the seats. "The test was positive for blood. But Esme, right now that's all we know. It could be anybody's blood—heck, it could even be a critter. These crime scene tests don't distinguish between animal and human." She pats the briefcase. "I'll get this to our lab; they'll tell us what we need to know. 'Til then, no point in getting in a fix about it, right?"

I have a dozen questions, but I mumble a "yes" as Graff pulls out into the road.

Blood.

CHAPTER EIGHTEEN

––––––

At the lodge we're greeted by a wet and wild set of parents with hopeful, staring eyes. They don't look too mad, but I'm not counting my chickens yet. They've got priorities. They want to know about Gaia's phone more than they want to tear a strip off me.

The fire is burning and the living room feels too hot, and way too full of people. Eli, Addy, Scott, and various friends have heard the news about the phone and are lingering, but Detective Graff quickly gets rid of everyone except my family. Bode and I are interviewed separately; me upstairs, him in the lounge. I hope he's sticking to the story.

Ma and Dad sit in on my interview. It feels totally nuts, the three of us perching on the end of their bed while Detective Graff sits awkwardly on the small stool at the dressing table, her long legs crossed, notepad on her knee. Thank god she's had a chance to tell my parents about the blood. I was dreading them hearing about it, and when we got to that bit, I keep emphasizing how it was A Really Small Amount. All things considered, they're dealing with it well. Ma looks a bit green, and there's this energy about them, a kind of coiled desperation, barely contained, but they are holding it together. Ma's phone keeps buzzing like an irate bee; she has it on silent, and each time it vibrates, she glances at it.

I learn a couple of things too. Detective Graff tells us she's going to organize a blood sample to be taken from my mother to compare against the blood on the keg. She warns us we may not hear "for some time," but she'll put pressure on for a quick result. Also, the police got in contact with Gaia's phone company and pinged the handset a short time before we did, and it showed up as being somewhere on Craig's street. Detective Graff took an educated guess and struck lucky first time when she showed up at the house. They pinged Craig's phone too, and his has come back as being local, but he's with a different provider and they can only narrow it down to a twelve-mile radius. It doesn't quite put him in Canada, but that's no small area to search.

After my time upstairs, I escape to find Bode eating a sandwich in the kitchen. There's a huge spread of food on a silver platter. *Go, Addisons.* Bode looks up at me mid-chew, guilty expression on his face.

"Sorry, they told me to eat."

I smile. "Look who's apologizing now, don't be daft. I'm starving." I pick over a sandwich tray, remove some cheese, and bite into a lettuce and tomato on whole wheat. *Oh shit, butter.* "Everything go okay?"

"Sure." He gives me a look. "You?"

"Fine," I say, going for a banana this time. "Bode, how come I didn't see Gaia's phone under the bed before, when I was there with my dad and Scott? It's bugging me. Do you think someone could have put it there afterward?"

"Who?"

"I dunno, maybe Lucille?"

Bode's eyes widen. "Why pick her?"

"She lives in that house. And I don't like her. At the party, she quite literally snarled at me."

"How come?"

I remember standing on the deck, waiting for Gaia at the end of the night. Craig had slammed the damn door in my face; I was pissed off, and a little scared, if I'm honest. The snow was falling, Addy had already left and was disappearing up the road, and I knew if I lost sight of her I wouldn't find my way home on my own.

"Lucille was outside, kissing some guy on the steps. I was in a hurry, and I slipped and nearly took them both out."

Bode snorts. "Least you didn't puke on them."

I shake my head. "I apologized, but she was as cold as ice, said something like, 'Gaaad, go to bed already, kid!'"

Bode titters at my attempt at the accent.

"The guy she was with was weird too…" I frown at the memory. "Not mean, but… He just smiled…and blew me a kiss." I shake myself. "Anyway, I don't trust Lucille. Perhaps she found Gaia's phone somewhere in the house, thought it made her look bad because she's the only one still living there, so she threw it under Craig's bed?" I sigh. "But then again, why not just ditch it in the woods?"

"Hayley's friends with Lucille." Bode takes another sandwich. "I guess I could ask her what she thinks her deal is."

"I don't want to make any more trouble for you."

"Oh, I'm always in trouble with Hayley. It's like a permanent state." He smiles ruefully. We both chew our lunch thoughtfully for a minute before he speaks again. "So, I was sitting here thinking about that social media 'Missing' page I mentioned?"

"Yeah," I pour myself an apple juice and take a gulp. "I don't know if my folks can face doing anything like that just yet. There's still a bunch of family and friends who don't know she's missing."

"It already happened." He holds up his phone.

I glance at the screen and nearly choke on my juice. A pic of Gaia—a gorgeous one, this time—Gaia in a strappy red dress I don't recognize, glitter on her cheeks, huge smile—stares back at me. And a page name below:

MISSING GAIA GILL!

I stare at Bode. "You did this?"

He looks horrified. "No way."

"Give me that," I take his phone, almost dropping it. I scroll down. There's text:

Nineteen-year-old GAIA GILL was last seen at a house party on Bluff Point, Moon Mountain Resort, New Hampshire, in the early hours of Sunday, April 15th. GAIA has been working at the resort as a VIP Guest Concierge since November of last year. Her family is very concerned about her and are seeking any information on her whereabouts. GAIA is mixed race (white/African American), 5'11", 145 lbs with a slim/athletic build, curly, shoulder-length black hair, brown eyes, and mid-brown skin. NB: GAIA speaks with a British accent. At the time of her disappearance, GAIA was wearing a dark green parka, a black beanie, a red sweater, and blue jeans.

Below, there's a pinned post marked UPDATE!!!!! with information about Craig, his description and how they might be together. And below that, comments…and comments…and comments. I recognize worried school friends, one of Gaia's teachers, my dad's workmates, a cousin…

"How long has this been up?"

"Not long, judging by the timeline…forty minutes?"

I think about my mother's phone constantly buzzing during the last part of the interview. People from home calling, worried, *frantic*, probably. I feel anger and panic welling up inside. My family was not ready to go full public yet.

"Who did this?" I shout at Bode, like it's his fault. He stands up.

"I can see who the admin is."

"Who?"

"Scott."

Of course. I scroll down. There's a pinned video post, the one from this morning. I click on it and see everyone gathered in the lounge. There's my sleep- and confusion-addled face, Scott's voice interviewing me. He *was* filming. *What a dickhead!*

"Where is he?" I growl, marching out into the lounge, looking out of the window across to the "command center" at Lodge 12. At the same time, my mother appears on the stairs, in an intense convo with someone on her phone.

"Esme!" Dad hisses at me. "Have you posted something on the internet?"

"No, I have not!" I put my boots and coat on, still clutching Bode's phone. "It's Scott, that arsehole! He's over there!" I fling the door open and run out into the cold. As I get to the lodge, the door opens, and Scott's standing there. And he's got his phone in my face already.

"Es! Can you tell me anything about finding Gaia's phone?"

I thump his arm away. "Stop it! Stop filming! How dare you do this? I can't believe you put that Missing page up. It's not your call!"

Scott looks horrified. "Es, I thought you were on board with everything I've been doing. She's my best friend."

"She's my sister!"

Bode arrives, followed closely by Dad, who starts berating Scott too, then Detective Graff is there and getting between them. My mother has hung up her phone and is screaming at my dad, I'm hugging her and shouting at Scott, and people are coming out of the command lodge onto the deck to see what the hell is happening.

"Simmer down, people!" Detective Graff shouts, but for once, nobody is listening.

Then I hear something, a noise from inside the lodge. I turn to look through the gap in the people and I can see a man on a walkie-talkie, his voice barely audible above the din around me. I hear the word *body*, someone says, "Alive?" and there's a murmur and a ripple of energy which turns into a wave of movement, and as I watch, someone pushes through the crowd in the doorway and launches themself out onto the deck.

"It's Craig Wilks! They've found him!"

CHAPTER NINETEEN

——

It's like someone dropped a bunch of $100 bills from the sky. People—so many people—erupt out of the lodge, shouting into walkie-talkies. Within seconds two quads and a four-wheel drive roar up the lane, spilling out yet more bodies. Detective Graff and the man from Mountain Rescue are attempting to organize the excited mass, and out of the corner of my eye, I see Officer Hernandez telling my parents to return to our lodge. *Good luck with that.*

"Hey, Es, this way." Bode beckons and we duck down the side of the building before anyone notices. "Heard my uncle's voice on the walkie. I know where they found Craig. We going?"

"Show me the way."

We race across the grass. Every second I'm praying that no one sees and calls us back, but we safely reach the woods that stretch down the mountain toward town.

"The moose shortcut we came up yesterday?" Bode pants.

"They'll be driving down there." He holds a low-hanging branch out of the way for me, and together we jump a ditch and bushwhack our way deeper into the forest. Bode forges ahead, looks both ways, and chooses a route. "I heard my uncle say they're at the deer tower." He starts downhill. "It's only 'bout a mile away by the trail, but we can beat 'em on foot."

"Shortcut for the shortcut." I scramble down the bank alongside him. "Like it."

"Wait up!" There's a shout behind us and we turn around. *Shit.* Two figures are following us: Eli and Addy.

"Pretend we haven't heard," I urge Bode; he nods, and we scramble on. I have no idea if they've been sent to bring us back, or are just along for the ride, but either way I'm not hanging around to find out. They're faster, but my advantage is I have someone who knows where he's going and how. I step where Bode steps, maneuvering around rocks and sliding down a steep bank on my backside. I can hear our pursuers crashing through the woods behind us, but I think we might be losing them. Ahead, I see Bode come to a halt. "Keep going!" I shout, loud as I dare, but then I see what the problem is: a river, white water in a gulch below, cutting off our path.

"Damn it." Bode scratches his head. "This is normally dry; I don't know if we can cross." He climbs down the bank toward the river and shouts up to me. "Too much meltwater, too deep. Tower is the other way, but to cross we'll have to go downstream and work our way back up."

Before I reply, there's a shout again.

"Wait!" Addy yells. "Didn't you hear us?" She and Eli career down the last slope and stop beside us on the bank, bent double with the effort.

"I'm not going back!"

"Nobody's telling you to," snaps Eli. "We only followed because I know *he* knows where they found Craig." He points to Bode.

"Too bad we won't get there before everyone else now." Bode frowns. "We'll have to follow this river to the trail; they'll beat us to it."

"No way," I say, climbing down the bank to the water's edge. "Eli, you can make yourself useful and help us cross here."

"What?" Bode says. "It's too wide, Es."

"Not if we move that." I point to a pine tree that has fallen, roots and all, halfway down the bank. The tree has lost quite a few branches and is small enough for four people to lift. "See, there, with the rocks?" I shout up to them. "We fling the tree across and we've got a bridge. Simple." I am sounding way more confident than I feel, and the boys are both looking at me like I've come unglued, but Addy is sliding down towards me, her face set with determination.

"Let's do this."

I nod at her, heartened, and together, we stride over to the tree and pull at it.

"Get down here, Eli!" Addy yells. Bode jumps, and Eli rolls his eyes and follows.

"It's a bloody Christmas tree," he says. "It won't hold our weight."

"Sure it will," Bode says. "Just think happy thoughts."

It *is* about the height of the Christmas tree the Addisons have in their enormous entrance hall every year, but that's pretty huge. Together, we drag it to the water. Bode thumps the bottom of the trunk down on a rock on the bank and steadies it with his boot.

"Haul it up!" he shouts. Eli, Addy, and I grab branches and pull precariously, hands rubbed red raw, raising the mighty timber—before crashing it down. It's pure luck that it lands over the rocks. Before I can say anything, Bode has started climbing across; with each step he has to thread through the branches, balancing on the trunk, but he makes it to the last rock like he does this in his sleep.

"Have to jump from here, trunk's too thin!" He shouts across, beckoning Addy, but she's already going for it, even quicker than Bode. She leaps, unaided, past Bode's rock to the bank, dusts herself off.

"Piece of cake, Es! You can do it!"

Oh shit, can I, though? Balance and coordination are not my big skills. But I'm damned if I'm letting anyone see that I'm scared. I take the first step off the nice, flat, safe rock and onto the slippery trunk, and it's tricky as hell because of all the branches, and oh sweet jingle bells, it's a-wobblin' and a-rollin' under my foot. Whose bright idea was this?

"Take it slow, you'll be fine!" Addy yells over the noise of the rushing water, which seems so much more menacing now I'm suspended over it. I bend from the waist, hanging on to any available branches, eyes searching for the next space to put my foot. *Don't look at the water. Just keep moving. Think Ninja Warrior.* A couple of steps, and I've found my next rock. I'm halfway.

"You got this, Es," Bode says, just loud enough for me to hear. It's the kind of thing that would irritate the hell out of me if anyone else said it, but he says it so casually, like *of course* I've got this, that it's exactly what I need to hear. I flash him a quick smile and step gingerly over the final, thinnest part of the tree, which bends alarmingly as I put my whole weight on it.

"Oh god, it's going to go!"

The trunk creaks. I crouch down, clinging to the branches, the water only inches below. "I can't think happy thoughts!" I screech at Bode. "I'm not Peter Pan!"

"So think angry ones," Bode leans toward me from the rock a few feet away, holding out a hand. He's right. *Screw this river,* I think. *Damn to hell this cold mountain that has swallowed up my sister. I will get her back and I will not let it claim me!* Somehow, I stand up again, put one foot in front of the other, and make it to the final rock, stick out a hand for Bode to hold—because, hell, I'm not proud—and with a giant lunge, I've made it.

I don't have time to celebrate before there's a crashing of sticks and water and Eli has launched himself across that Christmas tree like a cat tied up in tinsel. At first, sheer momentum carries him across, but as he reaches the rock where Bode is, a branch snags his foot, he goes down hard on his belly, arms and legs flailing, and for an awful moment I think he's actually impaled himself on a branch, as he wriggles there, nestled in pinecones. With sickening inevitability, gravity kicks in, and the tree rolls and topples over. Eli rolls with it and plops into the water, with barely a splash.

"Eli!" Addy screams, but remarkably her brother is on his feet, waist deep in the freezing torrent, his face stretched as he gasps in horror at the cold. Honestly, I'd laugh if I wasn't a nicer person. Eli's arms are waving, the current spinning him. Bode reaches from the rock, but Eli's too far gone.

"Dude, grab something!" Bode yells. "Keep on your feet!"

Addy is climbing down past me on the bank, and I can see why. The current is pushing Eli downriver.

"Eli! Grab this!" She's holding a branch and is flopping it toward him, he's trying to catch it, trying to keep his footing, and she's bopping him on the head with fronds of evergreen. After a few whacks and a particularly cringey eye poke, Eli seizes the branch, and Addy pulls him in. He climbs out on to the bank, ashen-faced and shivering uncontrollably.

"Get your trousers off!" I shout. "You'll freeze otherwise!"

"What?" Eli shudders back. "No!"

"You could die of exposure in minutes!" I yell.

"Really?" Addy says.

"Don't…be…ridiculous," Eli says, teeth chattering.

"Tell him, Bode!" I plead. "We only have seconds!"

Bode nods. "Dude, I've seen frostbite in that *area*." He waves a hand over his groin. "You do not want that, believe me."

Eli looks horrified, and quickly unbuckles his jeans with blue fingers. He kicks off his boots and strips off the wet denim, hopping on one foot and nearly falling in the drink again before tossing the jeans aside like they're soaked in acid.

"And the thermals." I point to his leggings. "Anything that's wet has to come off!"

Eli gingerly peels off his thermals. "I am not taking my underwear off!"

"Your call, I respect that," Bode says, turning to me. "Whaddya call that breakfast sausage you guys eat in the UK? Black pudding. Man." He shakes his head. "I'll never forget what that frostbite looked like."

"You little shits, you're having me on!" Eli roars, pulling at his boots and stomping, bare-legged, up the bank away from the river. "Now take us to Craig before I freeze my bloody bollocks off!"

Addy raises her eyebrows at us and follows him. Their backs turned, I hold up a palm to Bode, and he lightly slaps it.

"The deer tower."

Bode's led us out of the woods to a clearing. On the other side of the frost-bleached grass is a hut on massive stilts, almost as high as the trees behind. As we draw closer, I can see movement at the bottom. A stocky, gray-haired man in a checked shirt waves.

"Saul!" Bode calls, and we run. By the bottom of the ladder is a body on the ground. Everything good drains from me.

It's Craig.

Even though I knew it was going to be him, it's still a shock to see. Craig's lying on his back, with a coat—presumably Bode's uncle's—pulled over him. His face is dirty and pale, he has a blood-caked head, and both of his legs are turned inwards at an unnatural angle.

"Oh my god, Craig!" Addy drops down beside him.

"Is he alive?" Eli says.

"He's alive." If Bode's uncle thinks it's weird Eli is wearing a coat, boots, and nothing much in between, he doesn't say. "Reckon he's been out here overnight. Bode, you bring these kids?"

"Yeah, this is Es, Gaia's sister. And Addy and Eli are her friends."

Saul nods at me. "Where's the cavalry? Damn radio's flat. Good job I found him when I did."

"They're coming on the trail, should be here any minute," Bode answers. He looks up at the hut. "Did he fall?"

Saul shrugs. "Could be. Got a knock to the head, broken legs, maybe ribs. He's coming in and out of consciousness, was trying to talk earlier."

"He was?" I gasp. "Did he say anything about my sister?" I look wildly around the clearing. "Could she be near?"

"No sign that I could see, I was searching south of here before I came upon him. She could've walked out another direction though.'" Saul scratches the back of his head and looks down at Craig. "If he said anything worthwhile, I couldn't make sense of it."

Before I really know what I'm doing, I run into the middle of the clearing and yell.

"*Gaia! Gaia!*"

There's no reply but my voice bouncing back at me. I run another way. "Gaia! Can you hear me!"

"Cooee!"

I spin around; there are people heading across the clearing. Mountain Rescue carrying a stretcher, and behind, Detective Graff. As I watch them approach, the heavens open, and it pours. Within seconds, we all look like we've been in the river along with Eli. Everything speeds up, everyone on double time; Craig is lifted onto a stretcher, I'm ushered by Mountain Rescue back over the clearing to the woods and through to the moose trail. They give Bode, Eli, Addy, and me a huge umbrella to huddle under as they try and work out who's going in which vehicle.

"'Did you have anything to do with this, Eli?" I try to keep my voice down, but we're packed tight together, so everyone hears. Eli looks at me, his face white.

"Are you kidding me? Of course I didn't!"

"Why would you say that?" Addy stares at me.

"Because—oh, I dunno—he said if anything had happened to Gaia, he'd go after Craig!'" I spit out.

"I did not!" Eli abandons the shelter of the umbrella. "And if you go spreading that around, Esme, my family will sue!"

"Like I care!" I give up on the umbrella too, and Addy breaks away, leaving Bode standing holding it like the little man who comes out of the weather house to say it's going to rain.

"He's coming round!" A shout goes up. The rescuers are lifting Craig into the back of a four-wheel drive, and suddenly he's moving on the stretcher, trying to sit up.

"Craig!" I cry out, running over to him, the others hot on my tail.

"Esme!" Detective Graff shouts. Craig focuses on me. His eyes widen, and he groans.

"It's okay, Craig, you're safe," one of the rescue people reassures him. "We're getting you to the hospital. You can relax."

But Craig doesn't relax. He's agitated, he's trying to sit up, pushing against the restraints on the stretcher. Everyone is telling him to calm down, lie still, but he's staring hard at us all standing in the rain, with the weirdest look on his face.

"Where's my sister, Craig?"

"Come with me, Esme," Detective Graff says. "Let us deal with this."

"Where's Gaia?" I yell at Craig.

"Come on." Detective Graff takes me by the arm, and as she tries to lead me away, I watch Craig's eyes roll backward and his body flop, surrendering to the stretcher and the reassuring hands around him. I give in to Detective Graff's ushering, and for the second time today I find myself in a police car. Beside me, Bode is telling me the police will question Craig, that it's only a matter of time before they find my sister, find Gaia.

But I ignore him. Because it doesn't make sense. I can't get over the expression on Craig's face, so intense, but I couldn't read it—was it fear, or rage, or panic? And strangest of all, even though I was the one screaming at him, that look wasn't aimed at me.

Craig was looking at someone else.

CHAPTER TWENTY

———

I'm not sure I'll ever feel dry again. I never knew it could rain this hard for this long.

Craig's at the hospital in New Lanchester. An ambulance met him on the main road, and Officer Hernandez went with him. All we know is he's stable, and he's not talking. Whether that means he won't, or he can't, is unclear. I keep thinking about the strange look on his face when he was staring over my shoulder. Was he looking at Eli? For all his talk, I can't quite believe Eli would actually take Craig on in a fit of overprotective rage; he'd be so obviously out muscled. And Craig's expression wasn't anger. Was it…shock or guilt? Maybe he was looking at Detective Graff? Or someone else?

They couldn't keep me in the lodge for long. I was itching to get back into the woods. Part of the reason was wanting to escape Scott, who was waiting for us, cozy by the fire. He'd been ever-so-sorry about the social media page, but I was still furious.

"Mrs. Gill, I feel devastated that I've hurt you. He'd looked at my mother from beneath his long lashes. "Gaia will frickin' whoop my ass for that." I could see Ma's face soften slightly, and Scott chanced a smile. "I only want to find her, and time is of the essence. Detective Graff will back me up on that."

Detective Graff is the kind of person who I'd be willing to bet is wholly immune to Scott's charms, but she nodded. "Social media gets the word out better than we ever could, it's true. Scott here has an audience. And the sooner we raise awareness, the better."

"It should have come from us." My dad's voice sounded hoarse from lack of sleep. "Family and friends back home have been given a hell of a shock."

Scott's eyes welled up. "That was not my intention, Mr. Gill, you have to believe me. I should have asked you first. I thought it was something I could do to save you from dealing with it."

True enough. Nobody spoke for a moment. The rain was drumming on the windows, the fire crackled in the grate, and normally that would be one of my favorite sound baths, but it felt claustrophobic. Bode was lingering, awkward and damp in the kitchen with his uncle, and I resisted the urge to grab him and make a break for it, run to that perfect cabin in the woods, get far, far away from this upset, this mess, this exhausting cocktail of hope and dread that was burning my stomach.

Detective Graff stood, wiped her hands down her waterproof trousers. "I'm gonna suggest that you let Scott run with this, Mr. and Mrs. Gill, and add Esme as an admin on the page;

you hear me, Scott?" She looked over at him but didn't wait for agreement. "That way, the family has input and control. Let's face it, the younger generation are way better at managing these things, am I right?"

Well, not necessarily, I'd thought, but didn't say. Ma got her laptop, Scott added me, it was done. As I'd watched the comments growing in real time, Detective Graff leaned over my shoulder, straightened up, and cleared her throat.

"Now, let me make one thing clear." She looked over to Scott. "Work with us, not against us. Don't risk Gaia by going rogue. If you do everything with police collaboration, that's how we'll find her, you understand me?" We'd all nodded meekly. Scott may have squeezed out another tear.

Detective Graff told us she'd give us an update when they had a chance to properly question Craig. In the meantime, she recommended we stay put, but Family Gill wasn't having any of that, and there was nothing the police could do to stop us from joining the search party in the woods.

It'd rained all afternoon, without a break. The rescue people gave us a grid system to work, slowly and painstakingly, and we'd searched—my family, Bode and his uncle, Addy, Eli, and Gaia's friends, and a bunch of hardy volunteers. These folks are mostly older adults, like, retirees? All shockingly fit and unremittingly positive. They all knew who I was, clapped me on the back as we walked, shoulder to shoulder, so encouraging and optimistic it almost began to feel like I was worrying over nothing—Gaia would be over the next ridge, around the next boulder. Watching them, with their bits of kit and their smiling faces, it was obvious that on some level, they were enjoying this. It's a strange hobby. I can't be angry about that, only intensely grateful.

I stuck with it for as long as I could, walking the grid. Until you are in the thick of it, you have no idea how many places someone can get lost in a forest. There are ditches, gullies, banks, massive holes left by fallen trees, dark corners to explore. There are dense, springy beds of ferns and long clumpy grasses that knit together and form a kind of carpet that goes down a meter deep. It's almost impossible to walk in a straight line because of networks of thorny vines and clusters of seemingly impenetrable bushes, thorns, prickles, stinging things.

A call went up twice. Once, it was an old, gray ski glove, the leather bleached and hardened. Even I could tell that it'd been lying in the wood for a year or two. The second time, someone found a dirty magazine stuffed into a hollow by the side of the main trail. It looked recent, protected from the wet by a plastic bag. A bunch of people tried to stop me from seeing it—there was a real fluster. They bagged both items as potential evidence, but it all felt like a distraction from the main event.

I didn't want to find clues, I wanted to find *Gaia*. I wanted to run, yelling her name, until she yelled back.

So I did.

I escaped, launched myself deeper into the woods alone, my shouts all but drowned out by the constant barrage of rain hitting treetops. I stumbled on, grimly determined, fell over more times than I could count, and found...a dead deer.

A fawn was lying on the grass, delicate and perfect apart from a red gash to her neck.

It knocked the breath out of me to see death close-up. What—or who—did this? I spun around, my skin tingling and throat tightening, but the woods were so dark and dense, and the onslaught of the downpour overwhelmed my senses. The sensation of being watched, ever present, threatened to root me to the spot if I didn't keep moving. Panicked, I ran back toward where I thought the searchers were and, by sheer, stupid luck, spotted them.

Finding that sad, sodden little animal shifted something in me. The feeling that Gaia might be dead had been seeping into my head, slowly, sneakily, since I found her phone and saw the blood. But the deer changed everything. I *cannot* imagine my vital, luminous, infuriating sister as a lifeless body on the forest floor. She's still alive, I know it—and she's out there.

I sit on a fallen tree, blinking the rain away. Bode tramps through the grass toward me, water dripping off his face.

"Hey. They're done. We've searched everything between here and the trail and the spot they found Craig."

I frown. "What about the river?" I think about that rushing water. God, what if she was somewhere near the crossing, hearing us taking the piss out of Eli, lying there, trapped, while I'm making jokes and getting a thrill out of spending time with Bode? I feel sick to my stomach.

"Don't worry, that's next on the list." Bode says. "Saul's gonna take your mom and dad there, along with a couple volunteers. I'm gonna look there too, after I take you back."

"Back where?" I ask, but I already know.

Bode shifts, uncomfortably. "Your folks want you to get a change of clothes, eat something."

"No!" I stand, seeing Ma coming up behind Bode. "I can't go back yet…"

"I understand, love," Ma says, her face strained as if she's in physical pain. "But I need you there. I don't like the lodge being empty in case she comes back. Please."

"Bullshit, you just don't want me searching!" I shout at her. "Don't make me go back. It's unbearable to sit and wait. You said so yourself!"

"Darling." She holds my shoulders, her face a few inches from mine. "Remember what Gaia always says? Work hard, but work *clever*. That's where you come in. Check the page Scott set up, see if there are any clues, any tips or ideas." She glances at a group of Gaia's work friends who are gathering to leave. "Talk to any of those kids—there might be something they'll tell you that they don't want to share with the adults." Her voice chokes. "Dad and I can't do everything, Es. We need your help."

I nod frantically. I know I'm being played, but she's right. Bode and I walk back to the trail with some of the rescue people and get a ride to the lodges. Bode is up front, and Addy sits beside me in the back, looking wet and thoroughly miserable.

"Hey," I whisper to her. "When you've changed, come round, yeah? I could do with a talk."

"Def. Can you believe my parents have gone to Boston for a few days? Talk about timing, arseholes." She purses her lips.

"Pop left Eli here to watch over me, but he's got better things to do, thank god."

"Ads, did Eli ever tell you about that note he found?" I whisper. "In your room?"

"The quote?" Addy's eyes roll. "He's so stupid and overdramatic. It's from some set text Gaia studied for exams last year. She was probably using it as a bookmark."

"You don't think Gaia left it for us to find, or anything?"

"What? No!" Her face changes as she stares past me, out of the window. "Jeez. What's going on?"

There are bright lights outside our lodge. As the car draws level, I see a flash of white. There's a man standing on the covered deck, holding a camera, the light is mounted on top of it, a curtain of rain falling behind, illuminated in the glow. The camera is pointed at a woman with a microphone. She's interviewing someone on the deck.

Scott.

"Oh god, don't stop here, go on to my place," Addy tells the driver before turning to me. "You can dodge them."

"No!" I surprise her, and myself. "It's okay. I'll get out." *What am I doing?* I open the door, and as I do, the camera swings around to me, the interviewer moving to check me out. I walk up to the lodge, Bode behind me. The car with Addy drives on.

"Hi!" the interviewer calls out to me, as I walk up the steps. "Izzy Wizbowski from WNEC News! Who are you? Have you been out searching for Gaia Gill?"

I quickly look at Scott, then at Bode. "Hi, yeah I'm Gaia's

sister." I tuck a wet piece of hair behind my ear and instantly feel like the vainest person alive.

The interviewer practically squirms with delight. "That's amazing. Do you mind talking to us? What's your name and how old are you?"

A weird feeling rises in me; at first, I don't recognize it, but then I realize it's anger. Anger that my sister is missing. Anger that Scott is in the spotlight, and not hating it, by the looks of things. Anger that this woman in front of me is so damn... perky. I take a breath.

"My name is Esme. I'm almost sixteen."

Oh god. "Almost sixteen." How completely infantile.

"Esme!" She shouts my name back to me. "You must be Gaia's younger sister, right? And you've been out in this terrible weather searching—have you found any signs of her?"

I shake my head. "No, not yet. There are still people out looking."

"I see." She nods her head, reassuringly. "And, Ez-eem." She takes a noble stab at remembering my name. "We heard that police picked up your nineteen-year-old sister Gaia's boyfriend, thirty-three-year-old Craig Wilks, who was injured in the woods near here, and they've held him for questioning. What do you think about that?"

"Craig's not her boyfriend!" *Whoa, that came out way louder than it should have.* "He's my ski instructor." *And that sounds weirdly worse.* "He's in the hospital. They don't even know if my sister was with him."

"Oh really?" Izzy says. "So, Craig Wilks is denying everything."

My mouth opens. Bode touches my arm. "Do you want to go inside, Es?" he says quietly.

"And who are you?" Izzy asks him. "Are you Ezeem's boyfriend? What's your name?"

"My sister, Gaia, is five foot eleven inches tall!" I blurt out before Bode can say anything, looking directly at the camera. "She's athletic and strong, she's got brown skin, black, curly, shoulder-length hair, brown eyes—we look completely different… except we have the same nose!" I tap my nose, like a total dork. "Gaia loves her family, and she's super intelligent and kind and funny, and she totally wouldn't go missing on purpose. If anyone knows anything, they should get in touch immediately with Detective Graff at the New Lanchester police." I glance at Scott. "And we have a social media page called Missing Gaia Gill. So please if you know anything, even if it's something really small, get in touch. Now. Missing Gaia Gill. Thank you."

I march past Izzy, go into the lodge, and shut the door behind me. I kick off my boots and drop my drenched coat on the floor. Breathe. Sit on the arm of the sofa. Feel sick.

The door opens slowly and a head appears.

"Can I come in?" Bode says.

"Of course." I say. "Just not Scott, and definitely not those TV people."

"He's showing them Craig's house next. Tour of the 'hood."

Bode stays standing on the doormat. "You did amazing, if I may say so."

"Oh god, I didn't." I shudder, but I can't help being a little bit pleased that he thinks so. "And Scott's right. We need to get word out there. We have to do everything we can to give her the best chance possible." I look at Bode, still standing by the door. "Will you stay for a while? Help me?"

"Sure." Bode nods, takes his coat off. "Whatever I can do."

"Good." I stand up. "We need to check through the messages on the Missing page, think about what happened at the party, write stuff down, get organized. So Craig's not talking yet? Doesn't mean we wait for him. There's got to be something we've missed. Because—and this is kind of extra weird for me—" I blurt out a laugh, "I can't shake this feeling that the clock just sped up. Gaia's time is running out."

CHAPTER TWENTY-ONE

I'm shivering with cold and adrenaline. Got to warm the hell up and calm the hell down, if I'm going to be useful. I hit the shower, washing off the woods and the taint of the TV interview. I lean on the wall, water running down me, and breathe. *Just keep breathing.* It's almost like I can hear Gaia whispering in my ear. *Keep on keeping on, Es. That's all it takes.*

I dry myself quickly, flinging on jogging bottoms and one of Gaia's sweaters. It smells of her, but I'm done wallowing. I grab my mother's laptop and head downstairs.

"I made tea." Bode is sitting by the fire. "It's what Brits do in an emergency, I've heard."

I laugh. "That's certainly the ritual."

"Yeah, well." He hands me a mug. "Sorry if it's not made right."

"Ah, the traditional apology. You truly know my people."

We grin stupidly at each other; I risk my cup by balancing it on the hearth and dropping down onto the rug beside him.

While the laptop boots up, a picture of Gaia and me as little kids pops up. It's Ma's wallpaper. I remember the photo being taken on a hot day in our back garden. Gaia is about eight; long, brown limbs and a stripy swimsuit, leaping in the air, all athletic exuberance. And there's me, slightly behind her. Naked, with fat, pink shoulders, sitting on my blue plastic potty, grimacing—hopefully because I'm smiling for the camera, rather than trying to poop. Ma always says I was late potty training. Late everything. I didn't walk until I was eighteen months old, and I never crawled—Gaia would pull me around the house in a plastic laundry bag. *Oh god, I really don't want Bode to see four-year-old me having a dump;* I twist the screen away from him, but he's looking at his phone.

"Scott's posted footage of the TV crew already," he says. "And the search. I didn't even see him in the woods, musta made a flying visit."

"He's making it more about him than my sister," I say, through gritted teeth. "What's his game?"

"It's working, though." Bode says. "Take a look."

I log on to Missing Gaia Gill. There's a montage of Gaia pics shared by Scott.

"Wow. This has 243 comments." I scroll through. "It's been shared seventy-five times! That's a lot, right?"

"See the pinned post with her description? Shared 1,276 times. The page has gotten 6,657 followers and Scott only made it live five hours ago." Bode whistles. "Huge. I know you don't love it, but this could really help."

I scroll through the pics, carefully save a nice one of Gaia at the party, and insert it into a new post. Fingers shaking slightly, I type:

> Hi, everyone. Still no sign of my sister, Gaia. We are beyond worried because she wouldn't just take off and not tell us. Please share her description everywhere. If anyone knows anything, even if it doesn't seem important, please DM me. Thank you.

I press Post. It feels woefully inadequate and horribly exposing at the same time. It also makes it all the more real; likes and hearts and crying emojis instantly jump onto my post, and friends from school are commenting. I can't think about home right now. The fact that I can't just get on a plane and fly back to my normal, boring life where Gaia is still okay, is almost unbearable.

"The first time is the hardest."

I look up at Bode sharply. He nods at his phone; he's seen my post. I bite my lip and we sit in silence for a moment, until my stomach makes an excruciating noise and we both giggle a little, glad of the comic relief.

"Sorry. Think I'm hungry."

"*Very* hungry." He grins at me. "Want me to pick up pizza from the place in the resort?"

"They'll deliver, won't they?" I hunt through a bunch of menus in the drawer by the phone. A memory sparks. "Gaia mentioned wanting pizza. At the party. Do you remember pizza arriving?"

Bode shakes his head. "I always remember pizza."

"She was hungry, she hates being hungry," I say. "Maybe she left the party and went up to the pizzeria. It's open really late." I find the menu. "Until 2 a.m. Saturdays. She could have walked up there."

"So, we go ask?" Bode gets up. "Call and order, I'll go get the quad, pick you up."

I hesitate. Ma wouldn't want me to leave, especially because it's dark outside. And there's the whole quad thing; she did specify no more bike adventures. But this is hardly that. It's important we ask if anyone saw Gaia, maybe with Craig. I've got to go up there. What would my folks have me do, walk?

"You rescued the quad from the moose?" I raise an eyebrow at Bode.

He snorts. "My uncle towed it. Gave me hell." He moves to the door and flings his coat on. "Luckily for us, there's plenty more quads where that one came from."

"Okay. We won't be gone long." I pick up the pizza menu. "What shall I order for you?"

Bode pulls on his boots. "Whatever you're having."

"I'm a vegan special case. Did I tell you that?"

"No problem." He doesn't miss a beat. "I'm down with saving the world a few times a week. And there's no such thing as bad pizza."

Gaia would *not* agree. She's all about the Double-Cheese

Meaty McFleshfeast. Bode leaves to collect the quad, and I call the pizzeria and put an order in.

As I hang up, there's a beep on my phone; Bode must have forgotten something.

Hey hon, kind of in the middle of a sitch. Mind if I come round in an hour, or too late? xoxo

I squint at the message. What does he mean? I flush hot with a mixture of disappointment and that xoxo, then realize his name didn't pop up with the text, just the number. Not Bode. Yeah, *hon* is not his style. Then I remember: Addy got my number when I gave it to Ma. She said she'd be coming over, said her parents are in Boston. I press some keys and manage:

No probs see you then x

After a few mins a message appears that looks like two rectangles. Ah, this brick can't handle emojis, only emoticons.

"Hey!" Bode thumps the door, making me jump. "Your ride's here!"

I pocket the phone, grab a coat, and head out.

We set off on the quad, and you'd think with my previous experience that this time would be a breeze, but it's like I've never been on the back of the damn thing before. I cling to Bode's waist, but at least I feel a little less self-conscious about it now. Not sure if that's a good thing.

The road is slick. Bode goes slow, but it doesn't take long for us to reach the center of the resort. We draw into an almost empty parking lot, dump the bike, and walk past reception onto a walkway that runs the length of the buildings at the bottom of the ski slope. Everything is in darkness, except for the faux Victorian gas lamps that mark out the walkway. There's a high-end clothes shop, a coffee place, the equipment store, and the main buffet restaurant leading out onto the ski area. A huge building housing the gondola ski lift hunches motionless in the dark. Beyond that is the kid ski area and the learners' "magic carpet" conveyor belt that I managed to bring to a complete standstill every time I rode it. Down the other way is a chairlift, swinging gently in the breeze, and we walk in that direction toward the only signs of life—a bar called The Eclipse, with muted country music piping out onto the walkway.

"That's where Lucille works," Bode says. We peer through the tinted glass, and there she is, tending bar, towel in hand and laughing with a couple of patrons in baseball caps. "Gotta wonder what she'll do when she finds her house is covered in crime scene tape." He winces at me, and we continue to the next door. There's a big sign above, swinging in the breeze: a picture of a moon with red, white, and green lettering: Big Pizza Pie.

The bright light assaults my eyes as we walk in. There are a few tables with plastic chairs, and at the back there's a girl with a pink ponytail and a red uniform, leaning over the counter and playing with her phone.

"Hey." She puts the phone down and flashes us a quick smile. "Help you?"

"Hi," I smile, full-on friendly, walking up to the counter. "I phoned an order in? The, er, Vegetative State pizza and two Cokes?"

"Sure." She goes to a serving window behind the counter. "Ricky? You got that vegan?" she yells.

"In five!"

She shrugs at us. "Wanna have the Cokes while you wait?"

I nod and pay. Her name tag reads, "Paulina." She's probably the same age as Gaia. As she hands me the change, I make my move.

"So, are you open late every night?"

"Yep, through high season." She looks through me, taking Bode in. "Only tonight we're quiet, so we'll close up soon. Prolly be this way all week."

I glance up at the clock; it's 10:35 p.m., way later than I thought. Same time as my watch broke on Saturday night. That's kind of freaky.

"How about last Saturday? When did you close then?"

Paulina's eyes narrow. "That'd be 2:00 a.m. Why do you wanna know?" She puts her head on one side and looks at Bode again. "I've seen you in here before."

"Pepperoni-pineapple-extra-eggplant."

"Extra Eggplant Guy, yeah, that's you." Paulina's brow wrinkles. "You're Saul's nephew." She looks meaningfully at him. "My sister was in the same class as *Hayley*."

"Is that right?" Bode shuffles to a seat, pulls his can open, and chugs it.

"But she's English!" Paulina points a coral-tipped finger at me, and I can see the cogs working. "Hey, is this about Gaia?"

"Yes! You know she's missing? I'm her sister." I'm way too wired to sit. "You know her?"

"Sure I do, we hung out some." The girl is still frowning at me. "God, it's so tragic! Do you think she ran away, or did someone grab her?"

I feel the oxygen rush out of my lungs.

"Oh my god, do you think it's the Ghost of Mavis?" Paulina smacks her hands down on the counter. Her jaw is hanging open; I turn to Bode for an explanation, but he just looks a bit sick. "They say she comes back every ten years, is it ten years since last time?"

Bode shakes his head, looks at the floor.

"Ghost of...*Mavis*?" I ask Paulina.

"It's nothing," Bode says quickly. "Just, like, the local legend. Ghost of some girl who died on the mountain when the resort opened years ago. Little kids get scared by it, you know, parents say 'eat your vegetables or the Ghost of Mavis will get you!'" He's rolling his eyes so exaggeratedly it's making me believe it all the more.

"And she does!" Paulina says. "Every ten years!"

"What? People go missing?" I say, incredulous.

"Sure!" Paulina says.

"Not *ever*," Bode says.

"Dude, it's true," Paulina says. "Little Mavis was crushed by a Zamboni. Now every year on the anniversary she comes back to take another soul!" She's hugging the counter now, expression terrified.

"Every year? I thought you said every ten?" I say to Paulina, who holds out her hands in a "who knows?" gesture. "And what the hell is a *Zamboni*?" I look at Bode.

"It's, like, a resurfacing machine, for ice rinks? And you know what? I don't think they were even invented by then," Bode babbles. "Say, Paulina, were you working Saturday? Did you see Gaia in here late? Just before closing?"

Paulina still looks like she's afraid the Ghost of Mavis will materialize right here and take her.

"No, dude, at least, I was, but it was quiet after one, and I kinda snuck out for a smoke. Ricky was here—Ricky!" she yells. "You seen that girl Gaia here Saturday, late?"

There's silence. I think Ricky might have made off with my Vegetative State.

"Anyways, Paulina," Bode says. "You have cameras in here, right?" He points up to a corner CCTV, high on the wall. "Think you could have a look on there for us? See if she came in?"

"Oh man, I can't do that," Paulina says. "Not even for you." She gives him a smile.

"Look, I'll pay you!" I take out my wallet, go through the American notes that all look exactly the same and would have made life impossible if I'd actually had anything I'd wanted to spend them on.

Paulina smiles sadly, "Aw, honey, I would *totally* take your money, but these cameras aren't hooked up to anything. It's all for show. Nice to look at, but don't do any work—kinda like most of the rich kids who get jobs here." She leans over the counter, looking pleased with herself.

"What about Craig Wilks?" I lean right back. "You know him? You see him here that night?"

"Oh my god, someone said he was whacked in the woods!" Paulina's face is stretched in shock. "It makes sense! The Ghost of Mavis knocked him out and dragged your sister into…" she frowns while she thinks of the right words, "…her *icy lair*."

At this point, Ricky thunders into the room, bearing pizza. He's tall and built like a barn, with straggly brown hair under his chef's cap and dark circles under his eyes. He places the pizza box carefully onto the counter and wipes his sweaty brow with the back of his wrist. "Someone say they found Craig?"

"That's right!" I nod furiously. "Did you see him on Saturday night? Did you see my sister, Gaia? Were they in here?"

"They were not." Ricky leans on the counter heavily, and it groans slightly. My heart feels like it's doing the same.

"Are you sure?" I press. "Maybe when you were out in the kitchen?"

He shakes his head slowly. "*They* weren't here, but he was."

"Who, Craig?" I try to keep calm. "What time?"

"Tad before closing." He walks to the cash register, flips open a little hatch, and starts unreeling a long roll of receipts.

"Time stamp: 1:50 a.m. Musta been this one. Extra-large pizza, side of wings, two sodas. Last order of the night."

"That's a lot of food for one person, isn't it?" I look at Bode.

"Well, that's debatable." Ricky sighs. "But he did have someone with him. They called him when he was waiting for his order, I was out front talking with him while the pie cooked. His phone rings, he told whoever it was to wait in the car. Was kinda shady about it." He raises an eyebrow at me.

"What was on the pizza?" I ask.

Ricky squints at the receipt again. "Extra-large, thin crust, You Bacon Me Crazy."

"Bacon-sausage-double-cheese," Paulina reels off.

"That's Gaia's pizza." I turn to Bode. "That's completely what she'd order. It must have been her in the car."

"God, do you think that's when the Ghost of Mavis snatched her?" Paulina squeals.

I decide ignoring Paulina is probably the best way ahead and look at Ricky. "Are there security cameras in the parking lot?"

"Yes," Ricky says. "But you'll never get to see them without a warrant."

"Maybe the police have the footage already," Bode says. "Chief Seymour probably gave it to them; we should tell Detective Graff we know Craig was in here. They can check it."

"Yeah. Thanks, guys." I grab a menu and a pen from the counter and carefully copy the number off the back of my phone. "If you think of anything else, or hear anything, can you call me, please?" Ricky takes the number and pins it to the wall behind the counter. Paulina can't take her eyes off my phone; it's like real-life Jurassic Park for her. I pick it up, Bode takes the pizza, and we head for the door.

"Detective Graff. The really tall woman?" Ricky calls over as we leave. "Tell her I'll make her a free pie anytime she wants to come question me."

"Duh." I hear Paulina's voice as we open the door and walk out into the cold air. "Cops only eat donuts, stupid."

CHAPTER TWENTY-TWO

___

"I think I might have lost my appetite." I sigh, sitting down on a wet bench and burying my face in my hands. "I wish we knew for sure if Gaia was with Craig! Because if she was, why haven't we found her yet? And if it was her in the truck while he was picking up the pizza, why did he not want anyone seeing her? That sounds shady."

"He's gotta talk," Bode says. "He can't stay silent forever."

"What if he does?" I groan. "Maybe the Ghost of Mavis will come and finish him off!"

"Come on," Bode offers me a hand, and I find myself taking it and allowing him to haul me up. "Pizza makes everything better." He glances at me guiltily. "Sorry, that was dumb. Almost everything."

"It's okay, I know what you mean."

We trudge back along past the bar and through to the parking lot.

"Hey—better idea—follow me!" Bode says, taking off back to the walkway in the direction of the gondola building. There's a single light on the steps and I follow him up to a platform where a glass gondola pod is parked, waiting to go up the mountain. Bode grasps a lever and, with a flourish, opens the door for me. "After you." The pod moves ever so slightly as I step into it and sit down a little too quickly on the seat facing up mountain. Bode sits opposite. "Kinda dark, but warmer than sitting out."

"Not a bad view from where I'm sitting." I mean the mountain, but it sounds like I'm hitting on Bode. I rub my face, embarrassed. He laughs, flips open the lid of the pizza box, and offers it to me. I take a slice; hot and good, nothing so comforting. We wolf through the first couple of slices fast, in silence, both of us focused on the food and nothing else. I like that I can be quiet with him. I wonder if I'm the first girl he's taken to his "pod"; he knew it would be open. I decide not to think about that too much and scoff more pizza.

"What do I owe you?" he says, after a while.

"For the pizza? Nothing. Definitely on me."

"Big spender. I knew you pawned that fancy watch." He grins at me in the gloom.

"Oh my god, I totally forgot to tell you!" I say. "Addy's got it."

"Yeah? How come?"

"I showed it to her, told her we found it in Craig's truck." I stare at the pizza box a minute, unsure of how to go on. "The watch is genuine."

"Okay..." Bode says. "She's sure."

"Very."

"What's going on, Es?"

"So…" I take a breath. "Addy knows the watch is real because it's her mum's."

Bode sits up with a start and the pod rocks a little. "No way. What was Addy's mom doing in Craig's truck?"

I twist my lip, holding his gaze.

"Oh," Bode says quietly. "She wasn't in Craig's truck. Gaia was."

I nod.

"Addy thinks your sister stole the watch?"

"Gaia admitted it. Addy found it in her stuff, confronted her. She told Addy she had taken it in a kind of reckless moment, thought it was insured so it wouldn't matter. She was going to sell it for college money."

"You believe that?"

I sigh. "I… Addy wouldn't lie. She loves Gaia. College is expensive, Gaia has been so stressed at how she's going to pay for everything, 'specially hanging with Addy. Addy never cares about money—how could Gaia possibly keep up?" That comes out a little more forcefully than I'd planned, but Bode nods. "What I can't figure out is, this happened *weeks* ago. Gaia promised to give the watch to charity. But she must have still had it on her if she dropped it in Craig's truck."

"God, I'm sorry, Es." Bode sighs, his breath a cloud in the chilly pod. "Do you think that has anything to do with why she's disappeared?"

"I don't know how it could." I shrug. "Except that it shows Gaia was desperate. Shows there was stuff she was keeping hidden. Shows I don't really know her like I thought I did." I stare into the darkness, the pod rocking us gently in the wind, like it's trying to soothe me.

"Okay, so at least we're learning. And there's something I forgot to tell you." Bode reaches into his pocket. "The cops asked me if I could remember everyone at the party."

"Yeah, me too. Which was hopeless. I only knew a fraction of the people there, and I'm useless with names."

"I remembered most, but not all, and that bugged me, so I wrote them down." He flashes his phone at me.

"You did?" I take the phone. *A spreadsheet.* He's numbered each person and written a bunch of other info I can't immediately fathom. "You're thorough."

"It's just how I see it in my head."

"Lucky you." I look closer at the phone. "This thing I have—the dyspraxia—means I can't see stuff like that in my head at all. Time, dates, names—it's all a mash-up."

"Dyspraxia, okay."

I can't read his face. "You must have noticed I have the coordination of a toddler. And no sense of balance…direction…thinking ahead. All the basics, really."

"But like, who's neurotypical these days? It's *so* last century."

I bark out a laugh. "Look at you, with the vocab!"

He raises an eyebrow. "Do you have a wicked awesome superpower to make up for it?"

I kick out at him. "That would be telling."

He springs toward me, wrestling the phone out of my hand and pretends to be typing. "Advanced…skills…in snark."

I grab the phone back. "I can read too, on a good day." I trace my finger down the spreadsheet. "And count, sometimes… Yay, twenty people at the house. I guessed that right, go me."

"Basically, the party consisted of Craig's roomies at Bluff Point, Gaia and Addy's roomies from Abenaki Avenue, plus a few randos, your crew and mine."

"Oh god, don't call Eli 'my crew.'" I pull a face. "I'm not claiming him for the same species, let alone my crew… Okay, so there's you and your buddies, Jai and Keith; me, *Eli*," I scroll down, "…and then we've got Craig, Lucille, and the arguing couple that live with them, Greg and Shantay…" I read. "Shona and Stephanie—the twins with the black hair?"

"And subject of Jai's sickest dreams, but let's not go there."

I grunt, scanning further down the list. "Roy and Jessica, who the hell are they?"

"Older. Ski instructors, been here a few seasons. Live with your sister."

"No idea."

"They came late, left early. You probably didn't even clock 'em."

"Doesn't take much." I pull a face. "Okay, so…Brent, Don, Lachlan?" I read. "Ah! The Ski Lift Jerks? They were out with the search. What are they really like?"

"Whaddya think?" Bode's hazel eyes look gorgeous in this half-light.

"Testosterone-fueled bros who are probably decent but semi-formed; I don't understand them, and they remind me of the boys at middle school who used to make my life hell."

The hazel eyes narrow. "Really? You were, like, bullied?"

I smack my lips. "I was *teased*. Tormented, possibly. But hey, long time gone. There's this wonderful thing that happens when boys like that grow up: girls like me become invisible."

Bode sits there, rapt. I can't tell if he's horrified or deeply uncomfortable, but I don't care, because I'm speaking the truth. It feels good to open up to someone. I haven't done it since Gaia was living at home.

We sit and listen to the wind blowing through the gondola building. There's a faint, high-pitched whine—I can't figure out if it's the wind, or the pod swinging, or maybe it's ghostly Mavis crying, her voice echoing around the mountain.

Finally, Bode speaks.

"I don't think you're invisible."

"I know I'm not," I say quickly, looking directly at him. Because I *do* know. "I don't exist for other people to decide whether I'm worth bothering with or not. But I am invisible to guys like that. And I guess if I'm honest, that's a relief." I make a noise, like an exaggerated sigh, and risk a smile at him, and we both laugh and I pull a goofy face and draw a line under it. The pizza's gone cold, but I take a final slice anyway, and try and chew it casually. "Anyway, answer my question: what do you think of the Ski Lift Jerks?"

"They're harmless, I guess." If Bode's glad we're back on

safer ground, he doesn't show it. "Don's the oldest, he's been here a season or two, he's a failed frat boy, but whatever. Brent comes from money, his family are, like, Boston royalty. Lachlan had a thing with Addy around New Year's, but that's ancient history now."

"Do any of them fancy my sister?"

"Sure!" Bode says a little too quickly. "They all do. But like I said before, she never showed them any interest."

"There's one more—'Mystery Guy.'" I look at the last name on Bode's phone. "Hey, that doesn't sound suspicious *at all*."

"So, he's actually who I wanted to talk to you about. Lucille's date, who blew you a kiss when you left the party," Bode says. "I was thinking about them both, because you said she makes you suspicious."

"Oh god," I groan. "It could be dangerous to take me seriously, Bode."

"Well, I do." His eyes are smiling at me again. "I think you're right, Lucille's sus, and her sketchy bloke. I kinda recognize him, but I got no clue who he is. Definitely gonna quiz Hayley when I get a chance."

"Damn, Bode." I frown at the darkness outside. "We're gathering suspects, aren't we? Craig's still number one, but if he turns out to be an innocent victim, are we saying that someone else at the party is responsible for whatever's happened to Gaia?"

Bode folds his arms. "I think we're saying someone knows something."

I let that sit for a second.

"You said *bloke*."

Bode looks at me quizzically.

"'Her sketchy bloke.'" I laugh. "Sounds funny when you say it. But I like it."

I flick the pizza box closed and dump it on the floor, moving across to the seat next to him, kneeling and staring out at the darkness. "It was a full moon on Saturday night; Gaia talked about going up the mountain to see it one last time."

"Any chance she did?"

I shrug and slump down sideways on to the seat, facing him. "How would she get up there? The lifts wouldn't be running."

"She could hike it." Bode looks at me; I look back. "Kind of a major trek at 2:00 a.m. in the snow."

"I doubt she'd bother. But there's so much of this I can't figure out. I have no idea what she was thinking."

He nods slowly. My knees are touching the side of his thigh. He reaches out a hand to mine. It feels warm, and my whole body is suddenly on alert.

"Impossible to read someone's mind."

"Yeah." I have no idea if we're still talking about Gaia.

"Es…?" He leans toward me.

"I know," I lean right back. There's a flicker of something on his face, and before I can stop myself, I'm moving in and kissing him like I seduce boys on ski lifts every damn day of my life. I feel him hesitate when my lips touch his, *and then within a beautiful millisecond he's kissing me back and his hands are on my face and I can taste the salt on his lips and smell his slightly pizza-y fingers which sounds like it would be gross and it totally would be if this was not Bode and oh my god this kiss—*

Bee-beep!

Wha—?

My phone. We break apart. I reach into my pocket to get it and the little screen lights up green.

Darling, I hope you're in bed and Addy's with you. Are you okay? No news here, carrying on for now xxx

My head spins, caught in the act. "It's my mother." I can't meet Bode's eyes. "I better get back."

I type a quick and vague reply, and by the time I press Send, Bode's already gathered up our rubbish. My legs feel weak as hell as I stagger out of the pod; my mind is racing, full of guilt and embarrassment mixed with a whole heap of horny, which given the reason why we're here makes me feel like the worst person alive. I think Bode feels the same because we ride back to the lodge in solemn silence.

As he switches off the quad's engine I look up to the window, and I can see Addy pacing, on her phone in the living room. How come she's inside? Is Ma back already?

Shit. I will be in so much trouble. I speed up the steps and open the door.

CHAPTER TWENTY-THREE

———

"Hi, Es!"

As I open the front door, Addy spins round, hanging up her call.

"Are my parents here?"

"No." She smiles. "I let myself in when you didn't answer. Figured you'd stepped out for…" She eyes Bode behind me. "For…something."

"I…" I look round at him, not knowing what to say. "Wait, the door! Wasn't it locked?"

"Nope," Addy says. "Hey, have you got any food? I'm starving."

My hand dives into my pocket and closes around the key on the ring with long, wooden skis. I put it back into the door. "I must have…forgotten to lock it."

Addy nods absent-mindedly, walking toward the kitchen. "*Claire* only has wine in the cupboard, think it's been a few years since she did solids." She floats into through the archway and shouts back to me. "Your mum texted and asked me to stay the night. I brought my things."

"Hey," Bode calls from the door, not crossing the threshold, like suddenly that's too much of an invasion. "I should go."

I nod, avoiding his eyes. "Thanks."

"Sure," he says, his voice sounding surprised—or maybe he's not sure what I'm thanking him for. "Lock the door behind me, yeah?" He coughs. "God, sorry. I don't mean to sound like your dad."

"It's fine," I say quickly. "Sometimes I need reminding, obviously. See you tomorrow."

"You got it." He gives me a brief smile and a little salute, somehow managing to make it look cool, and walks away into the darkness.

I shut the door.

Addy is crashing around in the kitchen. I turn the key and stick it on the windowsill beside the door. When Ma and Dad eventually come back, they can get in with their key. I stare at the door. *I did lock it when I went out. I'm sure of it…*

"Hey." Addy slopes in from the kitchen with a huge bowl of cereal in one hand. "How you holding up?" She flops down on my armchair; a slosh of milk lands on the arm, but she doesn't notice.

"Yeah, fine," I say, automatically, taking my boots off and moving to the sofa. "You?"

Addy sighs and stares at her Rice Puffs. "This is going to come out all wrong."

"What?"

She sighs again. Takes a bite of cereal and chews gloomily. Then finally, "I guess I'm struggling, because I don't want to feel angry with her."

"With Gaia? What do you mean?"

She looks at the cereal like she's having serious second thoughts, either about her snack choice or this conversation. Finally, she dumps the bowl on the floor and locks eyes with me. "I'm like, Gee, did you do a runner? Duck out on us?" She tucks her legs up under her, pulling her sweater down to cover them.

"No way. She'd never put us through this."

"Hear me out." Addy holds up a hand. "The underwear run at the party? I could tell you were shocked, but she's been pulling stuff like that for weeks, stupid dares with Scott for the video channel. At the start, they were harmless—well, apart from the one where she ate bugs." She screws up her face. "I joined in with some of it, but I'm not eating a cockroach for anything."

"Okay. But that's nothing like this."

"I don't know…" She scratches her arm. "Over the weeks, they got more…extreme. Have you seen the clip of the silent disco?"

I shake my head. "I haven't watched any of them. I mean, I remember at the party some people were looking at Scott's channel on their phones or whatever, but before that night, I didn't even know about it."

"For real?" Addy's eyes widen. "Gaia never mentioned it?"

HAVE YOU SEEN MY SISTER?

"Never, ever."

Her face goes blank; she's mulling this over. "I suppose, it makes sense. Gaia's become very good at compartmentalizing." She shakes her head regretfully. "So, with the disco, what Scott and Gaia kept super quiet was that they broke into an abandoned building in town and got a bunch of people there, charged them for tickets. I mean, that's, like, really reckless. And illegal." She glances at me. "And then there was the watch thing, of course."

I feel myself get hot, embarrassed on my sister's behalf.

Addy fiddles with the hem on her sweater. "There's something else. We argued, week before you got here. Huge fight, like never before. I told her she had to stop doing the video channel, that it was going too far and she was starting to act erratic in real life too. I was only looking out for her, but she got really, really angry with me."

"God, Addy." I can't believe they'd fall out. "She loves you. That wouldn't make her leave!"

"I wouldn't have thought so, before the watch." Addy sighs. "I wonder if being here kind of broke the seal on something? She's kept stuff down for years, Es. Maybe this future she's mapped out for herself is too overwhelming and she's flipped?"

"I don't know, Addy…"

"Okay, well how about this? You and me both know she was nervous about meeting her birth dad's family in Boston." Addy says firmly. "Maybe she wanted to go there on the quiet?"

For once, I'm not in the dark. I do know about this.

At the party, not long before I left, Gaia was nowhere to be found. I'd eventually tracked her down to the kitchen. She was sitting, alone and subdued, on the countertop, picking distractedly at a Band-Aid on her hand.

"I've messaged the fam, we're going to meet before I start the beach job."

"What…? You mean your aunt?" I stared at her. "And the cousin in Boston?"

She nodded, eyes burning bright in the dimly lit kitchen.

When Gaia's dad, Ori, died, Ma left the United States and barely kept in touch with any of his family. Maybe it was too upsetting, or because Ma was white and Ori was Black and some of the extended families on both sides didn't exactly love that. But that was then.

"It could be great, amazing. There's this whole side of me I don't know." She half whispered. "But I'm scared. I hope they'll…accept me."

We'd hugged, I'd held her, any bad feelings from the night dropping away instantly. "Don't worry, they'll love you," I'd murmured, and meant it. How could they not?

But she wouldn't have left for Boston without telling us. Ma and Dad and I knew she was longing to connect with her American family and were supportive, no drama there.

Unless I'm wrong about that too…

Addy sees the doubt in my face. "Maybe Gaia went somewhere, for whatever reason, but she fell, banged her head, and doesn't know where she is?" She sits up, suddenly, positive again. "It happens. Sudden amnesia, I looked it up. There was this woman in New York who left her house to go to work and completely forgot who she was." Addy claps her hands. "Maybe Gee is out there walking around—in the city, or something— not even knowing there's anything wrong!"

"That's so random."

"Yeah? If we eliminate all the random possibilities, what's left?" I'm shocked to see tears in Addy's eyes. "Something way, way worse? Someone attacked her on the walk home? Someone took her against her will?"

"Someone like Craig?"

'Not him.' She tuts dismissively and brings out her phone. "I didn't want to have to share this with you. There was a teenager who went missing a couple years ago. Next town over. She was last seen running in the woods and there's been no sign of her since." She shoves the phone at me, and MISSING headlines swim before my eyes, a yearbook picture of a smiling girl with long, brown hair and laughing eyes. I feel a weight in my stomach. "Another case, over the border." Addy leans over me, tapping the phone until a page appears with a picture of a blond and a chilling headline. This woman is wearing athletic gear, she's a little older, perhaps, there's a child in her arms with their face blotted out. "See? Only six months ago. They found her *bloodstained clothing* on the other side of these mountains, Es!"

I don't speak for a moment. I can't.

"There's a pattern here." Addy takes back her phone. I stare at my knees but she grabs my hands, getting into my face. "Both were around the same age as Gaia! It's a hell of a coincidence. I have no doubt the police are taking it seriously."

I feel the heat rising in my chest.

"I don't know… It all seems too unbelievable."

"Is it more unbelievable than Gaia being harmed by one of her *friends*?"

I get up—I have to move—and pull the curtains across the window, suddenly feeling absolutely exhausted.

"Look, Ads, you're stressed and we're all stressed, but we've got to keep the faith she's okay and we'll find her." I hug her; her body feels tense and she breaks away before I do. "I'm going to bed. Sleep in Gaia's, if you want."

"Actually, think I'll wait 'til your ma gets back and push off, give you your space."

I nod, grateful that she's not leaving me on my own.

Addy picks up her cereal again and stirs it. "God, Es, I'm sorry, I'm supposed to be looking after you. You want anything to eat?"

"Bode and me… We had pizza." I turn around, not wanting her to see my face. Seems I can't even say his name without feeling my cheeks burn.

"What else did you have?" she teases. "You two happening, or what?"

"No." I say quickly. "Well, I dunno. We did…kiss." I have no idea why I tell her, and as soon as I have, I completely regret it. I wanted to live with it for a while; enjoy it, or agonize over it,

HAVE YOU SEEN MY SISTER?

or at least get used to the idea. I wouldn't normally tell anyone. Except Gaia.

"Nice." Addy, thank god, doesn't make it a big deal. She smiles, there's a little wink, but it's kind of warm, not teasing. "He's a good guy." She sighs. "Wish there were more like him."

"Yeah," I say, heading for the stairs. "So do I."

I double-check the locks on my window before I go to bed.

CHAPTER TWENTY-FOUR

For an out-and-proud introvert, I'm getting used to having a house full of people. It's quite the developmental benchmark. Gaia would say, "Ooh, well done, Es! Take the positive from this situation and run with it!" *Bleuch*. She's queen of making lemons into friggin' lemonade.

Emerging from my bedroom the next morning, it seems almost normal that there's a cop talking to my mother at the dining table and there are strangers standing around with cups of coffee.

What is not normal is that Gaia's missing. The day *that* feels normal is not something I want to experience.

I lean against the banister of the bottom of the stairs, and a wave of exhaustion washes over me. Dad's not here. He'll be out looking for her. How long can he go on like this?

Bode's uncle, Saul, is talking to a man in a resort uniform and pointing at a map. Bode's not here. I'm kind of glad. I need some time to get my game face on before I see him. The front door is ajar, almost in a hopeful way. I shiver. Doesn't anybody else feel cold?

"Where d'ya want these?" A man enters, balancing three brown boxes against his chest.

"Flyers?" Ma looks up from the table. "Great." She gestures to an empty bit of floor. "Anywhere is fine."

I sit on the bottom step of the stairs, invisible, and stare across at the boxes. The top of the pile has a sample taped to it. Gaia, wearing her favorite red turtleneck, grins out from the photo. The word MISSING is also in red, with a weirdly inappropriate curly-swirly border, like a cruel pastiche of a birthday banner above her head. *God*, that photo was only taken a few days ago. Gaia's got her arm around my shoulders; I've been cut out of the picture but an errant lock of my mousy brown mane has managed to worm its way into the frame. Ma snapped that picture right here, almost in the exact spot the boxes are now sitting. We were all going out for steak at The Apogee restaurant on the mountaintop, and I was rabidly outraged about the meatiness of it all, but how completely ridiculous that seems now.

The memory is so fresh, so tangible, it seems like I should be able to rewind to when Gaia was here. Such a short time ago she was standing beside me, solid. I could feel the warmth of her, smell her, be pissed off at her good mood and at being sandwiched between her and Dad, irritated at Ma wanting to take the pic. How can that be so real and yet she's not here now?

"Julia!" Scott's yell cuts across the memory. "We're up!" He's standing beside the huge TV, cranking the volume until the floor shakes.

On-screen there's a heavily made-up anchorwoman introducing the next news segment. My mother rushes to watch, everyone follows; I have to stand on the stairs to see above heads. Behind the anchorwoman, there's a picture, but it's not of Gaia, it's of Scott. Scott from his pop star days. *Of course.* That's why this is news. Then the picture changes to Scott beaming, his arm around Gaia, both of them in ski gear. It changes again, this time a close-up of Gaia. Whoever has taken the picture has caught her off guard. She's looking up, a surprised smile on her face; the picture is overexposed and the flash is making her eyes look almost green. It's an odd choice because she doesn't really look like her. She looks much younger than nineteen, slight, vulnerable. And then I realize: she also looks way *whiter.*

While that's still sinking in, the screen cuts to the rainy interview on the deck of our lodge yesterday. There's Izzy Whatsherface, the reporter, all determined and off-puttingly keen. She turns to Scott who is looking gutted but stoic, his beauty enhanced rather than diminished by the stark lighting and the rain running down his face. I can't take in what he's saying, but I'm aware that he's saying it all rather well. His voice is warm and he glows on-screen even more than in real life. Even the subject matter doesn't prevent his natural charisma from shining through.

And then the picture cuts to me, and it's more than enough

to shake me out of my skull. I jolt when I see myself, sweat pricking my armpits. A creeping dread, a cringe that begins in my stomach squeezes up my body until it completely envelops me.

On-screen, I look pasty and bedraggled and absolutely furious. My voice is thin and young and brittle. Is that how people see me? But I get the words out, even though it sounds like I'm spitting out nails. Come to think of it, the anger is probably working for me. I'm "feisty." I'm "plucky."

After the segment is over, some people clap. My mother stands, face blank; a couple of people are trying to talk to her, somebody has a hand on her arm, but she turns to me. Our eyes meet across the room, and Ma practically elbows everyone out of the way, and then I'm in her arms and she's hugging me and saying "Brilliant, brilliant," and I'm trying not to cry or pee myself or throw up, which all seem like options right now.

Over her shoulder, everyone is watching us. In Britain, people would be clearing their throats and shuffling feet and pretending not to look...while totally looking. At least the Americans are honest, although I half expect them to start applauding again. Right at the moment when I think Ma has held me a little too long to be comfortable, the front door opens. Detective Graff comes in. The look on her face makes my heart freeze. My arms drop and Ma instinctively swings around to see.

"Julia." Detective Graff crosses the room in a few long strides. "I need to let you know we've had a development. Craig Wilks is talking." She's speaking quietly, but you can bet everyone in the room hears her. "We've interviewed him at some length, and he's denying he was ever with Gaia after he left the party." Graff shifts her weight slightly. "Julia, I gotta tell you, there's some strong evidence to support that."

"He's lying!" Someone shouts, and there's a wave of protest and sounds of disbelief. But Ma just stands there, searching Detective Graff's face for answers.

"Calm down, people!" Detective Graff raises her hands. "Now, we wouldn't normally share this kind of information, so I'm trusting you. Nothing should stand in the way of the good work you're doing. Focus on finding Gaia. Let us deal with Craig Wilks."

Ma only nods, going out to the car with a box of flyers. Graff talks to a couple of people, and as she's leaving, I follow her out onto the deck.

"Craig went for pizza after the party. Did he tell you that?"

Detective Graff looks at me, her head on one side.

"Did he?" I hold her gaze. "He had someone in the car waiting for him, he was talking to them on the phone—and then he drove them to the motel. Did you find out who it was?"

"You've been busy, Miss Esme." Graff says evenly.

"How do you know that wasn't Gaia?" I press. "What's the evidence? Did you check the CCTV? Did whoever he was with come forward and verify his story?"

Her eyebrows raise.

"Do you know who Craig was with?" I realize I'm almost shouting. "Do you?"

"That is probably not relevant."

"How come?"

"Esme, let me do my job..." I've ticked her off, but then her face changes and her large hand falls on my shoulder. "You're one tough cookie. That's good. Right now, Gaia needs you to be."

I gulp, turning away. *So not fair of her to take the fire out of my argument like that.* Detective Graff claps me on the back and clomps down the stairs to talk to my mother.

But Craig is not off my Shit List. Not by a long way.

Ten minutes later we are in the car and headed down the mountain to town.

———

Ma, Addy, and I are standing outside the Screech Owl Bar and Grill on Main Street in Moonville. This is the place Gaia should have shown up to brunch on Sunday. Today she's here in her multitude, smiling up at us from the boxes of flyers.

"Are we going to call Dad?" I'd asked in the car. "We should tell him about Craig."

Ma shook her head. I'd wanted to push her further, but there were strangers in the car with us. And actually, Craig's denial changes nothing. Like Graff said, all we can do is focus on finding Gaia.

It's a freezingly crisp, dry day; we're clapping cold hands together, watching a trail of people walk down to join us through the morning sun. Someone from the bar has thoughtfully brought out cardboard trays of steamy coffee. I took one, and now I'm sipping the black, bitter hotness more because I feel like I should, rather than because I want it.

"Gather round, please, folks!" My mother has a clipboard and a mission, and this will be her saving. "Can I get you to organize yourselves into small teams?" Her voice is making clouds as she speaks, she's loud and assured. That's where Gaia gets it from. "Each group should have a team leader, someone who knows Gaia personally—I'll take names." Ma rounds up the people stomping their feet in the cold. I do a quick head count of the crowd, inevitably losing track twice, then giving up. Eighteen? Nineteen? Mainly locals, with a smattering of Gaia's friends. People who want to help but can't face another day poking sticks in the woods. Who can blame them?

"I'm going to give you each an area of town to cover." Ma scribbles on her clipboard; it doesn't surprise me she knows most of the people here already. "This morning we're hitting local businesses, municipal buildings, private homes, anywhere people are. I have lists of all the obvious places—if I've left anything out, let me know."

"Here ya go, Julia." A man whose name certainly I don't remember is shoving handfuls of Gaias into tote bags. She would think this is off the wall.

"Let's make every flyer count." Ma quickly hands out the totes and the lists. I shouldn't be surprised by my mother's skills. She's focused, efficient. "*Talk* to people. That's what's important here." She looks around, trying to hit everyone with a dose of direct eye contact. "Talk about Gaia, make them care. She needs their help." Her voice almost wobbles here, but she quickly brings it back. "This is not just about awareness, it's a fact-finding mission. Where should we be looking for Gaia? Everybody's got opinions, and let's face it, most folk like to share 'em." There's a titter of laughter at this. Ma's got it down. There's a tinge to her voice, a switch in her intonation and word choice that moves her away from British Stiff Upper Lip to something much more user-friendly. They not only feel sorry for her, they get her. Like I said, Ma's got skills.

"Partner up?" Bode is suddenly standing there, coffee in hand. He's got such stealthy moves, I hadn't even noticed him among the crowd. And you bet I looked.

"Hiya," I say, super cool and casual.

"Ms. Gill?" Bode strides up to my mother. "I'll take a bunch of flyers, head over to the high school."

Ma glances up, smiles tightly, hands over a tote.

"Thanks, Bode, I appreciate it."

"Es can come—she's great at getting people to open up, you know?"

I am? What is he doing? I'm stuck between being thrilled he's here and a little unnerved that we're not doing post-kiss awkwardness anymore.

Ma's face wrinkles into an automatic frown, but he's got her. "Yes, that makes good sense." She pierces me with a hard stare. "Just the school, and stay together." I nod, all serious; Bode tosses his coffee in the trash and we walk off. "Twelve o'clock back here, no later!" Ma shouts. "You finish earlier, you wait for me in the bar, you understand?"

I raise a hand, like I'm saying yes, but I know I'm not saying yes because that would be *a lie*. Once we get around the corner, I catch up with Bode.

"Hey!" I tap him on the shoulder. "We're not going to the school, are we?"

He keeps walking, eyes front. "Why would you say that?"

"Because there's nobody there." I say triumphantly. "Because it's spring break."

"Busted."

"So where are we going?" I say, struggling to keep up with him. "And why couldn't you tell my mother?"

"Okay. I heard about how Craig is talking, so—" he points to a bus stop up the street. "—we're going to the hospital."

I stop in my tracks and grab him by the arm. "Seriously?" I grin, half-shocked, totally excited. "I knew there was a reason I liked you."

"Only one? Come on, we gotta get moving!" He breaks into a jog; a bus is rounding the corner. "If we miss this, there's not another 'til eleven!"

We make it to the stop as the bus doors hiss open, and Bode climbs up ahead and gestures for me to go to the back. "Grab a seat, hunker down." The bus has maybe three or four people already on; most of them ignore me as I pass them. *Hunker down?*

As soon as the bus pulls away, I realize why. We're retracing the way back to Main Street, and *hello*, there are the flyering folks. I quickly shrink in my seat so they can't see me. The group has thinned out, but Ma is still there, talking to the woman who handed out the coffee, nodding to the man who brought the boxes. I sink further down in my seat. Oh god, last thing I want to do is add to her worries. Won't she realize it's the school holidays and Bode told her a barefaced lie? I shut my eyes, the motion of the bus mixing with the coffee in my empty stomach, making me feel sick.

Where is he, anyway? I poke my head out into the aisle. He's talking to a man with a flyer sitting halfway up the bus. Bode's spreading the word. This is good. This is smart. Not only can we talk to Craig, we can hand out flyers in the city. If there's any chance Gaia went somewhere other than Moon—unless she set off through the woods to Canada, which is completely nonsensical—she'd have to come though New Lanchester. If Addy's wild idea about amnesia has any truth to it, maybe this is where she'll be. We can paper the bus station, any bars or cafés on the way to the hospital—someone might know something.

I've got to believe they will.

CHAPTER TWENTY-FIVE

New Lanchester seems busy after sleepy ol' Moonville, and as we walk, I'm checking out any face that could be my sister's. It turns out, that's not many. On a first pass, New Lanchester looks pretty damn white. Gaia would certainly stand out here.

The hospital is on the outskirts of town and looks brand-new and shiny, with white walls and very dark glass. Reception has a glossy marble floor and pillars, and a smattering of people. *Yes.* Enough distraction to allow us to get up to tricks; a plan has been hatching in my brain on the walk over. I spy what I need on a windowsill—a plant with rubbery-looking leaves and large, pink flowers. To my delight, it still has a plastic card holder stuck into the soil. Perfect. Now all I need is paper. I tear one of the flyers and scribble on the back of it, tucking the paper into the holder.

"What's going on?" Bode whispers in my ear, his breath tickling my neck. I dump the plant in his hands and nod to the woman on the desk. "Huh?"

"I don't make a realistic delivery guy, but you totally do."

He feigns shock.

"Girl; you're such a criminal mastermind."

"So, we're both playing to our strengths."

His jaw drops in mock horror. Eyes twinkling, he turns and walks around the corner and toward the reception desk, and as he does his body language changes subtly, his shoulders droop, his stride slows, he pulls his beanie down over his forehead. My faith in him was well placed. *Method actor.* I loll behind a pillar and watch.

"Help you?" A middle-aged woman is tapping on a keyboard. She's wearing a mohair sweater featuring a jaunty-looking Easter Bunny, and a deep frown.

"Hey." Bode gives the woman a lazy smile. "Got a flower delivery for a Craig Wilks, says Ward 2?" Bode squints at the note I scribbled. "Wait. Ward 2 or 5? Gee, was this written by a kindergartner?"

The woman looks at him, impatient. "Lemme see."

"Would you? I'd appreciate that…" He looks at her name badge. "Denise. Here, let me—oh darn!" He fumbles the plant, drops the card holder before picking it up and surreptitiously rubbing soil on the note. "I was going with the 2, but once you see the 5…"

Denise sighs, takes the note, peers at it. "It says "Ward." I don't see a number."

"You don't?" Bode's devastated. "Oh, man."

Denise and Bode look at each other.

"I love your sweater," Bode chances.

Denise's face is implacable; she knows she's being played. But maybe she doesn't much care.

"Wilks? First name Craig?" She types. "Ward 3."

Bode looks shocked. "No way!"

Denise nods back. "Second floor."

"Thanks so much!"

"Uh-huh," Denise replies, her eyes back on the computer. "Visiting's over at 11." She glances up at me, peeking out behind the pillar. "And put the begonia back. I just watered her!"

"Denise has got our number," Bode ditches the plant as we jog toward the stairs, giggling.

"Yeah, but we got Craig's and that's what matters."

We find Ward 3. I punch a green button that swings double doors open. First thing we see is a nurses' station— unmanned—and a long corridor with doors.

"I guess he's in his own room," I whisper to Bode. "Do you think there'll be police guarding him?"

"Don't see any cops," Bode says. "Anyhow, they didn't arrest him, did they?"

"But he's a person of interest or whatever. What happens if he makes a run for it?"

We slink down the corridor, checking each door for a name. Fourth room's a winner.

WIIKS, CRAIG is written on the door in blue Sharpie.

"All righty. Here goes." I knock, wait for a second. "I'm going in."

As soon as we enter the room, we can see exactly why Craig is not going to be a flight risk.

Craig is lying on a bed with what can only be described as a crane above him. His eyes are shut and he's wearing earbuds. There's a neck brace, and one arm is in a sling. But it's his legs that I can't take my eyes off. The crane is suspending both of them—fully plastered to the knees, with hairy thighs akimbo—several inches off the bed.

"Oh my god." Bode says the only thing that can be said.

Craig's eyes flash open; he snatches at the earbuds with his good hand, while simultaneously trying to pull his blankets over his crotch with the sling hand. I was really trying not to look at *that area*, but with his legs in full-on birthing position, how can you not? There appears to be some kind of adult diaper thing going on, but it's not quite providing full coverage and *oh hell, no*.

"What are you doing here?" Craig rasps, eyes panicked, scrabbling for the bedsheet, but it's stuck fast.

"Dude, lemme…" Bode helps, unsnagging that sheet and covering him up as best he can. Bode turns away with a kind of horrified, apologetic, and semi-traumatized expression on his face, and I shoot him a thankful look.

"Where's Gaia?" I blurt. I had all this subtlety and preamble planned, but certain things make you cut to the chase.

"Get out," Craig grunts. He looks smaller, sallow and sunken in on himself, almost unrecognizable from the arrogant, athletic specimen of a couple of days ago. I take a step closer.

"We're not going anywhere." The steeliness of my voice

shocks me, and clearly has an effect on Craig, who sits up a little. "Craig, when I left the party, you said you were going to walk my sister home. Where is she?"

Craig licks his lips, his eyes darting to the side table. "I have no idea." There's a sour smell in the room, mixing with the tang of antiseptic. Craig Wilks is sweating bullets.

"What happened at the party?" I spit out. "She was supposed to be right behind me."

"She didn't want to leave then. End of story. Now get the hell out of my room."

"I will, but tell me what you know. I don't care about the police, just help me find her!"

Craig tries to shake his head, then pulls a face when the motion clearly hurts like hell.

"This is not happening. You need to leave." He darts his good hand out to the side, reaching for the nurse's call button. *Huh, look at that*—he can't quite grab it.

"Hey, Craig, nobody knows we're here. Es snuck away." Bode moves to the side of the bed where the call button is dangling. "Her family's out searching. They're hurting, man." He dips and picks up the button, puts it out of Craig's reach.

"Not my concern!" Craig's voice cracks. "I told the cops I left the house—on my own—and I didn't see her again!" He gestures wildly at the call button. "Gimme that!"

"You got pizza." I take another step toward the foot of the bed. "But there was someone in your truck, waiting. It was Gaia, wasn't it? You guys hooked up."

"No!" he shouts at me, like I've suggested something completely ludicrous. He gives up hope of the button and sinks, defeated, back down the bed. "She took a hard pass." Embarrassment flashes across his face. "Yeah, I've been trying to get with her all season, that what everybody's telling you? So sue me. But she wasn't interested, and guess what? I'm old enough to move the hell on. Last night's party? I'm gonna bet on a sure thing."

"And who was your 'sure thing'?" The words taste bitter in my mouth.

"That's nobody's business but mine. All you need to know is: not Gaia."

"Yeah, but that's a problem." I casually place a hand on the tether holding one of his legs up. "Because the mystery person is your alibi, aren't they, Craig?" I'm not sure where I'm finding the courage to put on this little show, but I guess that happens when your sister vanishes. I put some pressure on the tether, absent-mindedly leaning on it. Craig's left leg lifts up slowly.

"Careful!"

"Sorry," I smile ruefully, removing my hand. "You kept saying I was clumsy, right?"

"Who did this to you?" Bode changes tack. "Did someone push you off the deer tower?" Craig says nothing, his mouth fixed in a hard line. "Look, dude," Bode takes a step back, holds his hands up. "You were at the Eazy Stay, your truck was broken. So, what? You and your lady friend hiked back and she beat you up?"

207

"She beat me up? Don't be ridiculous." Craig tries a laugh.

"What about Eli?" I have to ask. "Did he come at you?"

The laugh is genuine this time. "Are you serious? Nobody beat anybody up. Yeah, the truck was screwed and I walked back, but I was on my own. Got turned around in the woods, climbed the tower to get my bearings and fell. The damn ladder was slippery."

"Where'd your date go?" Bode says.

"Don't know, don't care."

"Wow, you're such a catch, Craig," Bode says. "Too bad for you she won't come forward to back up your story."

"Guess you're going to have to take my word for it," Craig sneers.

"Gaia's out there!" I shout, and they look at me, startled. "All this time we're messing around, Gaia is *missing*. You give a damn about her, Craig? Help us." I lean toward him. "God knows why, but I believe you. I don't think you were with her that night. But I think you might know who was." I lean further still, and Craig's eyes widen. "You do care about her. You're in no shape to be out there looking, but you would, wouldn't you, if you could?"

Craig nods, almost imperceptibly.

"Where do we look, Craig?"

"No idea," Craig says. "She wasn't there at the end of the night, and I didn't see who she left with."

"Really?" I press. "I mean, if you're into someone, you normally notice."

"Maybe if you're a lovesick teen." He looks at me and Bode and I *will* myself not to go red. "The cops will verify; when I was picking up pizza, Gaia's phone was pinging off a cell tower in town. She couldn't have been anywhere on the mountain."

"Her phone was found under your bed!"

"So someone planted it there afterward." His face is blank.

The door behind me opens, and a nurse bustles in.

"Hey." She smiles at Craig. "Time for your meds. Your friends gotta leave, it's past visiting."

"Thank god." Craig sinks lower into his pillow.

"Let's get out of here." Bode walks to the door. The nurse leaves a little pot of pills on Craig's bedside table and breezes out again.

"One last thing," I say quickly. "Someone told me you were planning on following the girls to the Cape for summer. That true?"

Craig rolls his eyes at me. "Not 'following.' I work summers teaching sailing. A bunch of the ski guys do. Do your research next time."

Bode tuts like he wants to sock Craig in the face, but instead he grabs the tote bag of flyers that I'd dumped on the floor. "Es, I'll drop these at the nurses' station."

"Hold up." I grab a flyer from the bag as Bode exits. "If there's anything else… " I scribble down my number, "… call me, okay?"

"Yeah, right. I lost my phone in the woods." Craig looks past me. "Leave your number anyway. They say I'm concussed.

When I'm all better, who knows what I might remember?" He gives me a funny look, and for the first time, I wonder whether he's been fooling us all along.

"Strange, so many people lost their phones. You, Scott…"

"Wait, what?" Craig snaps. "Scott didn't lose his phone. When?"

"At the party. He went back to your house on the Sunday morning to find it."

"He's lying," Craig says. "I was there when he left the party. He had his phone in his hand like always."

"Are you sure?"

"I know what I saw."

"What time did he leave? Was Gaia gone by then?"

"Why should I remember?" He shuts his eyes, signaling the end of the conversation. I move to the door, wondering what I've missed. "By the way, don't make the mistake of trusting that guy. He's as fake as they come."

That guy. Scott? Or does he mean…*Bode?*

Before I can answer, the nurse pops her head in.

She fixes me with a disapproving look and strides away. "Don't make me have you removed!"

Craig sighs. "Hey, Es." His voice is suddenly softer. "Pass me my meds, will ya?"

I walk to the bedside table and give him the pot of pills.

"Water."

"You can swallow them dry, Craig." I ignore the jug and walk toward the door.

"Your sister climbed out the window."

I swing round. "What?"

"You heard me. She was in my room, before she left the party." His eyes glint. "We drank a beer. And then she climbed out the window."

"Why on earth would she do that? Did you put the moves on her?" Blood rushes to my head.

"I'm not that guy. It was kind of random. *So* Gaia. One minute we're talking, the next she's unlatching the damn window. That's one way to slip out unnoticed." He closes his eyes. "I was curious, so I climbed out too. She gave a little squeal when she jumped. I was kind of wondering if I'd find her laid out in the snow. But she'd gone."

"Did you look for her?"

He shakes his head. "Wasn't going to give her the satisfaction of chasing her. Dialed my date, hit the pizza place."

"Tell me who you were with."

"Not gonna happen." He nods to the table. "Water jug."

I groan, frustrated. "Get lost, Craig."

"I'll tell you something else, something worth way more," he teases. I stare at him, disbelievingly, then glance quickly down the hall to where Bode is standing at the nurses' station, handing out flyers.

"What?"

"I got something else, now we're on our own."

I feel frozen to the spot. Predator and prey.

Oh, screw that.

"Tell me."

"Scratch my itch first."

My jaw drops. I can't help it.

"Excuse me?"

"Come closer," he murmurs. "What? You were leaning over me a moment ago. Lost your nerve now? I got something you want and it don't come free."

My chin goes up. "Is that what you told my sister?"

He looks disappointed. "You know I didn't do anything to your sister. Come on, Es. It's easy."

I grit my teeth and walk back to the bed, hoping I look more confident than I feel.

"That's right." He smiles. "Now scratch."

"What?"

"My leg, above the cast."

I blink. "You literally want me to scratch your leg?"

He laughs. "Do it and I'll tell you something you wanna know."

I glance at the door, willing Bode to appear, but also dreading that he will.

"Quickly, before he comes back!" Craig urges.

I scratch his hairy leg, above the knee. It's firm, but clammy to the touch.

"Nuh-uh, higher." Craig says.

I roll my eyes and move up a few centimeters, digging my nails in and hoping I'm hurting him.

"Oh man!" he cries. "That feels good!"

"Enough!" I slap the bed and lean into his sweaty face, spit flying out of my mouth. "Tell me!"

He gets that blank look again.

"Telfer Cambridge. A guy who hangs around the resort like a bad smell. If anyone has done anything to Gaia, it's that loser. Remember the name, now, Es? Telfer Cambridge."

I push myself up off the bed and walk as steadily as I can to the doorway.

"Leaving? Oh, shame." Craig's voice is husky. "You scratched so good I was gonna have you yank my chain."

I swivel on my heel, stride back to the bed, and, with all my strength, pull down on the tether holding his nearest leg. Craig screams in pain as half of his body lifts up on the bed and crashes down again.

"Done."

I don't look back.

CHAPTER TWENTY-SIX

———

Telfer Cambridge, Telfer Cambridge, Telfer Cambridge…

We'd had to hustle to make the bus home, no time to write that name down as we hit the pavement running. With each footfall, I repeated the weird name in my head. *Telfer, Telfer, Telfer. Cambridge, like the university. Remember it, Es!* We reached the bus station as the last passengers were getting on, and now I'm in the back seat again, clawing in pockets for a pen, ignoring whatever Bode is saying and writing that sucker down before it flies out of my head forever.

Telfer Cambridge. What kind of a name is that? It sounds like code for something. Was Craig spinning me a tale? The thought of him lying there now, laughing, makes me want to scream.

"Hey." Bode leans over. "You okay?"

"I'm fine." I take a breath. "Gaia climbed out of Craig's window that night."

"What?" Bode stares at me. "He blurt that out when I left the room?"

"Pretty much." I fill him in on the details...but leave out scratching Craig's itch; I'm going to forget that ever happened.

"There's something else." I hold up the note. "Who's Telfer Cambridge?" Bode looks at my scrawl, confused. "Craig said we should look into him."

"Yeah, I bet he did." Bode sighs. "Telfer Cambridge is this... mountain man. My uncle knows him, kinda. I guess you could say he's your typical loner."

"He lives at the resort?"

"The other side of the mountain. Where nobody goes."

"Okay. And what's the skinny on him?"

Bode looks out of the window and stretches his legs. "The Cambridge family were old, old money, they owned all the land around Moonville. Before the Addisons got their hands on it, that is."

"How long ago are we talking?"

He shrugs. "Oh, way back, like, a hundred years. Story goes, Addy and Eli's—I guess, great-grandpa? Addison Senior Senior or whatever, he worked for Telfer Cambridge's great-grandpa, back when the resort was built in the 1930s. Addison was Cambridge's right-hand man. Anyway, old Cambridge had a thing for poker, and Addison beat him outta his money. Cheated, some say. The Cambridges lost everything. Had things gone different, Telfer woulda been the big man around here; instead, he lives in a beat-up shack, while the Addisons are millionaires."

"For real?"

"Who knows? People make stuff up, but that's how the story goes. Most of 'em in town think Telfer's a weirdo anyhow."

"Why?"

"He's different." Bode shifts, uncomfortably. "Sure, there's a bunch of rumors about him. Like *maybe* he was run out of town for creeping around people's yards or something. But none of it's based on fact; it's how folks around here label the ones who don't fit in."

"Craig said he was hanging around the resort." I stare at Bode. "Is Telfer Cambridge, like, angry at the Addisons?"

"What…so angry that he kidnapped their friend Gaia to get his revenge for what happened to his family all those years ago?" Bode pulls a face. "That's a stretch…and too daytime soap even for this town." He chews on his thumb for a minute. "What can I say? I've *never* seen Telfer at the resort. Maybe once in a while in town, at the grocery store. My uncle checks in on him if there's a bad storm, but the dude only gets around people if he absolutely needs to."

I feel the disappointment heavy on my chest. Craig didn't give me a hot lead, just the name of the local bogeyman. I groan and lean back in my seat, the bump of the bus making me feel dizzy. "You don't think he's involved."

Bode sinks down too, knees up on the seat in front. "Es, I don't know. If the cops are worth a crap, they will've thought of him already. He's, like, too obvious a suspect." He looks out of the window again. The streets of the city are gradually melting into suburbia. The bright sun of the early morning has given way to oppressive, nondescript gray. It's almost like England, *like home*, I think, and get a pang of longing for boring and normal. The bus rumbles on. Bode sits beside me, but feels far away, lost in his own thoughts.

"I get it. You want to be Telfer Cambridge when you grow up." I say, quietly. "Except with Wi-Fi and Chinese food."

His eyes dart back to me, looking dark in the low light of the bus, and for a moment I think I've pissed him off, but he laughs softly.

"Gotta have goals."

I nod, glad he's not upset with me. The bus hits the ramp for the highway, we speed up, and I shut my eyes, wanting to be back in Moonville before my mother can spring us. "Still," I say, almost to myself. "We check Telfer Cambridge out. Be stupid not to."

"You got it."

———

We walk into the Screech Owl Bar and Grill, the dimness of the room taking a second or two to get used to after daylight. It's one of those places that is decorated for the tourists to look like your friendly, all-American dive, with neon signs, jukebox, and a couple of locals propping up the bar. We pass the burger counter with kitchen behind, doing a busy lunch service of eat in or take-out Screech Burgers and Feral Fries. I weave through tables filled with flyer-volunteers drinking coffee, and past a small stage with a piano.

My mother's at the bar, perching on a stool; Scott is beside her. A guy wearing headphones is fiddling with a fuzzy-covered microphone, cord trailing out of a black bag marked WBC RADIO BOSTON. Wow. Looks like Ma and Scott are getting the word out to the big city. The radio guy looks up at the two TV screens above the bar and gesticulates to the barman to turn the sound down. The clock on the TV news reads 12:05 p.m. Okay, so we made it back close enough, without being suspiciously on time. Ma catches my eye and smiles, pointing at a big booth in the back of the room. "Ten minutes," she mouths, holding up ten waggly fingers. At least I think that's what she's saying. Either that or she wants me to give everyone a tune on the piano.

Bode turns to me. "Wanna drink?"

"Double vodka."

He cracks a smile. "Water it is."

At the booth, Addy is sitting nursing a coffee with a couple of other girls—and some of the Ski Lift Jerks. I'm thinking I might have to start calling them by their actual names; they can't be all-jerk if they're trying to find my sister. Alternatively, they're suspects, and I should *definitely* know their names. What did Bode say they were called? *Don? Brad? Bart?* Oh, man.

"Es!" Addy sees me, slides down the bench to the end of the table away from her friends, patting the seat next to her. The ski guys, who were laughing to themselves—halfway through a beer—sober up when they see me.

"Hey," Addy smiles. "You doing okay?"

"Yeah," I glance at her friends. "How's it going?"

"Well, we've got rid of the flyers your mum had printed." She takes a sip of coffee. "Hopefully it will do something. The boys were searching the train tracks."

"Oh? I didn't know there was a train station here."

"There isn't." She wipes away some coffee froth from her top lip with a delicate finger. "At least not anymore."

"Why would Gaia have gone on the train tracks then?"

"People go down there. To do…stuff." Addy's almost whispering, but then she shakes her head as if dismissing the thought. "If you want to walk out of town, the train track is one way to leave unnoticed, I guess. Easier than the woods."

Bode appears with a jug of water and a precarious tower of glasses, which he places carefully on the table. "They been on the tracks? Searching around the gold mine?"

"*Gold mine*? Are you serious?" I say, maybe a bit too loudly, feeling like I'm spiraling even further down the rabbit hole. "Could Gaia be trapped there?"

"Sealed up and filled in, has been for years. Except the first hundred feet or so, they take tourists in summer. Every kid in town goes at least once in school; you get to wear a hard hat, the whole deal. It's kinda neat." Bode pours water, pushes one toward me and I gulp it down.

"A gold mine. Gaia never mentioned it."

"It's not exactly Disney." Bode takes a slug of water. "The mine never came through. You can pan for dust in the river, but they didn't find the big seam they were looking for. The landowners—the *Cambridge* family—" He gives me a look. "They thought they were going to strike it big, but they had to wait another few decades for the ski resort to get the bucks rollin' in." His eyes flick at Addy for a second. "Not that they had *that* long."

"Gosh, you're pretty clued up on your local history. Those school trips weren't wasted," Addy says smoothly. "I guess I should know some of this stuff, family and all, but Pop has never seemed that bothered about our Yankee rellies until recently."

"Your dad grew up in England?"

"Born there," Addy says lightly. "Grandfather was never happy in the family business, apparently; he moved to the UK to strike out on his own."

Bode nods. "Great." He gives me a look. *So much for this being some kind of revenge kidnapping by Telfer Cambridge.* He scrapes his chair back. "Gotta pee."

As soon as he's gone, Addy leans forward.

"So? Where were you this morning?" She glances down at the empty tote bag I had slung on the floor. "I know you weren't dropping flyers off at the high school."

I wish I could be better at the whole lying thing.

"I won't tell." Addy says, playing with her spoon. "But your mother's not dumb, Es. Believe me, I know what it's like to have a parent breathe down your neck. You'd better have a cover story."

"Okay, thanks." I wrestle with telling her about Craig. I want some more time to think about it all before I share, but I'm not even sure why.

"I mean, hope you're being careful," Addy says. "Bode's a lovely boy, but it might not be the time to be getting down to some hot barn action, you know? Your mum's already dealing with so much, obviously."

"Eh?" I do that overly loud thing again, and the ski guys look round at us. "*Hot. Barn. Action?*" My face is puce, I know it. "We weren't at the barn! And we weren't doing any…action!"

"No?" Addy doesn't look completely convinced. "You told me you kissed last night."

"Yeah, but there's a humongous difference between that and…Hot Barn Action!" I can't believe we've coined a phrase. Gaia would love this.

"I'm sorry." Addy doesn't sound hugely sorry. "Scott said he'd seen you two there. I put two and two together…"

"Scott?" I practically yell.

"What's Scott done now?" Bode reappears from the toilets. "Or is this just Brit-speak again? 'Great Scott!'" He's loving it, laughing his own joke, and Actual Scott over at the bar is twisting around, checking out why his name is being taken in vain.

"We were with *Craig*," I mutter. Addy clatters her coffee cup in its saucer.

"What?"

"At the hospital. New Lanchester."

"My god, Es." Addy has two red spots forming on her pale cheeks. "What did he say? Is he okay?"

"He's got both legs in casts but he's fine, the bastard." I try not to picture the hairy thighs and Craig's *inner sanctum*, but the vision is imprinted forever. "He swears he wasn't with Gaia after the party. Says they talked up in his room after we went home, and she left. Kind of…dramatically." I take a breath, about to tell her about the window, but she laughs.

"Gaia, dramatic? Ha! That sounds about right." She looks at me. "God, sorry. That's really inappropriate." She plays with her cup. "Anyway… What else did Craig tell you?"

"He totally copped to going to the Eazy Stay, but he won't say who with, except it wasn't Gaia."

"Maybe he was on his own."

"Why go to the motel unless you're with someone you want to keep secret?"

"Graff said she had evidence it wasn't Gee. I guess that's good enough." Addy sniffs. "Did Craig say what happened in the woods?"

"He got lost." I lean back in my chair. "Climbed the deer tower to get his bearings, slipped on the ladder, and fell."

"Okay." Addy picks up her coffee cup and swirls her spoon around the cup, gathering foam.

"He did give me a name of someone we should look into."

"Yeah?"

"Telfer Cambridge. Know him?"

Her jaw drops. "The hermit guy? Craig thinks *he's* got Gaia?"

"He said we should look into him." I sit up. "You've seen him around, then?"

"Totally." Addy shoves her hair out of her eyes, looking more animated than I've seen her in days. "He was hanging round our house a few weeks' back. We were laughing about it."

"You and Gaia?"

"Yeah, and Lucille. He was in our garden—at least, where the woods start—and he was digging in the snow. We were having a smoke on the porch and he's there, bold as brass. Lucille made a joke saying maybe he's looking for his lost treasure!"

I glance at Bode and back at Addy. "Is that the first time you'd seen him?"

She nods. "Me and Gee had no idea who he was, but Lucille told us he's this weird loner. About a week later, we were skiing on our day off and we saw him again, up on one of the back trails that goes through the west woods." She shivers. "That time it was like he was watching us."

"Was Gaia there?"

"Yes." Addy looks worried. "Gaia, me, Lachlan, Shona… and Craig."

There are so many things I want to ask her, but Bode nudges me and as I turn, I see my mother walking over.

"Are you okay, darling? Hand out all of your flyers?"

I nod. *Nope, can't tell if she's on to me.*

She leans on the back of my chair. "Look, the radio man told me that their affiliate TV news station wants an interview tomorrow, so we're going to Boston."

"Great." I smile at her. "You and Dad?"

"Not Dad, Scott."

I can see Scott in the background, laughing with the radio interviewer and heading our way.

"Dad will want to keep searching, anyway," Ma says. "I'll have to get up very early—leaving at 4:00 a.m., it's the morning show—so will you be okay on your own at the lodge? We should be back by lunchtime."

"Absolutely," I say. "Don't worry about me."

"Hey, guys." Scott smiles at us. "Great opportunity to get Gaia's face out there, your mom tell you, Es?"

Yeah, and your face, I think but don't say. I smile back at him.

"Now—can I buy everyone lunch, to say thank you?" My mother delves into her backpack for her purse and looks around at the volunteers sitting at the nearby tables. "These people have been so kind. Screech Burgers all round?"

"Not for me, camera adds fifteen pounds!" Scott grins at my mother. "Seriously, though, slim pickings here for vegetarians like us, ain't that right, Es!" He rubs me on the back. "And Julia, you should save your bucks." He brings out a flurry of notes and puts them on the table. "I've gotta fly—but lunch is on me."

"Oh goodness, thanks, Scott!" Ma puts her purse away. "I'm heading up to the lodge." She looks at me. "Give you a lift? And Bode?"

"I'm good, thanks, Ms. Gill," Bode says.

She smiles at him. Yeah, she can't have realized we didn't go to the school. Or she's playing the long game. I watch her work her way over to the volunteers, thanking each one of them, shaking hands, hugging. She's so good at this. If we don't find

Gaia, it won't be because my mother didn't put everything into it. I gather up the water glasses, Bode grabs the jug, and we take everything to the bar together.

"Catch you later?" He sets the jug down. "What's our next move?"

"Tomorrow morning." I turn to him, my voice low. "Early. Get all the stuff we need. You're taking me up the mountain to find Telfer Cambridge."

CHAPTER TWENTY-SEVEN

———

"How often do people get attacked by moose around here?"

I'm trying not to pant too heavily as I clamber up behind Bode through the thickest, darkest, thick dark forest I've ever encountered. We conquered one colossal hill only to descend into a valley, and now we're climbing again.

"I mean, I've had my moose attack, do you think I'm good for a few years? Statistically. Does lightning strike twice? If lightning is a moose?"

Bode doesn't answer, or if he does, I'm grunting too loudly to hear him; this is hard work at stupid o'clock in the morning.

In darkness, we'd left the resort and driven up a dirt track which turned into mud and patches of snow. Telfer Cambridge's hut is only accessible by foot, so eventually we ditched the quad, flicked on headlamps, and squeezed into the woods. God knows if we'll ever get out again.

"Not much farther," Bode calls. "Worst of the climb is over, it flattens out here."

Flat? I haul myself up a bank, thankful for ski gloves allowing me to pull on the spiky fronds of *whatever* that are growing between trunks and latching themselves around my limbs. I'm kind of surprised anything grows here; the trees are so close together you wouldn't think there'd be any light hitting the forest floor. It's spooky quiet, only the white noise of wind in the canopy; no owl, no tweeters 'n peepers. I draw level with Bode; he's looking at a small round object in his hand.

"Old school." I wheeze. "A real, live compass."

"Man." He frowns at it. "Think the batteries ran out."

I look at him. "But surely it doesn't have—"

"Gotcha." He grins at me. "Come on. It's this way. Ten-minute stroll."

"Hmm, for you, maybe," I grumble. "An endless toil for me."

"Don't put yourself down! You're a lot more agile than you pretend."

"Agile? What are you, my PE teacher?"

"You got grit!" He does a kind of yee-haw accent, slaps me on the arm. "You got spunk, girl!"

Oh my.

Bode heads off again. "No moose here, to answer your question. Or if there are, they can't chase you. The underbrush is too thick in these woods. They try to charge, they get hung up on their antlers."

"Know how they feel." I mutter, unwrapping some random foliage from around my neck.

I can't fault Bode's navigation, however. After a short time, there's a break in the woods, a clearing. I can sense it before I see it, the change in air pressure. Bode switches off his headlamp, pulls me close and makes the *shh* finger in front of his lips, like I'm about to holler into the void.

"See the cabin?" he whispers. We're pressed together, leaning on a trunk, radiating heat. It's not unpleasant.

"Only just." *Gotta control my breathing.* The cabin is a black shape, barely distinguishable against the shadows of trees beyond. And yet, as I watch, a light flicks on at a window. I gasp. "Telfer's home. Bloody marvelous. Now what?"

"Now we wait."

———

Dawn is close; it's getting lighter, and crows fly over, cawing. We're scrunched down, tucked behind the tree trunk and some kind of evil bush, and my legs have fallen asleep. A couple of times a shadow moves behind a curtain at the window, but there's been no proper sighting of the inhabitant. I can make out the cabin better now, see the outline of a door leading out to a small deck with a rocking chair and steps to the ground. All manner of junk is stashed around the outside: a sled, coils of wire, piles of firewood, and a big ax sticking ominously out of a chopping block.

Bode's been silent for so long, I wonder if he's dozed off.

Yeah, if you think that we've been passing the time here in the undergrowth smooching, forget it. It's not like staking out your sister's potential kidnapper is conducive to getting it on.

Suddenly, the door swings open with an eerie creak. A figure—tall and slim, with dark clothes—emerges.

"That him?" I whisper. *Course it is.* Who else is it going to be, Huckleberry Finn? Bode nods, eyes on Telfer.

And he's mesmerizing. Telfer, I mean. He's bending down, putting things in a backpack, nothing particularly interesting. But he moves weirdly—super efficiently, smoothly, fluid like a dancer—no, a wolf? It's unnerving; he looks like he could turn on a pin with no warning and gobble us up.

"And they said Slenderman was a myth."

"They lied," Bode says. "Bizarre, isn't he?" He chews his lip. "Guess I haven't set eyes on him in a while, forgot that he moves…like he does."

"Still think he's misunderstood and harmless?" I can't suppress a shudder. Bode doesn't answer. As I watch Telfer gather up his things, I get a reality hit. This dawn adventure has been a bit of a lark so far, an adrenaline kick, creeping through the forest and tracking down a weirdo. But truth is, we're miles from help and there's a chance this man could have my sister. And while some sickos appear completely normal, this guy is seriously otherworldly. It's not the half-light of the dawn and the stillness of the forest—Telfer would look supernatural if he was buying a pint of milk in the supermarket. He gives off vibes. He scares me.

And then he's gone. He slunk away from the cabin without a second glance, absorbed into the trees.

"Do we follow?"

Bode doesn't answer me immediately, like he doesn't trust his eyes.

"He'd hear us. No point in trying to track a tracker."

"Come on, then!" I grab his arm. "Let's get into that cabin."

He nods. "Keep low. He took a pack; hopefully that's him good an' gone."

It takes me a second to feel my legs, but then the adrenaline kicks in again. We reach the deck and Bode hugs the wall, looking past the cabin in the direction where Telfer disappeared. I try the door and the handle turns easily.

"Not locked. I guess burglars aren't a thing out here."

"Also means he's not worried about anyone escaping." Bode gives me a look. "Unless, you know...they couldn't move or something."

"Going in." I score points for remembering the loud, spooky door creak, open it very slowly, and step inside.

It's dark, but the smell hits me immediately: warm, musty, and sweet. The kind of smell that wraps itself over your face, invades your nose and mouth until you can taste it. The kind of smell that makes the hairs on the back of your neck stand up. The kind of smell that makes you want to run.

"Oh my god, what *is* that?"

Bode doesn't answer me. He doesn't need to, we both know. It's the smell of death.

"I'm gonna turn on the flashlight." Bode's hand is on my arm. He shuts the door behind us and I brace myself.

His wide-beam flashlight flickers, and I flinch. There's a woodstove right there in the middle of the room, the chimney stretching up in front of me, and for a second it looks like a towering monster. Bode sweeps the flashlight beam around the cabin. There's a table and chair next to a window, a kitchen sink over a low cupboard in the corner, a sofa. I turn on my headlamp, walk slowly around the room, nearly bumping into a ladder reaching up to a…mezzanine, I guess? A platform, really. Bode's flashlight can't reach that far into the murkiness, but it looks like there's a bed up there.

He moves to the kitchen and opens the door of a small refrigerator.

"This isn't on. He's got a generator out back, prolly only uses it in summer. He'll have a cool box outside, maybe in a stream. Someplace outta reach of bears."

"Bears? Oh my god, and there's me worried about the moose!"

Bode shrugs. "Black bears here, no biggie. Not like the grizzlies they get out west." He opens a cupboard, finds mugs and plates. "Black bear will smell your food, though."

I have Bode in my beam. His jaw is clenched, his eyes a little wild. "Seriously, what do you think the smell is?" I'm desperate for him to say, *not a dead body. Not your sister.* "And where the hell is it coming from?"

"It's everywhere."

I walk over to the ladder.

"Up there?"

"After you." Bode gestures. "I'll be on your tail."

Great. Of course, now the challenge has been issued, I can't not go first. I put my hand on a rung, then a foot, gingerly, and haul myself up onto the platform slowly, my headlamp casting around for signs of my sister.

"Nothing." Bode has climbed up in half the time it took me. There's the bed, thick with piled blankets, but neatly made—kudos to Telfer, I would never bother if I lived on my own in the middle of nowhere—a small chest of drawers and a bedside table with a glass, a pile of books, and a pair of reading glasses. Somehow, the reading glasses make me relax slightly. Why I'd assume anyone who is a reader couldn't be a murderer, I don't know. I look at the covers. *Silent Spring* by Rachel Carson and *A Walk in the Woods* by Bill Bryson. The second one I recognize; it was on the shelf at the lodge. Gives me creeps now, to see it here.

"Es," Bode says from the ladder. "We should go."

I feel a surge of desperation—a feeling like we've totally missed something obvious and important.

"This can't be it." I look up, but there's no attic or storage space. "There's got to be more to this cabin. I mean, where does he even pee?"

"Potty under the bed." Bode points. "Saw him emptying something. That'll be the smell."

"That's not the smell and you know it."

"Maybe a possum died under the floorboards," Bode says. "Look, there's no sign of your sister. Telfer's a loner, and Craig was full of it. Come on, we'll search outside, then bounce; I don't wanna be here much longer now that it's light out."

I'm staring down at Bode on the ladder, and I'm really pissed off at him for giving up so easily because he doesn't want to be wrong about Telfer. He's not wrong about one thing; it really is getting light outside. The sun has come out—yay, first time since forever—and is streaming under the curtains of the windows and hitting the floor. I turn my headlamp off, and as I do, I see the lines on the wooden boards illuminated by the sunbeams. I point a finger downward.

"There."

"Huh?" Bode twists, almost falling of the ladder, like I've spotted a rattlesnake.

"Bode, there's a basement."

"What?"

"Turn around. Look directly down onto the floorboards. There's a trapdoor. Half-hidden by the rug." I can tell he doesn't want to believe me, but before he can say anything, there's a clattering sound outside.

I grab Bode by the scruff of his parka and haul him up from the ladder like a mama cat retrieving a naughty kitten. We fall back and scrabble onto our bellies. Over the edge of the platform I see the corner of the door open as we crawl, oh-so-silently, underneath the bed. The door shuts. I screw my eyes tight, press myself against the floor, the piss pot wobbles slightly beside my head. *Eurgh*. Footsteps, soft and smooth, pad over the floorboards.

"Pray he just forgot something," Bode whispers in my ear. The footsteps stop.

Silence.

Silence.

Silence.

For god's sake, what's he doing? I don't dare open my eyes in case he's there at the top of the ladder, smiling at us.

There's a kind of *flop* noise, then a wrenching sound. Footsteps again, but this time, different, heavier, descending. I slowly wriggle out from under the bed, Bode grabbing me this time, trying to pull me back, but the compulsion is too strong, I have to see.

Open trapdoor. I was right. And Telfer's disappeared down below.

I turn to Bode with triumphant eyes,. He's looking straight past me at the hole. Suddenly a wave of the dead smell wafts up to us, so strong I nearly swoon. I clamp a hand over my mouth and nose, my stomach lurching.

"Guess we found the smell," Bode whispers, his face pushed down into the neck of his parka.

You think? I want to say, but don't trust myself to open my mouth.

There's the sound of something being dragged—a large, heavy thing—and a series of clatters and a murmuring, as if Telfer's talking to someone. I grip Bode's arm. What the hell?

He's coming up! As one, Bode and I propel ourselves away from the edge, back under the bed, and I wince as my palm scrapes over a sharp piece of wood. We lie there, immobile, hardly daring to breathe. I feel the wetness of blood in my hand. There's a big splinter, but I don't care.

Telfer *pad, pad, pads* up the steps; there's a *whap* of the trapdoor being closed and a *flop* of rug over it. *Please don't come up the ladder.* The gods are listening; there's the creaking of the front door and a reassuring click when it shuts.

We lie there a minute. I mean, it could be five. Or maybe ten seconds. I have no idea which moment I'm living in.

I lift my head. He must be gone.

Shuffling on my front to the edge of the platform, I look down. Telfer opened the curtains; the room is full of warm light. The rug is neatly across the trapdoor. Bode's at my side, hand on my arm.

"We don't know if he's coming back."

"Nope. We don't." I scramble to the ladder.

"Seriously, Es!" Bode hisses at me, "We should get out—"

"We will." I start to climb down. "As soon as we've looked."

It's Bode's turn to look desperate. "Es, he could be right outside!"

"Yeah, I know." I reach the bottom of the ladder. "But Gaia could be down there." I seize the edge of the rug, flinging it back on itself, but it flops down stubbornly. "Stupid thing!" I haul it back again, stamping on it noisily until it relents and lies flat.

"Shit, Es!" Bode reaches down, his fingernails under the end of the trapdoor, trying to ease it. I spy a little rope knot nestled in one end, and I heave it upwards, the trap opening abruptly, almost braining Bode in the process.

Wow, and there's the smell.

I pause at the top of the steps. There's a light on. Huh. Maybe Telfer *is* coming back. Better make this fast.

I take the steps as quickly as I dare, the damp, cool air of the basement caressing my cheeks as I descend, carefully watching where I'm putting my feet. Once I reach the bottom, I look around frantically.

The basement is illuminated by a hurricane lamp, sitting on a clean, white counter that runs the length of the small room. It reminds me of Bode's setup in his barn, not just because of the long counter, but because of what's on it: a desktop, a laptop, and a tablet. Is that a satellite phone? A CB radio. Box files. A microscope, with slides beside it—*what*? Beakers of liquid. Maps, with notations and markings, spread out.

But then I turn around, and I see the bodies.

A gray, stainless-steel table—like you'd see in an autopsy TV drama—large, rectangular with a little drain around the sides to collect bodily fluids. There are four bodies, laid out on their backs, innards cut open, in various stages of decomposition. I feel the sting in my throat and slap both hands across my mouth to stop the vomit, or the scream, whichever is coming first.

"Jesus Christ!" Bode is at my side. "What the actual—?"

"What are they?" I croak, behind my hands.

"Woodchucks." Bode moves carefully round the table. "You know, groundhogs? Kind of like big squirrels."

I stare at the dead creature nearest to me; it looks like a cross between a giant beaver and a meerkat who ate all the pies. The poor thing has been split open from neck to navel, and although I'm no expert on anatomy of furry mammals, I'm fairly sure some organs have been removed. "This is…twisted." I glance back at the counter of equipment again. "Is he…experimenting on them or something?"

"Guess this explains the smell."

"Guess it does." I pick up a shiny tool on the metal table, turn it in my hand. A scalpel.

"No, *this.*"

I look up; Bode's standing in the corner under the stairs, by a large plastic barrel.

"Whatever he took outta them, he put it in here." Bode screws his face up. I move over to take a look…and that is a mistake. The barrel is almost completely full of blood and guts. It's when I see movement—maggots—that I lose the fight and heave onto the floor and Bode's boots. Luckily for him I didn't have time for breakfast this morning, so it's nothing more than a rank dribble, and compared to the abominable barrel of entrails beside us, that's almost pleasant.

"There's…so…much blood," I gasp, stretching out a hand to the wall to stop myself falling over.

"Yeah, those guys are obviously not his first victims."

"What's going on here?" I stare at him. "Who is this monster?"

Before he can answer me, we hear the sound of the front door closing with a slam, and the soft, deliberate padding of Telfer Cambridge walking toward the trapdoor.

CHAPTER TWENTY-EIGHT

———

We hide.

That is to say, we stay exactly where we are, because our options of concealing ourselves in this basement hell-laboratory are precisely zero. In the corner by the barrel of chum is as good as it's going to get, backs pressed against the damp wall.

The footsteps pad, pad, pad overhead…and stop. Maybe he won't come down?

But he does. The basement steps creak above us as Telfer descends, achingly slowly. I feel Bode breathe in beside me, his whole body like a spring, braced for flight or fight. *Yeah, buddy; if it comes to it, you might be on your own there. We all know I don't got the moves.*

Telfer's at the bottom of the steps, his back to us, completely still; I can feel my heart banging out of my chest. He's wearing a long coat and his hair is tied in a straggly ponytail with a polka-dot scrunchie, how random is that? For a terrible second, I wonder if it belongs to Gaia—*a killer's trophy?*—but no, *breathe, it's okay,* I don't recognize it. *Maybe he won't turn around. Maybe he won't see us. Maybe he'll just head back up the stairs.* I hold my breath.

"You'll excuse me if I'm unaccustomed to visitors stopping by."

I nearly throw up again. His voice is low, soft, educated. Is he talking to the groundhogs? *Please let him be talking to the groundhogs.*

"If I'd known you were coming, I would have cleaned up a little." It sounds like he's smiling. "I'd offer tea but I'm all out of Lapsang."

No, he's not talking to the groundhogs.

Bode clearly doesn't think so either; before I can stop him, he takes a step away from the wall.

"Hey, Telfer, man. Bode Ryan, Saul's nephew."

Telfer turns around. *Wow,* he's young—I mean, not our age, but maybe late twenties or early thirties, when I was expecting old. His face is thin and sunburnt, his clothes caked in dirt—but his eyes are bright, enjoying this.

"Bo-dee." He tests the name out, as if hearing it for the first time.

"That's right," Bode says, taking another step, holding his hands out in front of him. "Remember me? Look, man, I'm sorry we burst in like this. We wanted to talk to you. We didn't touch anything."

"*She* did." Telfer looks at me and *winks.* He nods to my hand and I realize I'm still clutching the scalpel from the table. I look at it, Bode looks at it, we look at each other. *Shit.* Should I, like, attack Telfer or something?

Telfer laughs; more of a giggle, really. I flinch as he snatches a stool from under the counter and sits, blocking our exit. 'You do know that New Hampshire has a stand your ground law?' He flicks his coat open with one hand, and there's a shotgun slung around his shoulder on a strap.

"Whoa, man!" Bode gasps, stepping back.

"What does that mean?" I look at Telfer, then at Bode. "A stand your what now?"

"He can legally shoot us because we broke in."

"But we didn't!" I stare at Telfer. "It was open!"

Telfer grins, his mouth is a little lopsided. Under different circumstances he might be kind of good-looking.

"You're on my property, without my permission. And…you have a weapon!" He points at the scalpel, and I drop it like it's hot—no, I fling it, wanting it out of my hand—and it flies into the air toward Telfer.

Bode cries, "Es!" as the scalpel whizzes past Telfer and clatters off the counter behind.

"Nice shot!" Telfer laughs, lolling back on his stool and scooping the scalpel up, waving it in front of him. "Nearly got me!"

I step backward, slam the chum barrel. The force makes a tidal wave of blood and gore slop over the side and splash down my jeans.

"*Ew*," Telfer says. "That's gonna be hell to clean. Hope you got stain remover."

"Oh god!" I stare down at my jeans. "Look, I didn't mean to throw the scalpel at you! I'm sorry." I chance a small step toward him. "And I'm really, really sorry we're in your house, but we're looking for my sister. Gaia Gill. She's been missing since Sunday morning from the resort."

"Missing? How awful." Telfer's brow furrows. "And what does that have to do with me?"

Ack.

"We thought… Well, someone told us you might know something about it."

"Aha." Telfer nods thoughtfully. "So, you awoke before sunrise, battled your way through the dark forest—for several hours, I suspect—and snuck into my cabin because you simply wanted to ask me if I knew anything. That's very dedicated."

Oh, to hell with it.

"I thought you might have her here." I glance at the dead animals on the table. "But actually, it turns out you're only cutting up woodhogs."

"*Ground*hogs," Telfer and Bode say at the same time.

"Oh god, okay, *ground*hogs!" I shout. "Like I said, Mr. Cambridge—"

"Telfer, please." Telfer smiles at me.

"Telfer, thanks. Obviously, your lifestyle is a little, um, different, with the…torturing furry animals thing… But now we know you're not a killer kidnapper, we'll be on our way…"

"Hold up." Telfer stands. "Let's get one thing straight. I don't torture these fellows, I study them. I'm an ecologist. *Marmota monax* at altitude is my specialty. I wrote a paper and everything; you can google me." He giggles. "*Killer kidnapper!*"

"Sweet," Bode says.

"Fab." I smile.

I'm not sure that we're buying this, but I think we're taking the tack of agreeing with everything Telfer says so that he'll basically not shoot us.

"But were you stalking my sister?" I blurt out. Oh dear. So much for the get-out-alive tactic. Telfer's frown is confused, rather than psychotic.

"I don't know your sister. If she's anything like you, however, I'm rather beginning to wish I did." He unclips his gun and lays it out on the counter. "I'm sorry that she's missing, however. That must be upsetting."

"Very," I stammer. "We were told you were sneaking around the resort; my sister's friends have seen you, um, lurking."

"*Lurking*," Telfer says, trying out the word for size. "*Sneaking around*." The frown is back. But then a smile flashes across his face. "Looking for dead hogs, probably! In the woods? Digging? Yes." He sniffs, rubs his nose with the back of his hand. "You're English? Aha, I *do* know who your sister is. Did you hurt your hand?"

"Wha—?"

He points. "There. Your left palm. It's bleeding." He leans over, reaches into a drawer under the counter and pulls out a roll of something and tosses it at me. "Catch!" I don't, of course, but Bode deftly snatches it out of the air. Gauze. Telfer, meanwhile, is assembling a small metal tray of items. "There we are." He stretches out and hands everything to Bode who balances it on the end of the metal table—a tube of antiseptic cream, tape, scissors. "Best to dress the wound. Lots of nasties in the great outdoors."

"Er, thanks." I fumble with the scissors, cutting some gauze.

"You're very welcome. Don't forget the antiseptic."

I nod furiously, squeeze a gloop on, stick it all in place, badly.

"Excellent." His eyes narrow. "Now, who told you I'd been 'stalking' your sister?" Before I can answer him—before I even know I'm going to—he looks up at the ceiling, closes his eyes and smiles. "Don't tell! It's Craig, of course."

"You know Craig?" I shout, knocking the metal tray and contents to the ground with a clatter. "Craig Wilks?"

"It was him, wasn't it?" Telfer smiles and shakes his head. "Oh, my dear cousin loves to drop me in it."

"Wait, you're his *cousin*?" Bode says.

"Guilty." Telfer walks toward us, bending to pick up the metal tray, scissors, and cream and placing them carefully on the table with a grimace. "Although as you've probably surmised, we're not awfully close."

"He was missing too," Bode says. "He's in the hospital now. That's where we talked to him."

"He is?" Telfer walks back to the counter, leans against it. "He'll live?"

"Yes, but he's broken his legs," I say. "He went missing the same time as my sister. Bode's uncle found him at the bottom of a deer tower, looked like he fell. He says he knows nothing about what happened to Gaia."

243

"Hmm, fascinating." Telfer drums the edge of the counter with his fingertips. "He won't have killed her, if that's what you're worried about." He rolls his eyes. "Oh, you weren't, were you? You were worried that *I* had. God's teeth, Craig! You little shit stirrer." He looks at me. "Excuse my French. He hates me because I inherited all the money and the looks." He winks again. "Families, huh? Nothing but trouble."

I can't tell if any of this is real.

"I do recall that I've seen him and your sister, hanging off each other, *sucking face*, or whatever the cool kids are calling it these days." He does a comedy pout, crosses his long arms.

"Kissing? Are you absolutely sure?" I say.

"Ooh, ya, I'm absolutely positive." He effects my accent. "Out in the woods, where they thought nobody could see them. I seem to remember your sister was getting a little bit huffy with Craig—totally understandable—and the next minute, ah, young love! They're making up and making out." Telfer shrugs and clears his throat. "But if it's gone sour, Craig's not the type to maim or kill; he's squeamish as hell." He nods at the table. "He couldn't tolerate looking at the boys there. Our grandfather took us hunting when we were children and Craig sobbed. He's an asshole, but he couldn't kill a rabbit, much less a person. Craig's got his fingers in all sorts of dubious business, but kidnap-murder is not one of them."

"What kind of business?" Bode says.

"Pilfering?" Telfer says. "Let's face it, what do I know? I'm not exactly a man-about-town. I listen in on the police channel sometimes," he nods to the radio on the counter, "but clearly not enough recently. I'm aware Craig has been moving some… goods, I guess you could say. A bottle of liquor here, a carton of cigarettes there…"

"You mean, he sells stolen stuff?" I feel like I'm losing the thread. "In an organized way?"

"A mere cog in a wheel is my guess." Telfer says. "Craig's not the head honcho. Not the big cheese, know what I'm saying?"

I really don't.

Telfer rubs his chin. "Aha! You'll want to talk to Jacques."

"Who's Jacques?"

"He's who Craig takes his orders from, I'm fairly sure. Canadian, runs with some of those youths your sister no doubt knows." He tuts. "And there was me thinking you supersleuths had been thorough. Haven't you interrogated all of them?"

"I've never heard Jacques mentioned. Does he work at the resort?"

Telfer snorts. "Not in the way you mean. He's lives in New Lanchester, I believe. Craig runs things here, Jacques rocks up to kick Craig's ass." He thumbs in the direction of the steps. "Follow the bread crumbs, kiddos. Just know that Jacques ain't playing." He moves away from the foot of the steps, gestures us to freedom once more. "Now scram. And don't come back."

We don't need asking again, scuttling past him and hitting the steps at pace. At the top I stop, turn around. Telfer is looking up at me with amused eyes.

"Thanks. And sorry, again. If you see any sign of my sister out in the woods, will you tell us?"

He nods. "I always have my eyes open."

"Thank you. I mean it."

"Bonne chance." He winks at me again. "And be clever. I don't want to be digging up your bodies next."

───────

We literally do not speak a word until we reach the quad. All our focus is on getting out of there. We don't look back either. It feels like if we do, we'll break the spell and Telfer or whatever malevolent forces are lurking in the woods will pounce and get us.

Finding the bike, and watching Bode retrieve the key from his pocket, I breathe a massive sigh of relief. I won't be completely relaxed until we get back to the lodge, but *wow* does it feel good to have safe passage home.

"Okay," I say. "I have to say it. I'm thinking...Jacques is—"

"Mystery Man," nods Bode, flinging a leg over the quad.

"Yes!" I practically jump on the spot. "Lucille's date at the party, the weirdo who blew me a kiss."

"Gotta be. Come to think it, dude's got a Canuck accent." Bode puts his gloves on. "And you know what? The Lucille connection makes perfect sense. She works at The Eclipse."

I rack my brains. "The bar at the resort?"

Bode nods. "Liquor was going missing around Christmas, boxes of the stuff. Lucille pointed the finger at a janitor, and they fired him. My uncle thought it was BS. He was an immigrant, an easy target. And that's around the time Jacques came on the scene."

"So you reckon Lucille and Craig were doing that? Passing stolen stuff to this Jacques guy to sell? I *knew* she was dodgy!" I'm practically shouting now. "But where does Gaia come into all of this?"

"No idea. But we should do like Telfer said, follow the bread crumbs. Anyway, let's get out of here," Bode turns the ignition. "Dunno 'bout you, but I wanna figure this all out in a place I'm not jumping at every shadow."

I nod, but don't get on the bike. Something, itching at the back of my brain...

"The watch."

Bode looks at me sharply.

"Bode, it fits." I put my hands on my head. "Gaia gave Craig the watch to sell through Jacques. Something went wrong. Maybe Jacques gave them money up front, but Craig lost the watch, so the deal went south. Jacques is pissed off, beats up Craig, takes my sister..."

Bode shakes his head. "Es, it sounds kinda...far-fetched—"

"Far-fetched like my-sister-going-missing far-fetched?" I climb on the quad behind him. "That watch was worth thousands; people have done more over way less. We need to get back. We need to track this Jacques down and find my sister!"

"We go to Detective Graff?"

"There's no evidence," I say. "I haven't even got the watch anymore. No, we need to check out Jacques first."

"I have an idea." Bode turns to me. "Something that might be useful."

"You've been holding out on me?" I search his face. "Spill."

"It's complicated," Bode says. "I can't explain it all here. I'll drop you back at the lodge, you ask Addy about Jacques, see what she knows. I need to call in at my place, then we go find him together." He sees the look on my face. "Es, please trust me. If there's anything in what I'm thinking, I'll let you know."

I nod. I do trust him. And right now, it feels like that's all I've got. He nods back and revs the engine. I hug his waist, and we roar down the trail away from the wild side of the mountain.

———

As we approach the resort, Bode slows.

"Want me to drop you off outta sight?"

"What time is it?"

He takes out his phone. "Ten thirty. God, it feels way later."

"It's okay, take me to the lodge," I say. "Ma and Scott won't be back from Boston until lunchtime. Dad'll be out searching; I've got the key."

But as we head up the lane and turn the corner, it's clear I won't be needing it.

Outside the lodge, standing at the bottom of the steps, are my parents, Scott, Addy, and Detective Graff. Bode sees them too, hits the brake, but it's too late. It only takes a second for them all to turn around to see us.

Shit.

CHAPTER TWENTY-NINE

My mother's face is a blend of relief and fury; Dad looks almost unrecognizable, so old it makes my heart ache. As Bode and I crawl up to the lodge, it's Detective Graff who takes the lead.

"Esme! You're back." She smiles tightly, her hand on my arm, helping me off the bike in a way that feels a little like she's going to arrest me. "You guys had us worried. Where'd you get to?"

"Sorry, hi—" I look past her to my parents. "Ma, I thought you'd gone to Boston for the TV thing with Scott?"

"We got bumped!" Scott interjects. "Some Red Sox player got caught doing stuff he shouldn't, so no room for us on the schedule." He rolls his eyes. "But hey, it's all good. Tomorrow they promised a way longer slot; gonna put some of my footage together, do a full segment on Gaia."

"That's great, Scott." Before I can get any more out, Ma marches up.

"Where on earth have you been?" The relief of a few seconds

ago has passed, and now she's just doing angry. "Have you hurt yourself?"

I realize she's looking down at my bandaged hand and bloodied trousers.

"No, you see—"

"And what the hell were you up to yesterday?" She cuts me off. "You told me you'd gone to the school. What's this about interrogating Craig at the hospital?" She turns to Bode. "Did you take her there? On that thing?"

Bode gets off the quad. "Ms. Gill, I'm so sorry, I—"

"No!" I shout. "Don't blame him. It was all my decision. And we went on the bus."

Detective Graff is at my side. "We had a call, Esme. From Craig's family's lawyer. They're threatening to press charges for harassment."

I snort. "I only asked Craig a few questions. He was the one who harassed me!"

"Well, he tells it different, and he's alleging physical assault." Graff says evenly. "They've issued a restraining order against you. You're not to go within fifty yards of Craig Wilks."

I laugh. I can't help it. The sheer idea of Craig being frightened of me is *golden*.

"Es, stop." Dad's voice is tired. "This is bang on what Detective Graff told you not to do. You're not helping Gaia."

I feel anger surge inside. *I am helping her. I'm doing more than all of you put together!*

"And where were you earlier this morning?" Ma says. "Addy

told me she called in at eight and there was nobody here. Did you sneak out in the middle of the night?" She glares at me, then at Bode. *Oh god. She thinks we're doing it.*

"I did leave in the night, for…reasons." *Damn, I so can't tell her about Telfer.* "Not those kind of reasons." I give Addy a furious look. "We were trying to find Gaia!"

"Have you any idea how much I've worried?" Ma practically screams at me.

"Okay, let's keep it calm, love. I'm sure she meant well." Dad places his warm hand on my shoulder, and I feel like I'm going to cry. "We can't cope with this, Es. A decision's been made."

"What?"

"Why don't we all take this inside, everyone," Detective Graff says, putting an arm around me and leading me up the stairs.

"What do you mean, Dad?" I squirm around, but Graff does a great job of keeping me on track into the lodge. Everyone troops after us and Dad shuts the door behind Bode.

"We're sending you home, love." *No, no, no.* "You're on the flight back to England tonight."

"I can't!" I look desperately from Dad to Ma and back again. "Please, please don't make me!"

"The flight is booked, Es." Ma says more gently. "I'm sorry. We need to focus on finding her, and you need to try and get back to normal."

"Normal?" I cry. "Are you kidding me?"

"This is doing you damage, Es. I want you safe back in

England, not tearing around on quad bikes and—" She gestures to my bloodied trousers. "God!—whatever that is."

"Particularly heavy period," I mutter.

Scott and Addy snort with laughter, Dad sucks in air through his teeth, and my mother looks like she's going to explode.

"Talking of blood." She glares at me. "The blood on the keg was Gaia's."

My heart stops beating.

"Julia!" my dad shouts.

"Now, folks." Detective Graff steps between us. "I told you we shouldn't get too concerned. It's a *tiny* amount."

"God—sorry, Es." Ma shudders, shaking her head. "Not fair of me to give you a shock like that. But can you understand why Dad and I can't cope with panicking about you too?"

"Yup," I nod solemnly. "I need to speak to Detective Graff. Privately."

Ma stares at me. "What's going on?"

"Just me and Bode." I point to the kitchen. "Two minutes."

"Esme!"

"Julia, let her," my dad soothes. Out of the corner of my eye I can see Addy and Scott wondering what the hell is going on, but Detective Graff has already nodded and I'm leading the way through the archway into the far end of the kitchen.

"Do you know Jacques?" I whisper to Detective Graff. "Lucille's boyfriend? He's Canadian. Was at the party on Saturday."

Detective Graff nods slowly. "We've talked to him, yes."

"You have?" My eyes dart to Bode, who isn't exactly looking encouraging, but I plow on regardless. "We were told, this morning, that he's involved in thefts around the resort. Craig too, possibly Lucille, but Jacques is the boss."

"Okay," Graff says carefully. "And you think this is relevant to your sister's disappearance?"

I swallow. "Perhaps. I think Gaia asked Craig to sell something for her. An expensive watch. Craig might have involved Jacques. And it went wrong somehow."

"Craig told you this?"

I shake my head. "No. Someone else told us about Jacques. They said he's bad news, dangerous."

"Who have you been talking to?"

"I don't want to say."

"It was Telfer Cambridge." Bode's voice is low. "Know him? Lives on the mountain."

"I'm aware." Detective Graff nods. "He's on our list of folks to talk to."

"Awesome. Well, we did it for you already." I stick my chin up. "Did you know Telfer is Craig's cousin?"

"I did not," Detective Graff raises her eyebrows. "But what I do know, Es, is that Jacques is not our guy."

I frown at her. "How come? Has he given you an alibi? Because—"

"I know because Jacques is working with us."

"What?"

Detective Graff glances toward the archway to the living

room. "Esme, I'm only telling you this because you're going home, and I know if I don't, you'll be tying yourself in knots on the plane tonight. And Bode—" She flashes him a stern look. "This is strictly confidential, you get me?"

He nods. We both nod.

"Jacques—it's not his real name, by the way—is one of us. At least he was. He's an ex-cop, Royal Canadian Mounted Police, to be exact."

"A Mountie? With the hat and everything?" I look at Bode. "I didn't know they actually existed."

"Well, they do, and Jacques was one. But now he works privately." Graff crosses her arms. "The resort hired him to investigate the thefts."

"The liquor?" Bode says. "They fired someone for that."

"And that may have been a mistake," Graff says. "There have been other thefts since: jewelry, electronics, and money taken from guests' accommodations. The resort wanted to handle it themselves initially to avoid bad publicity. Jacques was helping them. He was able to insert himself in the ring to get to the bottom of what was going on." She straightens up. "I can't say who's involved; this may go further, there may be prosecutions. I can tell you there's no indication it has anything to do with Gaia going missing."

"But what about the watch?" I say. "Wouldn't that be motivation? It was worth thousands."

"The people suspected of involvement in the thefts are absolutely in the clear regarding your sister, Es. We know their movements from phone records, among other things."

"So, where is she?" I stare out of the window. I feel exhausted, defeated. I'd been so sure we had something to go on. If this isn't the big lead, then where do we go now? *I go back to England, that's where.* I cannot believe it ends here. How can it?

Detective Graff holds my shoulders and fixes me with her green eyes. "I want you to know, Es, I will do everything in my power to find her. Going home is probably the toughest thing you'll ever have to do, but it's the right thing. Gaia would tell you that."

I'm not sure what Gaia would tell me. Would she go home if it was me missing? Not in a million years. But I am not my sister. She would be doing all of this way better than me. I pull away, slump into a chair, my head in my hands.

"Take care, Esme." Graff leaves the kitchen.

Bode is standing by the window; he's not looking at me and I can't guess what he's thinking. I don't know what I'm feeling anymore, apart from empty. Finished. This was my last play, and I didn't even know it at the time. If I had, I would have questioned Craig more, questioned Telfer more. I would have done...more. But now, it seems like I might as well give up and go home.

"I should pack."

Bode looks at me sharply. Maybe he didn't think I'd give in so easily. *Ha,* he really doesn't know me.

"I need to give you back your phone." I get up, retrieve the brick from my back pocket, push it across the table. He's there, his hand on mine.

"I don't want you to go." He looks away, uncomfortable. "I mean, *duh*."

"That's...nice."

He rounds the table, holds my hands. "I'll keep looking. When you're home, I'll give you updates, everything." He perks up. "Who knows? Maybe when she's found you'll come over again?"

I feel sick. I have no idea what the future might look like. I barely know what the next hour will look like. But I nod and look at those amazing hazel eyes, and...I go in for the kiss. If he's surprised, it only lasts a second. His hands are on my face, I'm pulling him close, and *oh god* I could stay in this moment forever, here, kissing in the kitchen like nothing matters—

"Esme."

My dad is at the archway.

Bode and I spring apart and my dad swears under his breath. Normally I'd be mortified, but as we know, normal climbed out the window with my sister back on Saturday night.

"I'm going out to search, love, so I'll say bye now." Dad looks dazed, like he can't process everything that's happening. I'm right there with him.

"I'll...leave you alone." Bode says. He exits, giving my dad a wide berth. Dad looks after him.

"You could do worse."

Wow. Didn't expect that. I clear my throat. "Yeah... He's been great, helping us, I mean. And you know, everything's been my idea. He shouldn't be blamed."

"Oh don't worry, I know you." A little bit of old Dad comes

back. He walks over and hugs me. "It may not seem like it, but I'm proud of you, Es. You going back to England is the right thing, but me and your mum are so very proud. Gaia would be too. She *will* be."

And of course, this last bit makes the sobs come. Huge, ugly sobs, in my dad's arms. And he stands and holds me, 'til they're gone.

"It'll be all right." He hugs me tight, like he'll never let go. "I—I can't make any promises, I wish I could. But I have a feeling it'll be all right."

"I know, Dad." I said, my voice sounding hoarse and too loud in my head. "I feel it too." Only, I don't. I did, a day or two ago. Deep down inside, I felt like it was only a matter of time 'til we found her. Now I'm not sure. The lie is there to comfort both of us.

"I have to go." Dad finally breaks apart. "Be gentle on your mum." I nod, and of course, I mean it now, although how much I'll be able to keep that promise is another thing entirely. Dad kisses me on the head one more time, and then he's gone.

I give myself a moment to get rid of the snot, splash my red face, and all of that. When I walk through the archway. Scott, Addy, and Bode are lingering in the sitting room. Scott's on his phone, laughing quietly at something, but he shuts it down quickly when he sees me. Detective Graff has gone, and judging by the banging of cupboard doors upstairs, Ma is packing my stuff already.

I say my goodbyes. It's so weird. Scott talks a bunch of promises in my ear, Addy says very little. We hug, they leave. I'll forgive them their trespasses. We're all doing our best.

Bode's sitting on the arm of my armchair. As I shut the door, he stands, scratches the back of his neck.

"It's your birthday tomorrow. I feel bad I didn't get you anything."

"Whoa." I walk over to him. "I totally forgot. Think everybody else did too. Probably just as well. Thanks for remembering though. It sucks even more that I'm not going to be here. You could have given me the bumps."

"The *what*?"

"Oh god," I groan. "Lost in translation. I'm not even going to try and explain, look it up."

"Will do." He smiles sadly, looks like he's going to kiss me again but thinks better of it. *Damn.* "Okay, so travel safe. I'll message you." He walks to the door. "Es, I don't know what more to say, except I'll keep looking." He reaches for the handle.

"Wait." I walk up to him. "What you said before, on the mountain. You were going to check something out."

Bode stares at me. "Yeah! God, I forgot. I guess it doesn't matter now we know Jacques is legit. Just something that was bothering me. I tell you what, I'll take a look, and if it is anything, I'll come back before you leave later, okay?"

"Esme!" Ma calls—kind of screeches, really—from a room upstairs.

"Better go," Bode says, his eyes searching my face like he really doesn't want to. We kiss. Break apart. Walk out onto the deck.

"And one for luck." I kiss him again. Then it's over.

He springs down the steps, starts the quad. Gives me one last grin and disappears down the lane and out of my life forever.

CHAPTER THIRTY

———

Eli draws the short straw of driving me to the airport. You can bet that's part of my punishment. Exactly what Eli did to deserve it is another matter. When he picks me up after lunch, the look on his face leaves me in no doubt that he's about as thrilled with this arrangement as I am.

Ma hauled my suitcase out onto the deck an hour before Eli was due to be here; I checked the time and everything. I was clock-watching, for once, waiting by the window to see if Bode was going to come roaring up the lane with news. But he never came.

"Auntie Susie will meet you at Heathrow." Ma finishes taping up the bandage on my hand and strides out on the deck to wave at Eli. She made a point of changing the dressing Telfer gave me; I think it's a kind of apology. "But don't panic if Susie's late. Hates driving on the M25; heaven knows she's been living practically on top of it for ten years, should have got used to it by now…"

Ah, younger sisters. What a frustration we are to our older siblings.

Eli has parked but is sitting in the car, staring down at his phones—or maybe it's his lap he finds endlessly fascinating. Like the cabbie who has already decided he's not getting a tip, there'll be no help with the luggage. I drag the suitcase and propel it down the steps into a small puddle. Ma swallows another sigh and heads inside, shouting.

"Back in a moment, don't go yet."

"Open up!" I lightly slap the car boot. Eli makes me wait a few seconds before I hear the click. Suitcase inside, I slam the boot, making the whole car rock. Shall I sit in the back? Eli's probably hoping I will. I open the front passenger door instead.

"Susie's number." Ma appears, holding out a piece of paper. "Just in case." She gives me a grimace of a smile. "She probably won't be *that* late."

I take the number. Did Susie ever get tested for dyspraxia? For the first time it occurs to me I might not be the only one in the family. I bet my mother's thought about it. Was Susie a pain in the ass for Ma, growing up? If dyspraxia is hereditary, does she blame her sister for me?

Ma goes in for the hug and I hold my breath. I can't let myself be in this moment. It's too hard. She says some stuff about not worrying, and that she loves me. I can't speak; there's too much to say. I want to rage at her, comfort her, cry with her. But if I start, I may not stop.

We part; I get in the car and fight with the seat belt. Eli makes a point of waiting for me to finish, then executes a painfully slow and accurate three-point turn, like he's doing his driving test. Ma taps on the glass and Eli opens my window.

"Here—extra cash if you need it in the airport!" She hands me notes. "I forgot to order you a vegan meal on the plane, so maybe pick up snacks?" She gives me a strangled, guilty look, blows a few kisses.

Eli sighs as he closes my window; god, I hate him. I give Ma the thumbs-up, and Eli takes us achingly slowly down the lane. I can see Ma in the mirror, standing there, a look of uncertainty on her face. Maybe she's doubting sending me away? More likely, she's wondering why Eli is driving like a grandpa.

We crawl down the lane to the junction with the main road. I have one last look for Bode. Nope.

As we descend the mountain, Eli taps his phone and starts his playlist. I glance at the screen. Power Ballads, Volume 1. *Oh jeez*. It's going to be a long drive.

***

I feel like I've aged twenty years by the time I walk into the concourse at Logan Airport, but the bustle jolts me out of my soft rock stupor. Crowds of people, umpteen flights on a board above me, so much noise and chaos after the calm of the mountain, but I don't mind that; it makes me feel small and insignificant in a good way.

Eli was silent during the journey, apart from the occasional middle-aged tutting at an irresponsible driver. When he dropped me off, I'd thanked him for the lift. He sat there, grinding his teeth, probably willing me to get out and leave him alone. I sighed, opened the door—but suddenly, he spoke.

"You're a good sister, Esme. Gaia is lucky to have you."

I almost fell out of the car. Tried to think of a response but could only make goldfish noises.

"If I went missing, I don't think Addy would be in a hurry to search for me." He laughed, bitterly.

Fair point, I thought, but didn't say.

"Gaia has so many people working hard for her." He turned and looked at me directly in the eyes, for the first time ever. "We reap what we sow."

Before I could think of a reply to that corker, a Boston driver leaned on his horn, reminding us politely that this is a drop-off area. Eli shook himself and I got the hell out before things could get any weirder. It does make me like Eli a little more, though. And feel sorry for him. Perhaps that's the weirdest thing of all.

It's lucky that I spot the logo of the airline I'm traveling with almost immediately. As I'm dragging my suitcase toward the long queue, a little thought dances in my brain, but I swat it out of the way.

"Oh, sorry!" I realize I've stopped walking, causing a massive pileup of people and suitcases behind me.

I lug my stuff over to a seat. Gosh, this suitcase is *wet*. Better unzip it and see the damage before I check in. Yeah, damp ski clothes on top. Next are a bunch of schoolbooks I forgot to even look at. I take out my sweatpants and T-shirt, ball them up, and push them into my backpack. Well, I might want to change on the plane, you know, it's the red-eye. I zip everything up and join the line.

After an age of shuffling forward, I reach the head of the line. The couple behind hate me. I kept drifting off and not noticing the line had moved, the woman sighing, passive aggressive. I felt like turning around and shouting, "You know what? My sister is missing! Cut me some slack!" But I don't.

When I reach the desk, I hand all my stuff over to the guy sitting in front of the computer and heft my suitcase onto the weighing thing.

"Traveling to London?" He looks at me above my passport. "Alone?" There's something about him that really reminds me of Scott: well-groomed, similar eyes.

"Yeah." I find the permission form my mother signed, because I'm underage. *Maybe they'll tell me I can't fly?*

"This is all great...Esme?" Not-Scott says. "That's an unusual name."

I nod. *You should meet my sister, she's called Gaia, which is even more wacky, but you can't because she's MISSING.*

"Did you pack all your luggage yourself?"

"Yeah." Nope, my mother did most of it. Hopefully she didn't add any bombs, drugs, or bushmeat.

"Got someone meeting you at Heathrow?" He smiles at me. I'd thought he was American, but he's got one of those pseudo-accents that British people acquire when they've been around Americans a lot. Like my sister did.

Does.

God, did I just think about her in the past tense?

I feel like I've been punched in the stomach, my legs numb and floppy; I have to hold on to the counter to stop myself from sinking. Around me, the airport spins.

"Are you all right?" Not-Scott gasps. I grip harder on the counter, breathe in through my nose, concentrate on seeming normal.

"Bit scared of flying." *Really?* First I knew about that. I smile, because that's what we psychopaths do when we lie.

Not-Scott returns the smile, but he's not convincing either.

"My god, are you Gaia's sister?"

"What? Yes!" I stare at him. "Do you know her?"

"Not IRL, but yeah, sure I follow them both. Are you kidding me?" He scrabbles beneath his desk, takes a quick look around, and shoves a phone in my face. On the screen is the video of Scott and me being interviewed on the rainy deck. "I knew I recognized you, I'm a *huge* Scott Mazzulo fan, loved him since back in the day. So stoked he's making it big again." He lowers his voice. "*God, how are you?* I've been mad worried about Gee! Rooting for Scott to find her! He said that he's on TV tomorrow. Pity I'm working, but he'll post a link on his channel, no doubt."

The interview on his phone is still playing, my rain-battered face glowing in the light, but suddenly I'm interrupted by some fit young beauties on a high-tech stationary cycle.

"Annoying ads," Not-Scott says, clicking on the screen to kill the commercial. "He has so many on his channel now. I guess that's how he makes money, but whatever, I'll still watch. I've been a follower since the really early stuff, like the scavenger hunt?" He looks at me, eyes shining. "Classic Scott n' Gee." He giggles. "To be honest, when Scott started with the 'Gaia's Missing' thing, I thought it was another stunt!"

"It's not a stunt." I smile. "My parents have barely slept. We've been searching the woods with dogs and phoning the hospitals."

Not-Scott looks at me, color draining from his face.

"I'm sorry. You must be so stressed." He whips his phone away and fixes eyes on his computer. "Lemme see what I can do." He click-clacks away on the keyboard. "I shouldn't, but I'm upgrading you to Business." He looks at me like he's giving me the golden ticket. "You can sleep, watch movies, keep your mind off things." I stare at him a second too long before I realize I'm supposed to be elated about this. "I really, really hope they find her." He sniffs, grabs a pad of paper. "Hey, when Scott drops the limited edition *Mazzulo and Miss Gee* hoodies, d'ya reckon you could score me one?" He scribbles and hands me a note. "My email. Size medium. That would be amazing, the merch will sell out so quick!"

"Merch?" I croak.

"Thanks so much." Not-Scott beams. "Awesome!"

"Awesome," I say, as he presses some button that makes my suitcase wobble away down a conveyor belt, where it flops over and blocks the hatch *because even my luggage is dyspraxic*. I turn on my heel and head in completely the wrong direction.

Security is a blur of plastic trays clashing and people

shouting, and I emerge feeling like I've been beaten up. There's a long concourse and I find a sign telling me where my gate is. I'm *so* early. Even with Eli's funereal driving.

Ma said something about snacks, but my stomach is churning. I should find a place to sit, try to read. There aren't many free seats, but I spy one next to white double doors with a sign on them saying: EXIT TO LANDSIDE. NO RETURN.

And then I see her.

Gaia's on the other side of the concourse. Her hair, her smile, her red jumper—unmistakable. I drop my backpack, drifting through the flow of the crowd, bashing into people hurrying for their flights, tripping over children and one of those annoying little wheeled suitcases—but I make it. There she is. Just a few feet away. She's looking right at me. My heart jumps into my mouth and I nearly choke on it.

MISSING: Gaia Gill

The flyer is front and center in the plexiglass-covered frame. Gaia has company—other Missing posters with curly edges, yellowing. There's an African American girl called Destiny, three, with cornrows and a frilly dress; a really faded picture of a Latino teenager called Salvador, fifteen, glasses and a stripy T-shirt. And my sis.

"Hey, missy!"

I turn around. Back at the seat, a security guard is holding my backpack. "This yours?"

I nod, slowly walking back to the other side of the concourse.

"You can't leave it here!" He frowns at me. "Wanna close the airport?"

"No." I take the bag back from him. "I don't."

He nods at me, his face a little kinder. "So don't leave your things lying around, okay?" He reaches down to the bench and hands me a newspaper. "This yours too?"

I stare at it. Local Star Scott Keeps Hope Alive for Safe Return of Friend, a headline reads under Scott's photo. There's a tiny insert of Gaia's pic too. I take the paper from the security guard.

"Thanks."

"No problem," he says. "You be careful, miss, or they'll remove you from your flight."

"It's okay," I say, shoving the newspaper in my pack and heading for the double doors. "That won't be necessary."

"Wait!" The man says, panicked. "Through those doors— that's a one-way exit, no return. You go through there, you can't get on your plane, you know!"

"Yes." I take a deep breath, before I walk through the door. "I do know."

———

It's amazing what you can do when your mind is focused, and I'm buzzed as hell but have never felt so calm. The idea, a week ago, of me finding the last bus north from the airport, let alone successfully purchasing a ticket and making it to the stop on time, would have been ridiculous. But when everything else ceases to matter, it's incredible what you can achieve.

The journey back to New Lanchester, now that I don't have to listen to Eli's power ballads, whizzes by.

Scott's making serious money off Gaia's disappearance. There are ads, merchandise. Somebody should be looking at that. That somebody is going to have to be me.

I stare out of the window as the sky darkens, and think some thoughts, make a plan. I have a little wobble when we finally pull into the bus station, as it's mostly empty and everything looks closed, but luckily there's a wodge of cash in my wallet and a lone cab driver who's happy to relieve me of it.

In the back seat of the overheated cab, even with the driver's country music station a little too loud to be comfortable, I almost drift off. I was wired in the airport and on the bus, but now the adrenaline has fallen away, I'm drained. Before I know it, we've hit the switchbacks and the slow climb up Moon Mountain.

"Where to?"

Good question. This was the hole in the plan. I glance at the digital clock on the cab's dash. 10:35 p.m. *No way. Third time.* Gotta be a sign I've made the right choice.

"Where you staying, honey?" The cab driver slows to a stop. *Argh.* Not the lodge, obviously. I only have until morning before my aunt realizes I wasn't on the flight, rings the alarm bells, and all hell breaks loose. Ma will be busy with the TV show in Boston early, so that might buy an extra couple of hours. Addy's place? Nope. I can't risk her running to my folks, and now I know she totally will.

"Here!" I recognize the entrance to the tunnel that leads to the staff accommodation. "You can let me out."

"You sure?"

"Yep, thanks." I grab my backpack, give the driver almost everything in my wallet, and step into the night air. I hurry to the tunnel as the cab does a U-turn and heads down the mountain.

Wow, it's dark. Dark, and still and quiet. My body tingles, every nerve suddenly firing, on full alert. *Deep breath.* Darkness is fine. I don't want anyone seeing me. It's only a short walk. I can do this.

As I exit the tunnel, there's movement up the road. *Shit!* Ducking into the bushes, I crouch as a figure heads toward me. It's Lucille, head low, talking on her phone.

"Lost signal, but I got you now." She's lingering by the entrance to the tunnel. "Anyhow, Gaia's still in the wind."

A chill goes through me.

"She's missing, she can't talk." Lucille listens to the person on the other end of the line. "Tomorrow, as planned? Yeah, everybody's busy looking for Gee, so…" She titters, turning her back to me. The breeze rustles the leaves and I struggle to hear. "Gotta go." She hangs up and walks off through the tunnel. I wait until the footsteps have faded, and slowly emerge from the undergrowth.

My god… *She's missing, she can't talk.* Can't talk about what?

About the thefts? Who was Lucille speaking to? Whoever it was, they obviously don't know where Gaia is.

Okay, lots to unpack here, but first things first… Sweating and clutching my backpack to me like a shield, I follow my nose and make it to Bluff Point. All the houses are in darkness, including Craig's. The yellow tape is still there; maybe that's why Lucille is going elsewhere. I cut through the shadows in Bode's uncle's yard to the barn. There are faint lights at the top windows. *Made it.* Sliding the door across, I take a deep breath and step inside.

CHAPTER THIRTY-ONE

The lights are on—a bedside lamp and a laptop, glowing—but Bode's not home.

I look around for his phone, his coat, a cup of warm something that means he'll be back in a sec. My heart sinks.

What now? All that excitement to get back here, and no big welcome. I take off my coat, dump my backpack. *God, I'm ravenous.* I never got those snacks. Bode must have some food here; I wander over to the kitchen area and spot the Cap'n Crunch. Splash of water, and we're done. Not the worst supper I've eaten.

I stand, munching, listening for Bode's return. The barn groans, there's a *drip, drip* that might be one of the tractors leaking below, and the sound of Bode's laptop whirring, snoozing on the counter.

I can't wait. I absolutely need to see what Scott has on his video channel. Like, *now.*

Abandoning the cereal, I sit in front of the laptop. As I move

the mouse, a password box jumps up and I type: EsmE_R0x.
Here's hoping he hasn't updated it. The screen changes—
yes!—I'm in.

I hit the Missing page first; Scott has made another photo
montage of Gaia, but this one is set to music. The song is a *Rival
Roomies* number, their version of "You've Got a Friend."

"Ew, cheesy."

*You just call out my name, and you know wherever I am, I'll
come running, to see you again ...*

A pic of Gaia celebrating her exams ending, arms around her
friends ...

Winter, spring, summer, or fall, all you have to do is call...

Gaia and Addy's selfie outside the Eazy Stay motel...

And I'll be there, you've got a friend.

The last photo taken of Gaia at the party.

"Talk about laying it on thick!" I bluster, closing the montage,
but the snark is keeping the lump in my throat at bay. "Wait a
minute..." I click, make myself watch again.

There.

The last pic of her on Saturday night. It's smiley and slightly
blurred, but there's something I hadn't realized before. In one
ear, a little gold hoop. In the other, an amber stud. I put my
hand in the pocket of my jeans, and incredibly, it's still there.
The matching amber earring, the one I'd picked up from Gaia's
room the morning we'd started looking for her. I stare at it in my
hand, and then at the photo. That's where the missing earring
is. It's missing with Gaia.

"Focus." I swallow the lump in my throat again and click on Scott's video channel, opening up the oldest clip, shot back in November. Immediately, I'm hit with ads and Scott's smiling face telling me about the limited edition *Mazzulo and Miss Gee* hoodie drop happening next week. $80 each.

I remember people playing some of these clips at the party, but now I'm way more interested. Scott and Gaia have chemistry together, and they're funny, playing exaggerated versions of themselves. Judging by the comments below, people love it. But maybe not enough people for Scott. Has he used Gaia going missing to push them toward the big league?

I shudder, glancing at the clock on the laptop—midnight. Can't afford to slow down. I boil a kettle for coffee on the gas ring, pace a little, try not to set fire to the barn.

Where is Bode? I'm trying to ignore it, but the initial relief of being here safe in the barn is giving way to feeling very alone in the barn. Should I go downstairs and lock the door? Does it even lock? No, sit tight. Don't want to repeat the trick of locking someone out in the night. For a second, guilt replaces fear, but only for a second. What if someone saw me come in here? They could just creep up those stairs and I'd be toast. Wish I'd kept that phone. I guiltily rifle through Bode's stuff looking for it, but no luck.

An idea! Ping him on one of my messaging apps.

"Get me, with my newfound tech savvy." I sing, moving back to the laptop and clicking on the file explorer to find the doc where I typed all my passwords.

I look down the list of things most recently opened, searching for "Espasswords," but I don't get past the first two folders:

Abenaki

Bluff

I frown at the screen.

Abenaki Avenue is Gaia's road; Bluff Point is *here*, this street. Why has Bode got folders named after them? I pause, my mouse hovering over Abenaki. I click.

The folder is chock-full of files, each one an icon of an arrow. Video clips? I hesitate for a second…open one.

"Wha—?"

It's black and white, but I instantly recognize Gaia and Addy's bedroom.

Gaia walks in, dressed in ski wear. She throws off a fleece and sits on the bottom bunk bed. The camera can't see everything from this angle, but her legs are visible; she pulls off socks, stands up, removes leggings and looks at her phone. There's no sound on this clip but I see her laugh and toss the phone onto the bed. She carries on undressing, taking off top and vest, and finally, her sports bra.

"Oh god!" I clap a hand over my mouth.

I watch, feeling the Cap'n Crunch rise in my stomach, as my sister tiptoes over to the dressing table in nothing but her panties, takes out a pot of face cream, quickly smoothing some over her forehead. She grabs jeans from her closet, a top, a new bra. Returning to the mirror, she applies lip gloss, and finally, *thank god*, dresses, retrieves her phone, and leaves the room. The clip only lasts two minutes and nineteen seconds, and quite a lot of that is boobs.

She definitely didn't know she was being filmed that time.

I click on another file; this one is Addy and...one of the Ski Lift Guys...Lachlan? They fall into the bedroom, giggling, drunk. They stand in the middle of the room kissing, fumbling...and, as the clothes start to come off, I close the file so fast I almost break the damn mouse.

"What the actual—?"

My heart is beating so hard, but I force myself to open the Bluff folder.

More video files, but this time not bedroom antics. It's Craig's living room. I watch Craig and Lucille come home. There's a view of the whole room; I see Craig walk up the stairs, pausing halfway to unpick a wedgie, watch Lucille slope down the corridor to the kitchen. Compared to the last video, it's totally innocuous, but it makes me feel awkward as hell. There's a pain in my chest. What is going on here? Bode is filming everyone? What kind of person does that?

Staring at the screen, I notice that one of the videos of Craig's house is named J? I open it.

A man enters the house; he stamps snow off his boots, but he doesn't turn around, so I can't see his face. He pauses a moment, then climbs the stairs and disappears.

J for Jacques? It could be. Is this what Bode said he had to check on?

The next video is time-stamped a few minutes later, but with no names. It's Lucille coming home with another girl. They take off their coats, and the girl I don't recognize lifts her face for a minute, shaking curly hair out of her eyes. *Hayley.* Bode's sister. He did mention she's friends with Lucille. They disappear upstairs—to meet Jacques?—and the clip ends. Does this mean Hayley's involved in the thefts too? Is Bode protecting her?

I push away from the counter, my mind reeling. *Why? Why? Why?*

Suddenly, I hear the sound of the door sliding open downstairs. *Oh god!* There's a girl's voice and the creak of the stairs. I glance around but I already know there's nowhere to hide. I back into the corner by the kitchen, breathing fast, mouth dry.

Hayley and Bode walk in. She's laughing, and she turns as she steps into the room, not seeing me. But Bode does. Bode sees me immediately and his face blanches.

"What's up?" Hayley notices Bode staring past her and swings around. "Well, look. She came back. That sure was a short trip."

"Es!" Bode takes a step toward me. "What are you doing here? I thought you'd gone!"

"Yep." I stay where I am, butt pressed up against the kitchen sink; if I move, I'll fall over. "Went to the airport, changed my mind."

Bode swears. "Really? Man, that's…awesome!" He pretends to look thrilled, but I can totally see his mind working. He knows something's not right. "What will your folks say?" He moves a little closer. "They'll realize you didn't get the plane, right?"

"Not 'til sunrise. Came here because I needed help." I move to the laptop, realizing I've left it open. "Maybe that was stupid of me."

"No! Of course not." Bode hasn't seen the screen yet. "Sure I'll help. And you can sleep here. I'll take the couch."

"What a gentleman," purrs Hayley.

"I didn't come here to sleep." I immediately flush hot, because it sounds like I'm here for Hot Barn Action. "I have to work out why my sister has gone missing. But maybe you know more about that, Bode." I turn the laptop around to face him. "I'm sorry. I know snooping is wrong. I was jumping out of my skin on the way back because I was convinced Scott was up to something. I needed to check his video channel, so I used your laptop. But then I found some other videos that are way more interesting."

If Bode was shocked when he first walked in here, it's nothing compared to now. He looks like he's going to projectile vomit all over me. At least that would make a change from me puking on him.

"What videos?" Hayley snaps. "What's she talking about, Bode?"

"Yeah, tell her, Bode." I smile brightly. "I'm sure she'd love to know."

"I… Es, I was going to tell you about this." He shakes his head. "God, I see how it looks. But it's not what you think."

"What do I think, exactly? That you were spying on my sister and her friends?" I snort, turning to Hayley. "You're on one of these clips too. Did your brother tell you that?"

Hayley gives me a look of pure scorn. "My *brother*? Bode's not my brother." She turns to him. "You loser, did you film me when I stayed over? And you told her I'm your sister?"

"I didn't, I swear!" Bode backs away from us both. "Neither of those things!" He runs his hands through his hair. "Es, Hayley is just my friend."

"Ha!" Hayley says. "With benefits!"

Bode glares at her. "That was one time, Hayley. We both said it was a mistake."

"Oh god!" I cry. "And you filmed her?" I look around. "You have cameras here too?"

"No!" Bode puts his head in his hands. "I don't have cameras anywhere, Es, You have to believe me."

"I don't have to do anything."

Hayley laughs. "From what I hear, you have to get your clumsy ass back to England, but whatever." She walks up to Bode, still staring me down. "Did lover boy tell you he got kicked out of school too? No?" She laughs. "You think you're Nancy Drew and you didn't even figure that out?"

"Hayley!" Bode shouts at her. "You need to leave. I'll call you in the morning."

"When you wanna use me again?" She shakes her head and moves to the stairs. "This is what I get for playing in the kiddie pool. We are *even*, Bode. Debt repaid in full. Don't come near me again." She clomps off down the stairs and we hear the door slam.

"Okay, first things first," Bode says. "She is not, nor never has been, my girlfriend." He grimaces. "Or friends with benefits."

"Except for that one time."

"That was not what she's making it out to be." He stares at me, face desperate. "And way more importantly, those clips on the laptop, I didn't make them. I found them on a flash drive."

"Right." I laugh.

"It's true, I swear!"

"So, whose?"

Bode rubs his hands over his face and moans. "My uncle's."

I wasn't expecting that.

"I know." He holds up a hand. "Look, can we sit a minute? I want to make sure I explain this right."

"You better." I cross my arms. "But I'm fine standing, thanks." Bode nods and perches on the sofa.

"Okay, I told you I got my uncle set up with a computer? He was given a bunch of hardware and I showed him how to use it." He glances at me, but I'm not giving him any slack. "There was a flash drive in the box with everything, and I copied it across to my machine as backup. I never looked at the files at first, but when I did... Of course, I assumed the worst. I thought Saul had been...watching people." Bode leans forward, his hands over his face. "I went looking and I found two tiny cameras, real sneaky, set into smoke alarms above the door in your sister's room and at Craig's house. It looked like they were still functioning, sending recordings to a hard drive somewhere. There are hundreds of clips on the flash. The cameras are motion-activated so they only record if there's movement, but you'd need to change a flash drive regularly or you'd run out of space…" He pauses, fixes me with those beautiful, sad, hazel eyes. "I want you to know I haven't watched more than a few clips, and even those, not all the way through. I felt…dirty. And *really* freaked out by my uncle."

"Understandable. I feel really freaked out now." I can't hold his gaze. "Go on."

"That night, at the party?" Bode says. "I was under the deck because I was looking for the hard drive—I knew there had to be one hidden somewhere at the house, to save the clips—but it probably wasn't going to be inside because someone would find it. I was right. It was in a box under the deck, but I didn't get a chance to grab it, because I stepped in that damn raccoon trap." He shakes his head. "Went back the next day, it was gone."

"What about at Gaia's house?"

"Whoever took the hard drive under Craig's deck no doubt removed the one from Abenaki too."

I move to the chair across from him and sit slowly, trying to process all of this. "You asked your uncle about the videos?"

Bode looks demolished. "Eventually. I'd been carrying this around for a couple weeks, not knowing what to think and how to ask my uncle. When he tore me a new one for trashing the quad, I lashed out and told him I'd seen 'em."

"And?"

"He said he found the flash drive on the street, had no idea what was on it... He was...shocked, to say the least."

"You believed him?"

"Without doubt." Bode's eyes bore a hole in mine. "First because he doesn't do tech. Second, he's too damn honest." He looks at the floor. "You heard what Hayley said. I got kicked out of school. I hacked their computer system, altered Hayley's attendance records because she asked me to, and at the time, I wanted her to like me. I got caught, my parents washed their hands of me, and Saul stepped in and saved my ass. He's the straightest man in this town and I'd trust him with my life."

"If it wasn't you or Saul, who rigged these cameras?"

Bode chews his lip. "You know when I told you this morning there was something I had to check? I realized where I'd seen Jacques before—on those clips. And what's more, I'd seen a clue that meant I could find out who hid the cameras."

"Jacques hid them?" I move to the laptop. "Do you think he did it to spy on the people he suspected were stealing? I mean, it's probably illegal, but would the resort even care if it meant they caught the thief?" I shake my head. "Look, I get it. Hayley's involved, isn't she? I saw her on the clip with Lucille and Jacques. You're protecting her."

"Whoa, slow down," Bode stands. "Hayley's no angel, but she's definitely not mixed up in this."

"How do you know for sure? Jacques set those cameras and you're worried she's implicated."

"Jacques didn't set the cameras." He's kind of twitching now, standing there, jaw clenching.

"How do you know that?"

"Like I said, I never watched all the files, but I did notice something change in your sister's bedroom. That made me curious, but I didn't really think about it again until this morning with Telfer. I had to come back and check."

"And? What had changed?"

Bode walks over my chair. "The view. In the later clips, someone has moved the angle of the camera so you can see the bottom bunk."

"Gaia's bed." I squirm. "Who?"

"Not Jacques." He moves to the laptop. "It's easier if I show you."

I lean forward. He scrolls fast through a bunch of files before clicking on one.

Addy walks in; she's talking to someone out of sight, in the doorway. There's no sound, but it's obvious that she's not happy with them. Her face twists between scorn and sarcastic amusement, her mouth moving fast and furious. She holds up her hand like she's trying to make the other person shut up. Eventually, she shakes her head and leaves the room.

"God, she was pissed off," I murmur. "Addy hardly ever gets pissed off. I wish I could lip-read."

"Wait, you won't have to."

A couple of seconds go by, and someone walks into the room. It's a male,. We can see the top of his head in a beanie, the back of his jacket. He turns around, but because he's still directly under the camera, we can only see a shoulder and one side of his body. It's like he's waiting for something. After a few seconds, with his back to us, he grabs a chair from the dressing table, stands on it, and looks directly into the camera.

"Oh my god," I mutter.

He stares into the lens, fiddling with something; the angle changes and we can see more of the room, the bottom bunk. He jumps down, goes to lie on the bed.

Eli grins and waves to the camera, before leaping up and walking out of the door. The screen goes dark.

CHAPTER THIRTY-TWO

———

"Where is he? Out 'looking for my sister'? The hypocrite! All this time he's been spying on her! To think I felt sorry for him this afternoon! I always knew he was a creep, but I never thought he'd go this far!"

I'm pacing up and down, the room is a blur of lights, and I don't think I'll ever be able to calm down.

"Where is he holding her?" I grab Bode. "What about in town? It's not like he hasn't got the money to rent a place. My god." I pace again. "Do you think Gaia's underwear run made him crack? Or has he been planning this for a while?" I'm shaking, clutching the back of the sofa, leaning on my arms. It might be shock or overload of adrenaline, but if I don't hold onto something, I'll faint.

"I thought it was Scott." I look up at Bode. "I was convinced. At the airport, someone showed me Scott's video channel with the ads and merchandise, and I thought—yes! It makes sense! Scott is keeping Gaia somewhere because he's making money off it! How ridiculous. I should have known it was Eli all along."

Bode stands up, cautiously, like he's afraid by moving he'll set me off again. "There could be another reason Eli set those cameras. He works for the resort; he could be helping Jacques. If they were investigating the thefts on the down-low, it would make sense to keep it in the family."

"What are you talking about?" I shake my head at the floor. "Eli was spying on Gaia! Why else would he move the camera so he can film her *bed*?"

"But what about the camera in Craig and Lucille's house?" Bode says. "That has nothing to do with Gaia. And we've only seen one flash drive. There could be a whole bunch of cameras we don't know about." Bode moves around the sofa and leans on it with me. "See, tonight I met up with Hayley because I wanted to check out the bar where Lucille works—The Eclipse, where the thefts began at New Year's. I figured that if Eli was trying to catch a thief, he would set a camera in the stockroom. My uncle has a set of master keys, so Hayley kept Lucille talking at the bar while I let myself in round back."

My immediate thought is that I'm jealous he's been playing detective with Hayley and not me.

"And?"

His face falls. "Nada. But that doesn't mean it was never there." He sighs. "Yes, Eli's sleazy, but I don't think this is all about your sister. There's something else going on."

Too much blood is rushing to my head. I can't think straight. What if Bode's right?

"I overheard Lucille, tonight, on the phone with someone. Saying it was good that Gaia was still missing because she can't talk." I straighten up slowly. "Okay, so either Eli's a perv and has my sister, or he's 'innocent' and maybe caught something on camera. Either way, no more guesswork, no more sneaking around—we go to the lodge, confront him." I get my coat. "Where's my phone? I want to have Detective Graff on speed dial."

Bode looks mildly terrified, but I think it's me he's scared of. And he's right to be. I'm filled with fire and fury. We're going to find Gaia before sunrise or…the sun won't rise. I won't let it.

"Still got those master keys?"

Bode slowly reaches into his coat pocket, pulls out a huge bunch.

"Something on there that will get us into the Addison's lodge?"

Bode hesitates only a second. "Guess we'll find out." He fetches my phone out of his lockbox, and we run down the stairs.

The Addison's lodge is in darkness. When we snuck by our place, there was a light on in the living room, as ever, keeping faith in Gaia's safe return. I have no idea what time it is, but it can't be long before Ma gets up to travel to Boston for that television appearance with Scott. I cringe when I think what she'll go through when she hears I wasn't on the plane. Can't do anything about that now.

"We're letting ourselves in." I reach into Bode's pocket and retrieve the keys.

"Hey! What? Oh god." He grimaces. "It's the gold key."

"Element of surprise." I spring up the steps to the front door and stick the key in the lock. "Addy said her parents are in town for a few days, so we don't have to worry about them." I open the door slowly.

"But what about Addy?" Bode says.

"What about me?"

"Jeez!"

Bode and I jump out of our skins. Addy is standing there in the darkness, as if she had been about to open the door from the other side.

"What the hell are you doing here, Es?" She stares at me. "Eli drove you to the airport hours ago. I thought you were on that flight!" She looks the bunch of keys. "You were breaking in?"

"It's a master key…" I stutter. Something about Addy standing here sparks a memory, makes me feel like we've been here before… I walk in and sit on the sofa.

"What are you doing?" she says, indignant. "It's 1:30 a.m., why have you come here?"

"We're looking for Eli." Bode follows me in.

"What?" Addy curls her lip. "Why do you want him?"

"Because he's been filming my sister, Addy." I look up at her. "Secretly. Did you know you had a hidden camera in your bedroom? Why don't we get Eli down here and see what he has to say about it?"

"He's not here!" Addy barks. "Es, you're going to be in so much trouble when your poor folks find out you didn't get on that plane, don't make it worse." She moves to the open door. "Come on. I'll take you back to your lodge now."

"Not going anywhere... I've got a deja that won't stop vu-ing." I get up, close the door and turn the overhead light on. "Bode." I jangle the keys in my hand. "Who else has master keys? Apart from your uncle."

"Er." He shifts uncomfortably, blinking in the light. "Security, obviously. I think there's a set at reception. And Concierge, they have keys. For running errands for the VIP guests, flowers, wine, stuff like that." He's looking from me to Addy.

"Concierge? That's your gig, isn't it, Ads?" I say as warmly as I can. "When you came round the other night, you let yourself in with a master key, didn't you? You said the door was open, but that really bothered me." I walk back to the sofa and sit on the arm. "Because I know I'm absent-minded and everything, but I definitely remember locking the door that night. Do you often let yourself into places? And lie about it?"

"I didn't lie!" Addy stutters. "I must have done it automatically!"

"Uh-huh." I nod. "While we're straightening a few things out, there's something else that's bothering me. Tonight, I was watching that photo montage Scott posted on the Missing page. Did you see it?"

"Haven't exactly had the time." She purses her lips. "What are you playing at Es? It's late; your parents have a right to know—"

"Oh stop!" I snap, and it's her turn to jump. "You lied about the Eazy Stay. Told me you'd never been there. But there's a selfie of you and Gaia standing in front of the motel's sign."

"So what? We probably passed by and took a pic. Why would I remember?"

"Know what I just remembered? Telfer Cambridge told us he's Craig's cousin. Did you know that?"

"No." Addy frowns. "Random. Why does it matter?"

"It doesn't really." I pull a face. "But on the way over here, I was thinking about how we all make assumptions. I would never guess Craig and Telfer could be cousins. And—this is a funny one for ya—I thought Hayley was Bode's sister, isn't that stupid?" I chuckle, reach over to the coffee table, where there's a pile of Gaia flyers, pick one up, and stare at her face, smiling up at me. "We look so different, Gaia and me. People who don't know us would never think we were related. But you know who does look more like me, Ads? *You*. Telfer told us he'd seen Craig and my sister arguing and kissing in the woods. Afterward, I got to thinking, Telfer's never seen Gaia, before or since—not a picture, nothing—all he knows is that she's English, and she's my sister. So, what did Telfer actually see? Craig and a girl with an English accent. A white girl. You."

"That's ridic." Addy laughs, but her eyes don't. I glance at Bode, who seems to be rooted to the spot.

"It never made sense to me why Craig would spend money on a motel. By all accounts, he's kind of cheap." I clear my throat. "I suppose we all assumed it was because he wanted to keep his flings secret. But he's a player, he wouldn't care. It must have been his date who wanted to keep it a secret. *You.*"

Addy shakes her head. "You don't know—"

"When we found Craig in the woods," I stand up, feeling blood pumping in my temples, "he was staring at someone—I haven't been able to get this out of my mind!—with a seriously weird look on his face. Staring at who?" I chew on my lip. "Not me, not Bode. I'd wondered about Eli, had those guys come to blows? Eli's too much of a coward for that. And Craig didn't look angry or scared, he looked…betrayed. Took me a while to work it out, but who was he staring at? You."

Addy turns on her heel, strides off into the kitchen.

"Daaamn." Bode stares at me, open-mouthed. "When did you figure this out?"

"Literally just now. I'm Agatha Christie–ing it."

"Man, if you're Hercule Poirot, you gonna start on me next?"

There's a thud; we both glance toward the kitchen.

"D'ya think she knows Craig's been stealing?" Bode whispers.

"Hold onto your seat. I'm moving on to that part next."

He snorts. "You scare me sometimes."

"I scare myself."

There's a loud slamming noise.

"Reckon she jumped out of the window?" Bode says.

"Seems to be a thing." We leap up, but Addy appears in the

doorway, bottle of wine in one hand, glass in another. She sits at the table, pours herself a very large glass, and drinks.

"Ha! Can you tell I'm related to my mother, Esme?" she mutters, drinks again.

I move to the table and sit down opposite her. Bode scuttles to sit down next to me like he's caught in a game of musical chairs.

"It is so shitty loving someone who doesn't love you back. Demeaning." She takes another drink. "Especially when you could have pretty much anyone else you fancy." She gives me a little smile. "And I can. But not him. Not Craig. Because Craig's obsessed with Gaia. Oh, I'm a good second best when he's desperate, but that's it." She picks at the corner of the wine label with her fingernail. "After the party on Saturday, surprise-surprise, I was drunk." She rolls her eyes. "Thanks for walking me home, Es. Wish you'd come in, because if you had, I would've ignored Craig when he texted me. But I didn't." She sighs, drinks again. "We met, drove to the pizza place, ended up in that crappy motel. I paid, by the way. I always do." Her eyes are watery. "The next morning, his truck's dead, we argue, I go to brunch and he... He went back to bed, but afterward—so you told me—he tried to walk home and hurt himself." She glances at me through wet eyelashes. "God, I feel so bad about that."

"That's not your fault," Bode says. Addy looks at him sharply, like she's forgotten he's there.

"The watch." I say gently. "This is the part I can't get to fit. If you were with him that night, how could Gaia have left the watch in Craig's truck?"

"She didn't," Addy gulps, a single tear streaking down her porcelain cheek. "I did. Gaia didn't steal the watch, Es. Craig gave it to her."

"What?"

Addy sniffs. "A present, to prove he "loves" her—and she showed it to me! Can you imagine? She had no idea it was my mother's!" Her voice cracks, and she sobs. "Gaia tried to give it back to Craig, but he wouldn't accept it. So I said I'd see if I could get her some money for it. She had no idea what it was worth, would have been happy with fifty bucks!" She wipes the tears away with the back of her hand and sighs through gritted teeth. "And when Craig and I argued, I hid it under the seat in his truck. Was going to call the police and tip them off. Oh god, I feel sick. I don't know if I'd have actually gone through with it."

Anger rises inside me. Anger that Addy lied to me about Gaia, but way worse, anger that I'd believed her.

"Addy, did Craig steal it?" I say. "We know there have been a bunch of thefts. The resort has been investigating. Craig and Lucille are under suspicion, you must know some of this...?"

"I know nothing." Addy pours more wine, her hand shaking. "My mother probably lost the watch on the slopes and maybe Craig found it. Look, Es." She leans toward me and I can smell the wine on her breath. "People like Craig and Lucille might bend a few rules to make ends meet or whatever, but they're not hardened crims." She purses her lips. "I don't judge. It doesn't concern me."

We sit in silence a minute, my mind racing. Bode sits up suddenly.

"Addy, there's something I just realized."

"Oh great!" she says, laughing bitterly. "It's been good cop/bad cop, but now you're going to get stuck in too?"

"Es told you about Eli putting the camera in your room," Bode says carefully. "You didn't react. That is not news to you."

She looks at us, her blue eyes shot with red. "I'm not ashamed of being with Craig. That isn't why we went to the motel. We went there because I knew my brother was filming me."

"But… he was watching Gaia!" I practically shout at her. "We saw him move the camera to see the bottom bunk, her bed!"

"That's *my* bed, Es." She chugs the wine and clatters the glass on the table. "Who's making assumptions again? And it's not Eli who's the freak, it's my father. Control freak. Eli was following orders. His job was to report back to Pop: who I was with, what I was doing."

Bode gasps. "Your dad spied on you? Why?"

Addy sighs, like it's completely obvious. "Because he didn't spend all that money buying me into the best university in the world for me to go and ruin my life before I get there." Her face crumples.

"How did you find out?" I ask.

"Easily. Eli's not the brightest. He left boxes from the cameras in the bin in our backyard." Her laugh sounds hollow. "One of the few times I actually take out the trash, there it all was. He'd even made notes on the instruction book. What an idiot! Right away, I knew. They've pulled crap like this on me before. That school trip to Paris two years ago? Pop hired a private eye to tail me. Overprotective? He's off his head."

"Are there more cameras?" Bode says.

Addy shrugs. "I only knew about the one in our bedroom. I assumed there'd be one somewhere at Craig's. Eli knew we were hooking up."

"Did you tell my sister there was a camera in the room?" I stare at Addy, who looks blankly back at me. "My god, you didn't, did you?"

"Wasn't about her," Addy slurs. "It was about me."

"Didn't you think she'd want to know? Or was it your way of paying her back for Craig?"

"Oh shut up, Es!" Addy slaps the table.

My brain can't keep up. I'd been riding a high 'til now, sure I was unraveling some of this mystery. But what has any of this got to do with Gaia going missing?

"She climbed out of the window. Why would she do that?" I look at Addy. "Why would Gaia climb out of Craig's window at a party on the last night here?"

"That's what happened?" Addy's eyebrows disappear into her red fringe. "Maybe Craig was…being a dick?" She blurts out a laugh.

"Big deal. You said it yourself. Gaia's dealt with worse." I stand up, the chair scraping. "No, I think we've ignored this bloody massive clue: my sister climbed out of the window.

Craig said, *That's one way to slip out unnoticed*. He climbed out too." I lean forward on the table. "Who were they avoiding that night, who unnerved them *so much* they didn't want to be seen leaving the house?"

Bode and Addy sit there in silence. I'm not sure if it's because they're thinking about it, or because I'm way off track.

"Lucille and Jacques?" I look at Addy. "They arrived at the party as I was leaving. Tonight I heard Lucille telling someone on the phone that it was good that Gaia was still missing, because that meant she *couldn't talk*. Addy, did Gaia know something? Was she scared of them?"

"Haven't got a clue." Addy bats her lashes. "She doesn't exactly confide in me these days. Super awkward with the whole love triangle thing, ya know?"

Bode speaks. "So if Gaia was scared, who would she tell?"

"Scott." Addy and I say at the same time.

"What time is it?" I ask Bode, who glances at his watch.

"Nearly 2."

"We're going to Scott's house." I jump up. "We've got to catch him before he leaves for the Boston TV interview. Now!"

"I'll drive you," Addy rises unsteadily.

"You're kinda drunk to be behind the wheel," Bode says. "Let me?"

"This isn't close to drunk." Addy makes a stink face at him. "But sure, whatever. Are you even legal?"

Bode takes the keys from her. "I think we're way past worrying about that."

"I call shotgun!" I run to the door.

"Do you even know what that means?" Bode says to me as we race down the stairs to Addy's car.

"No idea." I grimace at him. "Don't you know by now? I just make it up as I go along."

CHAPTER THIRTY-THREE

———

"Oh my god."

I gasp as we pull up outside Scott's house in Moonville. "I know this place. On the final episode of *Rival Roomies*, Scott came home to tell his mother he'd got into the band." I frown at the memory. "It was so sad because she'd had her cancer diagnosis."

"You were a *fan*?" Bode side-eyes me.

"Course I was a fan, why do you think I'm so shy around him?"

"Most of the time I see you shouting at him. There ya go, we have something else in common. I was *obsessed*."

"Shut up."

"Hey, I was ten. He was from my town. Their sound *rocked*." Bode blinks. "I quite literally had the T-shirt."

"Posters on the wall?"

"*Signed* posters."

"Show-off." I look at the house. "They dedicated a song to his mum when she died. This is so weird."

"Tha's lovely. But tick-tock, peeps," Addy slurs from the back seat. The red wine has kicked in hard. "Dontcha wanna catch him before he leaves? I'll stay here though, s'warm."

We leave her stretched out on the back seat, face pressed against the window like a spaniel. I ring the doorbell, and, surprisingly quickly, a light flicks on in the hallway.

Scott's dressed in sweats; he looks like he's been working out. His face is even pinker than usual, and he's breathing hard.

"Esme! You didn't catch the plane?" He glances at Bode, and beyond to Addy's car. She grins and waves lazily at him. "Something's happened?"

"Can we come in?"

"Absolutely." He beckons us into the hallway, and I glance around. There are photos on the walls, knickknacks on shelves, a Persian rug on the floor. His mum's stuff he can't face throwing out? Scott shuts the door behind us. "So you guys okay? Addy...?"

"She's drunk, but she'll live." I give him a quick smile. "We need to ask you about Gaia. Urgently."

Scott's eyes go wide. "Sure! But I don't have long. The car with your mom is coming to pick me up, Es. Does she even know you're here?" He walks through to a kitchen and we follow.

"Nope."

The kitchen is more Scott's style. Minimal, shades of gray, showy appliances. Scott perches on a stool beside an island and gestures to us to sit opposite.

"What's going on?"

"Gaia trusts you, Scott." I take a breath. "Confides in you. Is it possible she was avoiding someone at the party? Lucille, for example? Jacques?"

"It's possible." Scott frowns, but his brow barely wrinkles. "Lucille and Gee never saw eye to eye. Jacques? Barely know the guy. You think she was avoiding them? Or Craig? I kinda assumed she climbed out the window because he was getting touchy-feely with her." He springs up from the island. "Where are my manners? I mean, sure, it's—" he glances at his watch. "—2:26 a.m.! But we could all use some coffee, right?" He busies himself with a huge, black and chrome coffee maker, filling it with water, grinding beans.

I suddenly feel a wave of coldness, like if I just hold this moment, the tornado in my mind will evaporate and everything will be clear ...

"Soy or oat?" Scott stands at his enormous fridge, milk cartons in both hands.

"Black," Bode says.

"Scott, I'm so jumpy already." I smile. "Do you have tea?"

"Sure, hon! I keep it here for Gaia. You like it with the bag in, like your sis?"

I nod, although I don't.

Scott shuts the fridge door, and I notice he has one of those sensor trash cans that opens when you wave a hand over it. Sticking out of it is a food wrapper, caught in the lid. The wrapper is orange, with a green design printed on. It looks familiar, but I'm not sure why.

"You know." Scott is pouring the hot water for my tea. "That

Jacques guy *is* kind of shady. I remember Gaia said one time she had seen him with Craig, moving stuff into a pickup? She asked Craig about it later, he clammed up." Scott passes drinks to us. "Could be something? Anyway," he glances at his watch again, "you're welcome to finish your beverages, but I gotta hustle. That car's gonna be here! And I've lost my phone, so annoying." He disappears through the door and we hear footsteps going upstairs.

"Lost his phone again," Bode whispers. "Dude probably only put it down twice in his life and each time he loses it."

"Craig said he was lying about losing his phone at the party." I take a sip of tea.

"We know Craig's full of it."

"God, we're no further forward. Looks like Eli is our last hope to find out more." I fish my tea bag out of the mug with a spoon, walk it over to the trash can. The food wrapper is there, looking at me. I wave my hand over the trash can to open it, but it won't. Perhaps the wrapper is jamming the mechanism? I wave again.

"You casting a spell?" Bode quips, getting up. "Come on, let's go think in the car. Hope Addy hasn't puked."

I nod, ditch the tea bag in the sink. But something is pulling me back to the trash can. I tug on the corner of the food wrapper until the lid opens and look at the greased paper in my hand. An owl winks, a bubble coming out of its mouth that says: Screech Burger.

"Whatcha doing?"

I ignore Bode, reaching into the trash can for a brown paper bag with a delivery receipt stuck on the front of it. Inside there's a chicken wings box.

"You hungry?" Bode chuckles, his voice tired.

"Someone was, but not Scott. Cheeseburger and wings."

"Huh?"

I waggle the wrappers like a madwoman. "Call yourself a superfan?"

Bode stares, confusion on his face.

"Meat. Scott's *vegetarian.*"

"Are you sure?" Bode frowns. "Maybe he secretly stuffs himself with burgers when no one is watching?"

"Hey, guys." Scott appears at the doorway, his face in a grimace. "You know, I'm getting a fever. Gonna have to cancel on your mom, Es. You should leave in case I'm infectious…" His voice trails off as he notices what I have in my hands. If I had any doubts, they are gone in an instant when I see his face change. Scott's an actor, but he's not that great. He can't hide his reaction quick enough. I drop the wrappers, turn around, and scream at the top of my lungs.

"*Gaia!*"

I run to the back of the kitchen, there's a door out to another room.

"*Gaia! Answer me!*"

"Es?" Bode's behind me. "What are you doing?"

I push past him and see a huge, expensive-looking block with shiny knives sticking out of it. I grab the biggest one.

"Where is she? Where are you keeping her?" I flourish the knife at Scott, who leaps backward.

"Jesus, Esme!" he yells. "Have you lost your mind?"

"She's here, isn't she?" I take another step toward him. "You're holding her somewhere. *Gaia!*"

"Sweetie, I understand you're upset." Scott holds out a hand. "You're traumatized, nobody would blame you, you're cracking up!"

"Don't! Gaslight! Me!" I poke the knife at him, only just keeping my grip. "I've never been saner! I know she's here. Get out of my way!"

I run at him in the doorway, and he must step aside, because I'm through and standing at the bottom of the stairs, shouting her name. I run up to the landing and I'm vaguely aware of Bode shouting at me, but then it changes, and he's shouting Gaia's name too. I fling open doors, charge through rooms, and she's not there, but suddenly Scott is and Bode is and there's a push and a scuffle and a cry and the knife goes clattering down the stairs and I'm running after it and slipping and falling and scrambling to my feet in the hallway, grabbing that knife and suddenly realizing I know exactly where Gaia is.

"Basement," I mutter.

The episode of *Rival Roomies* where Scott visits his mother, they're laughing in the "Cozy," the basement room Scott's mum had kitted out as a studio for her wannabe pop star.

"Gotta keep Scotty shut down here for the neighbors' sake!" she'd joked. "It's soundproofed!"

Where better to lock up my loudmouth sister? *Plus, I*

think as I run to the door at the end of the hallway, *it's always the basement.*

I fling the door open, frantically slap the wall to turn the light on, and propel myself down the stairs.

"Gaia!"

There's nobody here.

The room is exactly as I remember it on TV, the leather sofa, the karaoke machine, a mirror ball. The only difference is, there's a mattress in one corner with a mess of sheets, a plate with half a cheeseburger on the floor, and a *Screech* soda cup, lying on its side. I walk into the middle of it all, casting around for anything that's hers, but I don't need to. I can *smell* her. I sink to my knees. Her hair oil, her shower gel, her stinky feet, her *Gaia-ness.*

"She's not here, you stupid bitch!"

"Hey, man, don't call her that!"

I look up. Scott and Bode have arrived at the bottom of the stairs.

"What? You think that because there's a burger, that proves she's been here? I had someone over," Scott shouts.

I shake my head. "I know she was here. Up there in the kitchen just now, you said Gaia *climbed out of Craig's window.* How did you know that? You couldn't have known unless Gaia told you."

Scott shakes his head. "You mentioned it…"

"No, I didn't!" I scream at him. "What have you done with her, Scott? Have you killed her?"

"You're ridiculous!" Scott yells at me. "I'd never lay a hand on your sister!"

"Es." Bode walks toward me very slowly. "We need to go. Gaia's not here, there's no real proof she ever was."

"She was!" I shout. "He's done something with her!"

"I swear I don't know where she is!" Scott's voice comes out in a wail.

"Es, there's, er, another reason we have to go," Bode says. "You kinda stabbed me."

For the first time I realize he has one hand inside of his coat.

"I mean, it's not so bad," He opens his coat, takes his hand away and there's red, glistening on his fingers. "But I think if we don't go now, it might…get bad."

"Oh my god, Bode!" I glance down, realizing I still have the knife in my hand and tossing it away so that it falls on the mattress, making a small clinking sound. "How did I do that to you?"

Bode winces, I move to get up off this floor and go to him, but wait—a small clinking sound? Knives dropped on mattresses don't make that noise… I crawl over, swipe the knife away, and there, nestled in the sheets, it is.

I carefully pick up the small, amber earring. Beside it, partially hidden by the bedding: handcuffs.

"What happened, Scott?" My voice sounds calm, but as though it's echoing in my head, like when your ears don't pop on the plane. I stand slowly, holding the earring out in front of me, and walk past poor, wounded Bode to where Scott is standing, hugging the doorway.

"Gaia's stayed over so many times," Scott babbles. "She must have lost that last time she was here."

"Along with the *handcuffs*?" The calm has gone. "I gave her these earrings, Scott. I have one of them; the other she was wearing at the party."

"You must be misremembering,"

"There's a photo that shows her wearing it that night. You should know. You took it."

Scott walks past me, his knees bend, and he falls forward onto the mattress in a ball making a weird, keening noise—almost like the singing he used to do back in the day.

"Where is she, Scott?"

"I don't know!" The sobs come, racking his whole body. "She was here, but I never hurt her. You have to believe me."

"Get up." I swallow. "Tell me everything."

"Uh-huh." He rises, trying to control the sobs. "After the party I waited for her, gave her a ride here. It was *planned*, she was in on it, Es!" He looks at me, eyes frantic. "We were gonna do a Hide-and-Go-Seek for the kids before brunch, have everyone track Gaia down, for laughs." He wipes a hand across his face, brushing away tears. "But the next morning she got sick. She needed to sleep so I gave her some of my pills." He shudders and a clear glob of snot runs from one nostril. "She slept and slept...and I—I got...obsessed with this idea of something big happening, Gaia going missing, just for a couple days—I knew she'd play along. We'd get so much attention for the channel, and the money from the clicks and the merch would solve all her problems—she's been *so* stressed about money! I told your mom she was missing…and there was no going back."

"Gaia's been sick all this time and you didn't do anything?" My voice sounds like it's not coming from me, somehow.

"No." Scott waves his hands. "By Monday, she was better. She got really angry with me when she realized what had happened, but I couldn't let her go because I needed time to talk her round. I knew I could, Es! I always can."

"The phone," Bode croaks from the other side of the room. "How did her phone get into Craig's room?"

"I put it there," Scott says. "I couldn't leave it at my place. They'd trace it. I dropped it under the bed; it was all part of the plan."

"To frame Craig?"

"No!" Scott howls. "To throw everyone off the scent for a sec, give me time to play this out."

"Play?" I snarl at him. "This wasn't one of your stunts! What about the blood on the keg?"

Scott rolls his eyes. "Okay, so that was a little much, I admit."

"What did you do—?"

"I didn't hurt her! She cut herself on a soda can at the party. I took the Band-Aid off while she was sleeping, rubbed it on the keg."

I remember the Band-Aid on her hand. She'd been playing with it when we talked in the kitchen at the party.

"I regret that now," Scott says. "Kinda overkill."

"You reckon?" I bellow at him. I look around the room,

imagine how Gaia must have felt, locked down here, feeling ill and worried as hell about what we were going through. "You're her best friend. She trusts you. She must have been so scared." The knife is right by my hand. It would be so easy to grab it and drive it deep into Scott's chest.

"I was gonna 'find' her, soon, real soon. I'm not a monster, Es; I could see what you were going through. It gave me so much pain." He puts out a hand to touch my arm, I snatch the knife, and we spring back from each other. "You have to believe me! This afternoon, Gaia was okay. I gave her food. I came back just before 2:00 a.m., she was here, but I went to shower, and she stole my phone and my car and escaped. I have no idea where she is, and I'm so worried...!" His tears flowing, snot streaming down into his wailing mouth.

"She has your phone?" I turn to Bode, who is propping himself up against the wall. "We have to call her, now!"

There's a rapping noise from the front door, and the sound of someone bursting in.

"Hello!"

Scott takes flight, rushes past me, and pushes Bode out of the way, pelting up the stairs. I hear a scuffle, and shriek. Then the voice comes again—

"Esme? Where are you?"

I run to Bode, who's lying on the floor groaning, and scream up the stairs.

"I'm down here, Ma!"

CHAPTER THIRTY-FOUR

——

We wait for the ambulance in the hallway, Bode dripping blood onto the Persian rug.

"They're coming soon, hang in there." Ma is in charge. She's found something to put on Bode's wound, and she leans over him, putting pressure on to stem the flow, her hand burrowed under his sweater in a way that would freak me out forever, if I wasn't already at Peak Freak. "The driver says he'll look for Scott, but the police are on their way." She glances out of the front door for the fiftieth time. "God! I thought Addy was drunk when we drove up and she said you were inside, Es."

"She is drunk."

"She's also gone," Ma says, straightening up, her fingers red with Bode's blood. "Car door's open. Maybe she chased after Scott?"

"Nothing would surprise me now." I glance at Bode. He's very pale, his breathing is shallow and too quick, but at least the bleeding has slowed. I kneel beside him. "I'm so, so sorry for the stabbing."

"When we first met under the deck you warned me you were lethal with a blade." He cracks a smile. "Reckon you missed all the important stuff. Try harder next time."

"What time did Scott say Gaia was last here?" Ma paces.

"At 2 a.m. We must have only just missed her?" I look at Bode, who nods painfully.

Ma checks her phone and strides to the door. "So she's been gone over an hour and she's driving his car; where the hell is she?"

Ma leaves messages with Bode's uncle and Addy's parents, tries to raise Detective Graff again, dials Scott's number in the hope that Gaia will pick up.

Finally, the ambulance arrives, Officer Hernandez with it. Bode gets checked over, put on a gurney, and wheeled out of the house. While they're fiddling with the ambulance doors, he whispers to me.

"I'll say it was an accident, so don't go taking the blame for any slicing and dicing." His eyes crinkle into a smile. "Go find her."

I clutch his hand briefly, and they whisk him away in a blaze of sirens.

Officer Hernandez is on his radio, issuing searches for Gaia, Scott, and Addy. He questions me and I give him a tour of Scott's house, replaying everything. More cops arrive, and one of them drives Ma and me back to the lodge, where Dad barrels in, with a screech of brakes. There are tears, a few choice words about me skipping my flight, but the feeling in the air is nothing like we've known for days. The hope is real. It's agony to have been so close to finding her, but *she's alive*. Ma and Dad race away to search, and as they've run out of people to look after me, I'm here on my own.

"Get some sleep," Ma orders me as she stands at the doorway, new life in her eyes. "When you wake, we'll have found her."

Sleep? *Please.*

I text Bode, but there's no reply. I try Scott and Addy's phones. I log onto Ma's laptop and see if anything new is on the Missing page. Officer Hernandez told me not to spill about Gaia yet. As much as I want to post an update, how could I tell everyone we've found her and lost her again?

And there's something horrible going around in my head, something that must have occurred to my parents too. If Gaia is free, wouldn't she knock on the nearest friendly-looking door for sanctuary? Shout from the hills that she's safe? I can't think of any good answers to that question.

It's cold in the lodge. The clock on the wall says 6:05 a.m. Time is more meaningless than ever, but I do know that I'm hungry. I go into the kitchen to scrape a snack together. Before I flick the ceiling light on, I can see the darkness outside begin to lift. As I pounce on bread and peanut butter, there's a banging on the door.

"Gaia!" I throw everything to the floor and run, flinging the door open and staring at the person outside.

"Es, they're in deadly trouble." Eli stands there, panting. "Can I come in?" He doesn't wait for me to reply, pushing past into the room and closing the door behind him.

"You! How—"

"I know." He holds out a hand to stop me. "I was with your dad when your mum rang; I know about Gaia at Scott's house, and my sister running off." He licks his lips. "I think she's in serious danger, Es. That's why I'm here."

"Which 'she' are we talking about?" I glare at him. "My sister, who you were filming, or your sister, who you were spying on?"

I expect him to look furious and deny it all, but his face is passive.

"Okay, so Addy told you about the cameras. Given the circumstances, I didn't think she'd hold out this long. Not until I realized what she's really involved in, that is."

"We found the flash drive." I didn't think I had it in me to still be angry, but guess what? I have. "You were spying on Addy for your dad, but oh-what-a-shame you had to watch Gaia half-undressed, eh? That must have really sucked for you."

Eli's eyebrows knot together in a frown. "Yes, I saw things that I shouldn't have. I didn't enjoy it, believe me. It was Addy I was interested in. And that's why I'm here now. My sister is in danger, and I think Gaia knows it and that's why she's disappeared again. Gaia is trying to save her."

"What?" My head spins, and I grab a chair from the table. "That makes zero sense. Gaia left Scott's hours ago. Addy was with us, she was drunk, she wandered off down the street."

Eli moves over to the sofa and sits, head in hands. When he looks at me again, the muscle in his chiseled jaw is working overtime.

"I was filming Addy, yes. But my dad had me do other things Addy has no idea about. I have passwords for all her accounts. There's a tracker on her car."

"Oh my god, my mum actually joked about your dad doing that!"

"It gets worse." He brings out one of his precious phones. "This is hers. At least, a clone."

I feel my mouth drop open.

"I see who she calls. I read her texts." He sighs. "Es, she's in way over her head."

"I know!" I sit opposite him on the sofa. "She admitted she was with Craig at the motel, and we know about him being involved with thefts in the resort, like your mum's watch."

"Craig didn't take the watch." He looks at me. "*Addy* did. She passed it to Craig to sell, but he gave it to Gaia. Addy was furious when Gaia showed it to her."

I feel sick.

"Craig used Addy and her concierge key to steal from guests, but that's small fry compared to what she's got herself mixed up in now."

"Lucille and Jacques?" I lean forward. "Listen, I know about him. Detective Graff told us how Jacques is working for your uncle—"

"Jacques is shady as hell." Eli fixes me with big, brown cow-eyes. "I've seen and heard enough to know he's playing both sides. I couldn't go to Graff with it all, obviously; the things I've been doing aren't exactly legal either."

"Jacques is a bad guy? How can you be sure?"

"Let's just say, if the wind is blowing in the right direction, I can listen in on Addy's calls." He scowls. "They're moving stolen goods, yes, but Jacques is bringing stuff in. *Drugs.* Over the border from Canada. Addy's car has been used. I've followed her."

"Oh my god."

"Craig wanted out, thought they were going too far. He argued with Addy on the Sunday morning. Later, she texted and told him she'd meet him at the deer tower. But she set him up. I think Jacques met Craig there and pushed him off the tower."

I stare at Eli. "Why didn't you say anything at the time?"

"Because the messages weren't obvious; there was a time and a coded reference to a place. It only made sense to me when we found Craig. And I didn't say anything then because I'd be dropping Addy in it."

"And yourself," I growl at him. "So what makes you think Addy's in danger now?"

Eli shifts in his seat.

"It was Addy who was supposed to go missing."

"*What?*"

"Jacques had a plan. I caught snatches of conversations I didn't understand. Something about a final job before summer. Took me ages to piece it all together. Addy was going to 'disappear,' and our family would pay to get her back. I think Gaia found out and confronted Addy. Gaia had an inkling all along about the stealing, but this was different. She wouldn't stay silent about something like a fake kidnapping."

My head is hurting, but I shake away the fog. "They argued, Addy said as much. And at the party, Gaia jumped out of the window to avoid Jacques and Lucille."

"Makes sense." Eli nods. "Addy warned them Gaia knew. When she went missing, I think Addy assumed Jacques had shut her up. My guess is Addy's been terrified he'd do the same to her if she talked."

I get up and walk to the window. "I overheard Lucille on her phone last night. Said something about a plan going ahead. Today."

"She was probably talking to Jacques." Eli holds up the phone. "And then Addy called Lucille at 3:00 a.m. What's the betting she's tricked Addy into meeting Jacques and he's holding her somewhere?"

"But... You said that Gaia's gone to save her? How would Gaia know where she is?"

"Addy's phone is switched off now." Eli swallows. "But before it went dead, she received one last call. From Scott's phone."

"From *Gaia*."

"Exactly." He shrugs hopelessly. "Don't know where to look for them I'm flying blind."

I stare at him. "All that technology, and you have no idea where they could be? Think, Eli! God, I'm surprised you didn't implant something in Addy's neck so you could follow her everywhere!"

"I wish I had," he says solemnly, "but even Pop wouldn't go that far."

Dawn is breaking outside, and there's a movement down the lane. I turn and look out of the window, my heart exploding as I see a quad bike zooming up to the lodge. I run to the door as Bode pulls in and gets off the bike carefully.

"You're back!" I feel like running down and flinging my arms around him, but I don't. "Are you okay? What did they do to you?"

"Patch-up job." He grins briefly. "Sorry I didn't reply to your texts; battery ran out. And I needed to see you urgently. Have you checked the Missing page? Oh." He spots Eli, sees the look on both of our faces.

We go back inside and I bring him up to speed as quickly as I can, Eli chipping in helpfully with all the really incriminating stuff.

"Man." Bode looks at us, slack-jawed. "You really think Jacques and Lucille are going ahead with the plan to fake kidnap Addy?"

"Addy's a loose end," Eli says. "If Jacques is serious enough to push Craig off the tower, who knows what they'll do to my sister?"

And mine.

"Where would they hide out? Eli, there's really nothing in the messages?" I look at Eli desperately, but he shakes his head.

"Guys, we might have someone helping us; I came here as soon as I saw it." Bode holds up his phone. "Check it." I look at the screen, it's the Missing page discussion thread. "Last comment. Posted twenty minutes ago."

I squint at the thread. There's just a tag, Esme Gill. But it's the person who's done the tagging that gets my attention. *Scott Mazzulo*. I feel my legs go weak beneath me and stick out a hand to grab Bode's arm.

"She's… Gaia's done that?"

"Let me see!" Eli crowds in.

I swear loudly. "Come on, Gaia! Tell us where you are!"

"She's telling us she's okay," Eli says. "Subtle."

"She knows I don't do subtle!" I shout. "Where the hell are you, Gaia!"

Bode sways slightly, like he's going to faint.

"God, you need to rest. Sit!" I point to the chair. "Watch that phone like a hawk. I'm getting you a glass of water." I take off into the kitchen. The sun is coming up, hitting the mountain, bouncing off the white peaks in the distance. I said I wouldn't let the sun rise until I found her. I failed. But maybe she's giving me another chance. I fumble a glass under the tap, hand shaking, tripping over slices of bread I'd dropped when Eli bashed on the door.

"This." Bode is suddenly at my side, thrusting his phone in front of me again. "Look."

"I thought I'd told you to stay put…" My eyes swim over the screen, eventually focusing on a clip just posted.

Posted by *Gaia*.

There's a blur of carpet, a quick pan of furniture and a dark wall with pictures on it, a blank...ceiling? And a voice. My sister's voice, a whisper.

"The app."

The clip cuts off.

"What the—?" I turn, frantic, to Bode, and Eli who is standing beside him. "Where is that?" I press Play again. The carpet, dark with a white pattern, the furniture is...chairs, a table...the wall, the ceiling...

"The app."

"What is she saying?" I press it again. "The app? What app?" I search Bode and Eli's faces.

"An app on her phone?" Eli says.

"She's gonna message you on an app?" Bode frowns.

"She knows I don't have my phone; that's why she's posting this on here. It's her only way of communicating with me!" I thump the table. "Come on, Gaia! Give me more!"

"Looks like she got interrupted," Bode says. "God, that carpet is scrambling my brain. I've seen it before, I know I have."

I keep pressing Play, keep watching, looking for the clue that will make everything fall into place, but it doesn't come. The carpet, the chairs, the pictures on the wall—it's all too fast—and the whispered words. The sun reflecting off the mountain is getting in my eyes so I can't see the screen well enough. I put a hand up to stop the flickering light.

Wait...

The sun is not reflecting off the slopes. It's reflecting off the windows of the revolving restaurant, up high on the mountain, light blinking off the glass.

"It's moving," I mutter. "It's supposed to be closed. Why is it moving?"

"What is?" Eli says, irritated.

"The revolving restaurant."

"The Apogee?" Bode asks.

"The Ap," I whisper back. I play the video one more time, and when the camera moves up the wall, I freeze it as it passes over the picture hanging in its frame. It's an old black and white photo of Gaia's place. The one she showed us when we went for the steak I moaned about. I look up the mountain. The Apogee has stopped.

"Gaia's up there."

CHAPTER THIRTY-FIVE

———

Bode and I are standing at the bottom of the ski slope. We'd roared away from the lodge on the quad, as Eli frantically leapt into Addy's car to track down my parents, the police, anyone who can help. We're going to need it.

Outside the gondola station on the muddy grass: Scott's car. Gaia's bad parking.

"She went up on the lift." Bode takes off at a trot. "Quickest way to The Apogee."

I run after; *oh god, it's back to the pod.*

"Is it safe?" I shout over to Bode, who is flinging open panels on a steel-gray pillar and pressing buttons. "Strike that, who cares? We've got to get up there even if it means monkeying along the friggin' cables."

"That's the spirit." Bode hits another button, a motor whirs, and we leap onboard as the door closes and the pod lurches off the platform. I kneel on the forward seat, hanging on for dear life as we quickly ascend, the bare ground falling away, looking way harder and scarier than the pillowy snow that lay below the last time I made this journey. The line of the gondola takes us up the mountain steeply, pine trees on either side. I look across the mountain; the restaurant's out of sight. The forest will conceal us for now, but once we clear the tree line we'll be exposed.

"They're going to see us coming,"

"Speed over stealth," Bode says. "And hopefully they'll think it's a maintenance run, not the gruesome twosome, come to save the day."

"Gruesome twosome." I chuckle nervously. "That's what my mother used to call me and Gaia. God, I hope Gaia's got a plan. I sure as hell don't. Do you think they'll have guns?"

"Everybody's got guns." Bode shrugs. "God save America."

"You have one?" I stare at him. "Didn't you think it might be a good idea to, oh, I dunno, go and fetch it?"

Bode gives me a look. "Hey, I was hoping we'd hit them with your piercing British sarcasm." He rubs his stomach lightly. "Or maybe a carving knife."

Yeah, that shuts me up. "Eli better round up the troops or we are toast. Any chance he'll bottle it?"

Bode frowns. "No idea what that means, but he's got your back, Es. Whatever he's done, he loves his sister, and Gaia. And he'll do what he has to because you did a great job of guilting him out."

"Go, me." I grip the seat tighter. The tree line is approaching. Bode sees it too.

"Get down, they won't see us. We reach the platform? Door opens, we jump out without stopping."

I nod, and we scramble to sit on the cold floor, pressed up against each other, arm to arm. "Seems I've done a lot of hunkering down with you recently," I side-eye him. "That hasn't been the worst part."

"Happy you think so." His eyes do their twinkle, in spite of the exhaustion, the stab wound, and the fact we're riding into a fight with no ammo apart from my advanced skills in snark. He looks up sharply. "Here we go, get ready to roll." He moves on to all fours, but there's a screech of metal on metal and the pod lurches backward.

"What the hell?" I gasp. "Did you stop it?"

"Nope." Bode slowly lifts his head to look out of the window.

"Is it broken?"

"Nope."

I pull myself up. We've come to a halt short of our stop by a bus length. The ground below us slopes away very steeply, too high to jump down. There, standing on the platform, is Lucille, holding a shovel. She looks shocked when she sees us, then amused. So damn tickled, in fact, that she tosses the shovel aside, doubling over with laughter. She finds it so funny that she doesn't see the shadow sneaking up behind her, a tall, rangy, beautiful figure who emerges like a conquering Amazon, scoops up the shovel, and smacks her over the back of the head.

"Yes!" I punch the air, instant tears running down my cheeks. "Oh my god, *Gaia!*"

Gaia looks at me, surprise and irritation on her face. Shouts something I can't hear.

Bode jumps onto the seat, opens a window in the roof, and sticks his head out. "Hey, Gaia, it's amazing to finally find you!"

"What are you doing here?" She really does look very annoyed. "You need to go, now!"

What the—? "We saw your video and we've come to sodding save you!" I shout back.

She shakes her head vigorously. "I don't need saving! Jacques has got Addy. I have to stop him."

"We know!" I clamber up and stick my head through the roof. "There are police coming; they'll help."

"Great job!" Gaia shouts. "Now I've got to go!"

"Wait!" Bode shouts. "Can you get us to the platform?"

"Lucille smashed the controls." Gaia holds out the shovel. "I'll come back for you."

"Gaia!" I scream at her, but she's running back into the shadows of the gondola station, out of sight. "Typical!" I swear loudly.

"Found it."

Bode has jumped down and is holding a webbed thing with buckles, which he puts over his head and fastens between his legs. *A harness.* I swear again.

"Tell me you're not going to do what I think you're going to do."

"Emergency escape." He looks up at me, grinning.

"I was joking when I said I'd monkey along the cable. Don't you Americans even get sarcasm?"

He ignores me, but the grin's still there. "Piece o' cake, seen 'em do it before. What, you wanna stay here?" He jumps up beside me, pulls himself through the window with a groan, reaches up, and proceeds to attach two ropes to the cable above us and to himself. He tosses one of them to me. "So you can pull the harness back when I've made it to the platform."

"Are you actually kidding me? You do remember you've been stabbed and everything?"

He crouches down, the amber-flecked eyes as serious as I've ever seen them. "You wanna help your sister, or quit at the last minute?"

"You are nuts." My voice is shaking.

"So are you. That's why we get on so well. Now don't drop the frickin' rope, because I can't do this on my own." He grabs the cable, swings his legs up, and pulls himself along, hand over hand, grunting with the effort.

"Oh my god, Bode!" I whisper, more to myself than to him, feeding the coil of rope out as he goes. I can see he's hurting, but he's doing it. The downward slope on the cable is helping, and he's almost at the platform. There's a set of rollers that the cable runs through, and he has to hang from his hands and swing his legs onto the ladder on the tower that supports the cable. After a couple of tries, he's there. He undoes the harness, letting it dangle off the rope, and turns to me, victorious.

"Your turn!"

I know, with absolute certainty, that there is no way I can

do this. But *I'm nuts*, so I clamber onto the roof of the pod and pull on the rope so the harness stutters along the cable toward me.

"Atta girl!" Bode shouts. I glare back at him.

"Why do you always have to be so bloody positive?"

"You bring it out in me!"

"God, that's such an insult," I mutter, tugging on the rope. *Damn.* The harness is caught on something. I jerk the rope, trying to unsnag it.

"Wait!" Bode shouts. "It's twisted." He leans out from the ladder with one hand, reaching to grasp the cable and trying to shake the rope free. The cable's too thick and taut for him to have any effect. He jumps, grabbing with both hands and swinging his legs up to hook over the cable, making my pod bob a little. He's holding himself up with the crook of one knee, kicking away at the snagged rope with the other foot. "Got it!"

I pull the rope again, and this time the harness races along smoothly.

"Yes!"

I reach out, pulling it down, slipping it over my head and fastening it before I have time to think. I glance at Bode and he grins back encouragingly, moving hand over hand back to the tower. But maybe he's a little too quick, or the cable is greasy—his legs slip, his grip fails, and suddenly he's falling.

"Bode!" I swallow a scream, looking down at his motionless figure in the bank of snow below.

I glance toward The Apogee; there's no one else in sight. This one's on me, and me alone.

I bite my lip, check buckles with shaking hands and reach up to the cable. It's freezing, and too wide to get a proper grip. *Gonna have to improvise.*

Tightening the harness as much as I can, I cling onto the rope and kick my legs up toward the cable. Once, twice, three times… This is useless. I'm not even close.

Oh god, Bode. He's not moving. *Have to do this.* I look at the angle of the cable. Gravity is on my side. That's what Craig used to say when he was trying to teach me to ski.

Everything inside you might be screaming, but gravity is on your side, Esme. Take a leap of faith.

Yeah, that worked out so well before, Craig.

I leap anyway.

For a split second I'm free-falling but the bindings tighten, cutting into my flesh with a jerk, and I zip-line toward the platform. The rollers stop my ride and I bash, hard, into the ladder on the tower. I unclip, climb down, jump onto the drift of snow and skid on my arse to Bode.

"You made it." He turns his head, coughs. "Look at what I had to do to get you motivated."

"You jerk!" I'm gulping and crying and kind of hitting him too, which is probably not a good thing. "Are you all right? Can you stand?"

He nods and I haul him to his feet, but as he tries to put one foot in front of another, he sinks.

"Ankle," he looks at me, pale as the snow.

"I'll get something—" As I say the words, a scream cuts across the stillness, coming from The Apogee.

"Go."

I'm running faster than I ever thought I could, feet skidding on patchy crusts of icy slush and slippery mud, heading for those windows, the harness still around me, the scream ringing in my ears. The main entrance is closed. I rattle the doors, but they're chained. The scream comes again, around the back, and I make a dash for it, keeping low, until I reach another entrance. There, in the doorway, is my sister. She's panting, blood dripping from her forehead. In front of her, is Jacques on a quad, a stricken Addy sitting behind him, hands tied. Nobody has seen me because everyone is looking at the object in Jacques's hand, the gun he is pointing at my sister.

I've always been told off for not thinking things through. I genuinely believe, in the heat of the moment, something in my brain just clicks. Dyspraxia? *No.* Teenager? *Maybe.* And it's like that now.

I dig my hands into my pockets and pull out the only thing I have with me, my phone. In a single movement I fling it with all my might at Jacques's head. I watch, in slo-mo, as it flies through the air, with incredible topspin and unrepeatable accuracy, and smacks him in the temple with a sickening crack.

Beautiful, brilliant brick.

He falls, eyes closed and mouth open, hand releasing the gun which skitters down the slope for me to grab. Jacques is out cold before he hits the ground, toppling into the dirt. Addy leaps off the bike, pulls back a foot, and kicks him in the other temple for good measure. Gaia staggers toward her, turns the ignition on the bike, and somehow we're all piling on and she's driving us away, back to the gondola, where Bode has climbed to the platform and is trussing up a drowsy Lucille with plastic cable ties he probably had in his pockets, because that's who he is.

"We won't all fit on the bike," Gaia says.

I look down the mountain. "We won't need to."

There, coming toward us, is our army. Quads, a police four-wheel drive, a whole bunch of red-faced hikers, charging up the slope.

"Eli came through."

My mother and father burst out of the police car. They could have run the whole way if they needed to, but they don't, just these last few feet. Their faces, when they see Gaia, I can't begin… The hell of the past few days falls away, and in its place is sheer joy and relief. She's in their arms, and me too, and we're all crying, and snot is flying everywhere, and it's the happiest I've ever been.

When I finally break away, Addy's gasping about Jacques, and from the cries that go up from the direction of The Apogee, he's somehow managed to disappear. Detective Graff is radioing, Lucille is wriggling, and a whole horde of cops are shouting. There's a minor police kerfuffle when I bring out the gun, but I toss it in the mud without incident and they don't shoot me.

"Glad you did that, not me," Gaia mutters. "Es, Addy said you went to Scott's. The bastard had me trapped there, you know."

I nod. "I worked it out, eventually. He ran off."

Gaia swears. "He spiked my tea. When I finally came round, I panicked because I knew Jacques and Lucille were planning on hurting Addy."

"Did you tell Scott that?"

"I couldn't. I didn't know if he was involved; after all, he had bloody kidnapped me!"

"None of them deserve you." I wrap my arms around her. "You picked the handcuffs with the earring, though? Respect."

"Great present, thanks. Beautiful *and* practical." She laughs softly into my hair. "Happy Birthday, by the way."

"Best present ever, getting you back," I croak. "Well, apart from that amazing robot dog I got when I was seven, obvs."

"That was a bear."

"*Dog.* God, you're such a loser." I hug her tighter, breathing her in. A medic appears, breaking us apart and leading Gaia away, dabbing at her bloodied head.

I spot Eli.

"Thank you. For coming to me at the lodge. And for the rescue."

He shrugs. "You Gill girls had it under control. You always do."

I go to walk away, turn back. "Hey…that note that you found in Gaia's room?"

Eli clears his throat. "Gaia gave it to me weeks ago. Out of some book she'd studied. I was depressed about how my father rules my life, how I was too scared to walk away from the family, poured my heart out to her. She slipped that note into my pocket. 'Throw the whole book in the fire!' Guess she was telling me to grow a pair."

"Why did you pretend she'd left it in her room?"

He shrugs. "To drop Scott in the shit, because I hate him. It felt like it could have been a clue for one of their stunts."

"You were right about him."

Eli nods. I give him a smile, he returns it. I turn away before we can have a moment or anything.

"Guys?" Bode is sitting on a rock, looking at his phone, bad ankle being wrapped by a paramedic. "Scott kept his appointment this morning."

He turns the screen around so we can see. Live-streaming TV: Scott is sitting on a sofa, his face red and puffy, talking through tears. Breaking News: Star Confesses "Kidnap" Stunt Gone Wrong runs along the bottom of the screen.

"Whaddya reckon?" Bode whistles. "The driver found Scott, who persuaded him to give him a ride to the TV studio? That dude can talk anyone around."

"No, he can't," Gaia murmurs, beside me. "And he's not going to talk his way out of this one, believe me."

EPILOGUE

———

England is so dull. Everything is small and boring after America. I love it.

Gaia's here too, and I really love that. She's doing great. She's deferred her college place a year, but she's definitely going back to America, maybe as soon as summer, to finally get to know her aunt and cousin. I understand, totally, and I'm proud. Ma and Dad haven't heard about it yet, and they might take a little persuading to let go of her again so quickly. But ultimately, they'll know it takes more than a bunch of psycho-losers to dampen Gaia Gill's spirit.

Not to say it's always an easy ride.

One time I find her on the floor in her room, phone in hand, and at first, I think she's laughing because her broad shoulders are shaking so much. But there's no raucous cackle.

"Gaia?"

I kneel down beside her, tentatively. She's sobbing quietly, scrolling down the Missing page Scott created.

"I feel…sorry for him."

"For Scott?" I say, incredulous. "Are you out of your mind? You should be furious!"

"Oh, that too. Big-time." Her eyes glint. "Hey, it's one hell of a roller coaster." She tosses the phone to the floor. "I switch between angry, scared, humiliated, guilty—wondering if on some level, it was my fault—"

I go to protest, and she raises a hand, a small smile on her lips.

"I know I'm not to blame. I did a lot of dumb stuff with Scott, but I *did not* ask him to drug me and hold me captive." She exhales deeply, staring out of her bedroom window. "It was all him. He's addicted to attention; he doesn't even feel like he exists if he's ignored. Gotta be relevant. And that's what makes me pity him; he only lives through others' eyes." She shrugs. "Most of us do that, I suppose. Everyone cares way too much about what people think of them." She pauses for a moment, then turns and holds my gaze. "But not you."

"What?" I bluster. "Of course I care about what people think!"

"Only people who matter." She smiles. "You're not obsessed by what random acquaintances or strangers on the internet think. I envy you, so much. You're the most authentic of any of us. Don't lose that, ever."

I snort. "I don't think I could."

She laughs, ruffles my hair in a way that has me batting her hand away and pushing her over onto the floor, and we're back to glorious normal, squabbling, enjoying annoying the hell out of each other. Our own special kind of therapy.

Addy has the best psychotherapist money can buy. We don't see her. Her family somehow got her out of the United States, and I doubt she'll be going back anytime soon. Certainly that college place isn't happening. I hope she's okay. In spite of it all, she was a victim too. She needs to ditch those parents, but family can be hard to shake. Gaia says she'll reach out to her once the dust has settled. Eli's been here, once. He's cut the ties to his dad, he told us, finally *threw the whole book in the fire*. I hope it works out for him.

Bits of news drip through from America. I follow it closer than I let on, pretend to be surprised when the parents tell us stuff. Lucille, Craig, and Scott were all arrested, but Scott got bailed, for now...on the condition he doesn't post anything on social media. It must be killing him. Bet he's working on the book deal.

Jacques escaped. In those moments on the mountain when we were drowning in hugs and relief, he gave the cops the slip. He got halfway to Canada, apparently, before he was apprehended. And not by the police. A mountain man caught up with Jacques, took him down. The man hog-tied Jacques and left him to be pecked by the crows until he'd hiked into town to report it. I wish there was a way I could thank Telfer, but I doubt he does video calls.

Bode does do video calls. It's kind of crappy, but it's all we've got for now and I love seeing his face on my screen. *Yeah, I got a smartphone, so what?* We chat every day. We game a little, sometimes a lot. And there's the messaging; my banter is getting better. Bode's uncle has promised if he gets his school diploma—whatever that is—he'll buy him a plane ticket over here. Would be kind of fun to see how he does in the city. Can't promise any moose, but there are some hella vicious stump-footed pigeons here. And maybe, when Gaia goes back to the United States, I'll visit him. Maybe I could work at Moon? I reckon I'd be a dab hand at operating the gondola.

God, I miss him. But, you know, you gotta have hope. Missing doesn't always mean gone forever. Sometimes we find each other again.

DON'T MISS ANOTHER
TWISTED THRILLER
FROM KIRSTY MCKAY:
THE ASSASSIN GAME

CHAPTER 1

———

It is about 4:00 a.m. when they come for me. I am already awake, strung out on the fear that they will come and the fear that they won't. When I finally hear the click of the latch on the dormitory door, I have only a second to brace myself before they're on me.

"Do as we say!"

A rasping voice, sudden and violent, in my ear.

I swallow my scream as a hood—a pillowcase?—is shoved over my head. A large hand clamps across my mouth and nose, mashing my lip against my upper teeth, and I taste blood. Weight presses down on my pajamaed chest, and panic rises as I wriggle a little to clear my nostrils to breathe. Silently, I'm lifted from my bed. Efficiently. They've done this before.

They bundle me to the floor and flip me on my stomach, yanking my hands behind my back. My gut lurches with panic. A pinch of plastic, and my hands are trussed so tight that I can feel the blood thudding out a frantic heartbeat back and forth from wrist to wrist.

"One noise from you, Cate, and this is over."

I want to puke. I try to nod, but my neck is twisted at an awkward angle, and that hand is still clamped over my hooded face. But they must understand my compliance, as the hand is removed; I'm forced to my feet and pushed forward, one bare foot stumbling after the other. The urge to pee is extreme, but I have to fight it with everything because, hey, if I wet myself, I'm dead for sure.

We walk; there's the shove of shoulders to either side of me, and the hands are there again, on my arms this time, pulling me to one side then another. Light seeps into the pillowcase from somewhere, but I still can't see anything other than shadows. My feet tell me we have exited the dormitory as the carpet briefly gives way to a strip of bare boards before they find the hall runner and turn left, left toward the short staircase down to the ground floor. The staircase! Will they push me? Will I fall? My fears are unfounded as suddenly my legs are swept up from under me and, with a grunt, someone carries me downstairs.

I know that grunt. He remembered to disguise his voice when he spoke but not the grunt. Does the fact that it's him carrying me make me feel better or worse?

Dark again. The cool September night air hits me; we must have left the building by the side door. And then I'm lowered, surprisingly gently, and I feel cold, damp metal beneath my PJs. A hard rim under my shoulders and knees. A box? Some kind of coffin? Would they go that far? The panic comes back. I'm tilted, and I draw my feet inside to brace myself against the rim. There's a wobble, a crunch of stone, and then a squeak.

OK, a wheelbarrow. The squeak gave it away. I breathe again. I'm being pushed in a wheelbarrow, my bum rubbing in earthworms and soil. This is their idea of funny.

Slowly we travel over the gravel, silently except for that tiny, little squeak every rotation. I'm sure someone was tasked to oil it, but not well enough. They'll get into trouble for that.

There's a slight bump as the terrain gets softer. I sink and wobble again, and then we take off, much faster than before, a wild ride. The squeak becomes a constant whine. I wish I could hold on to the sides, but all I can do is push down on my feet to wedge myself in there as we bump along, my abs burning in a half crunch. I hope the ride will be short. Which way are we heading? North to the woods or east to the causeway? Please, please, not south to the cliff path; surely they wouldn't risk that? I don't have much idea, no sense of direction, but as we jog on, I hear a few muted giggles and pants, even a whisper that is quickly shushed. Three of them with me? Four? One pushing, the others running alongside.

We stop. I strain to hear the sea, but all I can hear is the blood in my ears. And then:

"Woo-woo!" goes the world's least convincing owl.

"Twit-twoo!" No, strike that. The second one is worse.

"Coooo-oo!" The third sounds like a drunken dove, and suddenly the first two seem very realistic.

Muted giggles. We're off again, faster this time, and I hear a rumble to my left, a rumble to my right. More wheelbarrows? Yes, without doubt, and we're racing. I'm not the only one who has been taken, and that's reassuring. The race is almost fun at first—apart from the sheer terror, of course—but it's exhilarating at least. Just when I'm thinking I can no longer hold on, my knees are burning and my feet are turning to ice, I sense my kidnappers are tiring as well, and we slow. There's more panting, unabashed and unconcealed this time. Someone mutters, but I can't hear what's said. Almost there. The fear comes back.

We stop again, this time for good. I'm lowered with a thud, pulled out of the wheelbarrow and on to my cold, bare feet. Blood wells up into my face, and I sway a little. I squeeze my toes, trying to find my balance.

I'm standing on sand. Cool but not damp. And yet, no sound of the waves hitting the rocks...where are we? There's a smell too, but it's not of salty air—at least, no more than this whole island smells of the sea. It's an acrid, oily smell. Something is burning.

I dare to open my eyes, and through the pillowcase, there's light out there. Orange, glowing balls of light, suspended off the ground. Of course. Suddenly, I know exactly where we are.

My hood is whipped off. Shadows slink away into shadow. I squint and try to stop the ground from spinning.

An amphitheater, carved into the side of a hill, and I am onstage. Oil lanterns hang from stands, lighting the scene. There's also the full blood moon—but it only winks at us as blue-gray clouds blow across it, obscuring its light. My kidnappers gone. I turn around to see my fellow captives, blinking and swiveling their heads, all of us nodding dogs, taking it in.

Martin Parish is next to me, bent over, panting and grinning his goofy, gap-toothed grin. He's just stoked to be selected; he doesn't care what they might do to us. Tesha Quinn stands to his right, eyes wide and also swaying on her bare feet, her dark-blond corkscrew curls standing out in shock from her head. She doesn't look at me—trying to hold the panic down—because if she does, she might break. Both kids have tied hands, both in night attire. I thank luck and good judgment that I'm wearing modest pajamas; Martin is shivering in boxers and Tesha's not much better off in underwear and a cami. They're cold and vulnerable. At least I have flannel to hide behind.

Only three of us harvested tonight? The final selection for this year. The Game can begin.

ACKNOWLEDGMENTS

——

Every year an average of 600,000 people go missing in the USA. Most of these cases are resolved relatively quickly, but around 2,000 annually remain unsolved. It was hearing the heartbreaking accounts from some of the families of the missing that prompted me to imagine Gaia and Esme's story. The bravery, persistence and hope exhibited by ordinary people looking for their loved ones was inspirational to me for this book, and way beyond.

I'm so happy and excited to be writing for Sourcebooks Fire again. Huge thanks to my editor Annie Berger for her vision, incisive focus, and endless patience with the Brit-speak. Also, thanks and respect go to Gabbi Calabrese for help and encouragement, and to all the fantastic and hardworking team at Sourcebooks.

To my agent, Veronique Baxter, and Sara Langham at David Higham Associates for believing in this book and helping me to bushwhack it into shape. I could not have navigated my way through the dark woods without you.

As always, thanks to John, Didi, Xanthe, Louie, and Tilly for their support, endless understanding, and belly laughs. Love you all muchly.

Finally, thank you, my wonderful readers. It still blows my mind that my books are out in the world, and that's only because you're reading them. Please keep doing that. Cheers, folks.

ABOUT THE AUTHOR

Kirsty was born in northeast England and worked as an actor in London before moving to Boston, Massachusetts for several very happy years of adventure, including writing stuff and having kids. Constantly exhausted yet puzzlingly invigorated, she now lives with her family in the beautiful hills of Northumberland, England. She can be contacted via kirstymckay.com or on as many of the social media platforms as her addled brain can manage.